COVENS, CAKES, AND BIG MISTAKES

COVENS, CAKES, AND BIG MISTAKES

THE WITCHES OF PINECROFT COVE BOOK TWO

NICOLE ST CLAIRE

Apple Blossom Press
Bolton, MA

ALSO BY NICOLE ST CLAIRE

Don't miss the entire Witches of Pinecroft Cove series of
paranormal cozy mysteries!

Spirits, Pies, and Alibis

Covens, Cakes, and Big Mistakes

Magic, Lead, and Gingerbread*

*Coming soon

Visit NicoleStClaire.com to discover more titles coming
soon!

Covens, Cakes, and Big Mistakes
The Witches of Pinecroft Cove Book Two
Copyright © 2019 Nicole St Claire

Developmental Editing by Em Stevens
Edited by Kelly Hashway
Cover Design by: Victoria Cooper

Find out more: www.NicoleStClaire.com
Contact the author: Nicole@NicoleStClaire.com

ISBN: 9781697684971
This is a work of fiction. Any resemblance of characters to actual persons, living or dead, is purely coincidental.

Apple Blossom Press
PO Box 547
Bolton MA 01740

CHAPTER ONE

"Are you sure you'll be okay while I'm away?" Though she said it in her usual kind way, Aunt Gwen couldn't hide her doubt at my survival abilities.

Immediately, I went on the defensive. "It's not like I'm going to burn the place to the ground while you're gone." As soon as I said it, my aunt's eyes widened, and I knew my word choice was a mistake. Considering my woeful lack of kitchen skills, burning the house down was not an unreasonable fear.

"I wouldn't even think of leaving, only the coven has been on the waiting list for this cruise for three years, and if we pass up the chance, we may never have it again."

Standing at the bottom of the porch steps, Aunt Gwen rested one hand on the handle of a battered suitcase that was almost as big as she was. She wore a short-sleeve, ankle-length cotton dress covered with larger-than-life hibiscus flowers in a variety of colors too garish to exist in nature. A pair of oversized sunglasses shielded her eyes from the bright summer sun, and a floppy straw hat covered her hair, which glowed crimson from the fresh application of dye she'd given it in honor of her upcoming vacation.

"I'll be fine," I assured her, seasoning my words with heaping spoonfuls of enthusiasm and confidence that did not necessarily reflect how I felt. "With Labor Day weekend behind us, the summer rush is officially over."

"True, but that doesn't mean the work is done. Guests will be arriving Friday for the start of the Summerhaven Literary Festival, don't forget." She shifted her weight, raising one foot as if to climb back up the steps. "It's too much. I'll tell Bess and Sue Ellen to go without me."

"Absolutely not." I scrambled down to ground level and placed my hand on Aunt Gwen's shoulder, applying gentle pressure until she'd turned around and was facing the expansive front lawn. I knew how much the Bermuda witches cruise meant to her and her coven, and there was no way I was going to be the reason they missed out. Besides, after a solid month of witchcraft lessons from my perfectionist aunt, this below-average student was ready for a break.

She took all of three steps at my prodding, her suit-case barely starting to roll, before she came to a sudden halt. "But what about the baked goods for the authors' tea on Saturday?"

"The currant scones and tea sandwiches? We've been over those recipes a dozen times, and I haven't had a single magical mistake in a week." Full disclosure, it had been closer to three days. That particular spell I'd chosen from our time-worn grimoire had been splattered with a liberal layer of kitchen goop, and after accidentally skipping a few of the most obscured words, I somehow turned an entire box of dried currants into tiny black pebbles. I discovered this fact after popping a handful of them into my mouth as a snack and nearly cracking a tooth, but I managed to replace the ruined fruit with a fresh box without my aunt's knowledge, and the finished scones had been delightful, so I didn't see any reason one tiny error should be counted against me. "Don't worry, Aunt Gwen. I can handle it."

"I suppose you're right. I'm just being silly." Aunt Gwen took a deep breath and adjusted her grip on the suitcase handle. "You've been making fine progress this past month, and it's only fair you get a chance to test your skills."

"I'm looking forward to it," I told her as I looped my arm around her elbow and escorted her along the path toward the driveway where Bess and Sue Ellen were waiting in the island's only taxi.

That I was lying about looking forward to running the inn on my own for three weeks was not something she needed to hear. Her cruise to Bermuda with the other members of her coven would be her first vacation in years, and I wasn't about to spoil her fun. Besides, my apprehension over flying solo as an innkeeper wasn't exactly the only secret I was keeping these days. It paled in comparison to the fact that, for the past five weeks since Lillian Bassett had materialized in my bedroom on Lughnasadh Eve with her cat, Gus, on her lap, not only had I been seeing the ghost of the feisty flapper and her immortal feline companion everywhere I turned, they'd pretty much been keeping me awake 'round the clock with their incessant chatter. Yes, Gus chattered, too, in his own cat-like way. Not in real words, mind you, but frankly, sometimes I wasn't sure which one made more noise, Lillian or her darned cat.

Now, if Aunt Gwen caught wind of *that* secret, she'd never step foot off the island again. Kitchen witches did *not* see spirits, and as far as everyone else was concerned, a kitchen witch is exactly what I was. All the Bassett women were. We had been for generations upon generations. It was simply how things were supposed to be. Only, well, I wasn't. And I was terrified someone would figure it out.

If the witches of Pinecroft Cove discovered I wasn't the type of witch they thought me to be, what would happen? My heart beat faster at the thought. Would I be sent away? Would my powers be stripped from me?

Whatever I was, it wasn't normal. I would probably be shunned.

Fearing what might happen if my aunt or the members of my own coven discovered I communicated with a dead woman and her cat on a regular basis, I'd kept my lips tightly buttoned. I planned to keep doing just that until maybe, just maybe, my uninvited guests from the great beyond drifted into the light or whatever it was they were meant to do. In the meantime, I was going to learn to cook if it killed me. Which, if you've ever seen enchanted blueberry pie filling explode, was not so far-fetched. Let's just say there were a few things about me that were better for no one else to know, and they'd be a whole lot easier to hide if Aunt Gwen were gone for a while. Hence, my rushing her out the door.

Albert, the island's only taxi driver, hopped out of his vehicle and opened the rear door as we approached. I wiggled my fingers in a cheerful acknowledgment of the two old witches who already occupied the back seat. They'd both dressed in their own signature fashions for their tropical adventure. Auntie Bess wore a gauzy skirt with a paisley print, her multiple black braids cinched back into a single pony tail, while Auntie Sue had on what might best be classified as resort wear, with coral linen pants and a lightweight cashmere twinset. Different as night and day, how all three of these old ladies had been best friends since time began was a true magical mystery.

As poor Albert attempted to cram my aunt's luggage into the minuscule space that was left in his trunk, swearing under his breath at the two massive bags that belonged to her companions, I gave Aunt Gwen a kiss on the cheek. "Don't worry about me, or the inn, while you're gone. I've got it under control. I'll see you in three weeks."

Instead of getting into the car, Aunt Gwen rested an arm against the car door and frowned. "I feel so guilty. I'll be missing your first Mabon."

I'd been hard at work studying every aspect of witchcraft since I'd had the bombshell dropped on me that I was an honest-to-goodness witch. Even so, I paused for a moment, trying to recall exactly which of the numerous unfamiliar holidays Mabon happened to be. It had to do with the harvest, maybe. Something like that. I shrugged. "It's okay, Aunt Gwen. If you were trying to deprive me of a Thanksgiving turkey and homemade pie, I'd probably feel differently, but I didn't grow up with all these holidays. Mabon's just another day on the calendar as far as I'm concerned."

"Oh, my dear." Aunt Gwen's eyes sparkled with a mist of tears as she traced a gnarled finger along my cheek. "You've missed so much of what it means to be a witch. When Samhain rolls around, I'll make it up to you, I promise."

Now, even as a total newbie, Samhain was a holiday I knew something about. Better known by the name Halloween, it was the pinnacle of the witch's calendar, a night for gathering with loved ones for feasting and celebrating, and a night when the spirits of the dearly departed roamed free upon the earth. It was, in other words, the one night of the year upon which my ghost-whispering self had every intention of coming down with an unfortunate cold and hiding in bed. One lonely ghost was quite enough for my nerves, thank you very much. I didn't need to be badgered by a whole town full of them. I smiled weakly, hoping to hide my dread. "I can hardly wait."

With a final round of goodbyes, the ladies were off to the ferry, and I was free to make my way back inside the house. For the first time since I'd arrived, the Pinecroft Inn was completely empty, without even the need to prepare for new guests for a couple days. Though I'd been looking forward to some downtime, I couldn't help but think, as I entered the kitchen, that the silence was—a girlishly shrill voice pierced my eardrum like an ice pick, interrupting my train of thought.

"Look at you, you dewdropper!" The once empty kitchen was suddenly occupied as the figure of a woman in a flapper's dress shimmered into existence in the middle of the room. Almost immediately after that, I heard a meow and saw a pair of emerald eyes blinking in the shadowy space between the refrigerator and the pantry.

Short-lived, I thought. With a ghost in the house who hadn't had the chance to engage in conversation since 1929, that blessed silence I'd been savoring a moment ago had been *extremely* short-lived.

"Hi, Lillian," I said, holding back a sigh. Not only did my new best friend never stop talking, but her addiction to archaic slang meant I frequently had no idea what she was trying to say. "What exactly is a dewdropper?"

"A lollygagger, you dumb Dora," she explained with a breezy laugh. I'd never heard of a dumb Dora before, either, but I managed to get the gist of that one without asking. "A dewdropper is someone who sits around all day and has nothing to do."

"Oh, well then, I guess I'm guilty as charged."

"Guilty as charged?" Lillian frowned. "They haven't made it a crime to have nothing to do, have they?"

"Uh, no." I pressed my lips together to keep from laughing. For as much slang as the woman dished out, she sure didn't know how to take it. "Still perfectly legal."

"Well, that's a relief. I love doing nothing," she assured me, as if somehow it had escaped my attention these past five weeks that, despite her cat leaving fur and mayhem in his wake, my new roommate hadn't lifted a finger to help clean up a single mess. "You gonna call that fella of yours, Dr. Caldwell, and tell him you're finally ready for your date?"

Ignoring her impertinent inquiry into what passed for my personal life, I breezed by her and searched the countertop for the leather-bound recipe book that was our family grimoire, or book of magic spells. The last thing I needed was commentary from a ghost on the awkward way I'd handled my relationship with Noah Caldwell. *It's not a relationship*, I quickly chided myself.

That was definitely not the right word to describe whatever was going on that caused all of my brain cells to power down the moment I was within ten feet of the formerly shy and awkward boy who had, once upon a time, had a crush on me. Noah had become a confident and extra-hunky doctor while I was away, making my stomach flip-flop every time he was near. But surely his feelings for me, a failed accountant who lived with her aunt, were strictly based on pity and nothing more these days.

When I did finally speak, there was no disguising my whining tone. "Where did Aunt Gwen put the grimoire?"

"Come on, Tamsyn. I'm not going to let you duck out of answering me that easily. He's phoned at least three times in the past week, and you've been coming up with excuses right and left not to call him back. If you don't do it soon, I wouldn't blame him for thinking you don't want to see him."

"But I *don't* want to see him," I replied, then cringed at how harsh the words had sounded as soon as they were outside of my head. "I don't like being felt sorry for. The island's most eligible bachelor is certainly not interested in dating me, and I have no desire to spend an evening mentally cataloging all the reasons why over a pity dinner. Besides, I have way too much on my plate."

Lillian's eyes made a pointed sweep of the pristine kitchen in which not a single item was out of place or in need of attention. "Sure you do."

"Next time I see him I'll—oh, there's the grimoire." I retrieved the book from a shelf and plopped it on the countertop, rifling through the pages until I reached the recipe for currant scones. "If you'll excuse me, I have a recipe to practice for Saturday's authors' tea."

Just as I said it, my phone rang. I squinted at the name on the caller ID. Jan Prince. She was the new organizer for the literary festival. Why would she be calling me? I suspected she might have dialed incorrectly. Even so, I gave Lillian a warning look as she opened her mouth to speak. "I'd better answer this. Hello?"

"Tamsyn, it's Jan from the festival. Sorry to bother you, but Ms. Gwyneth isn't picking up her phone."

"She's probably on the ferry by now," I told her. "She's off on a little vacation, but maybe I can help since I'll be taking over her duties at the inn while she's away."

"Vacation? Oh, dear." There was no mistaking her utter dismay at this news, but I tried not to take it as a reflection of her lack of confidence in me, even as my palms grew slick with sweat.

"It's okay, Jan. If you're calling about the authors'

tea, I can assure you I have the menu completely under control." *Scones. Tea sandwiches. Boiling water.* I could manage that, right?

"Well, that's just it. I've had some excellent news. Sebastian Grenville is traveling to Maine on a book tour and has just agreed to give the keynote address on Saturday." For a woman who claimed to be imparting good news, she sounded more troubled than elated.

"Sebastian Grenville. You mean the one who wrote *Magnolia Sunset*?" It had been nearly two decades since the book had come out, but even now, Grenville's groundbreaking work was hailed as a modern-day classic and was required reading in just about every college in the country. As far as I knew, it was his only published work, so the fact he was embarking on a book tour was surprising news. "I had no idea he was still on tour for that book."

"No, not for *Magnolia Sunset*. It's just been announced that his next book, *Azalea Nightfall*, is publishing next month. Understandably, the literary world is going wild."

"Well, how exciting." I stifled a snort as a mental image formed of all the members of the island's literary society attempting to go wild. There was a good chance someone would break a hip. "But what does this have to do with the tea?"

"Oh, yes, the tea." Jan let out a frazzled laugh. "That's the whole reason I called. You see, Mr. Grenville has some dietary restrictions, so the menu will need to be tweaked. When is Ms. Gwyneth due back?"

"Not for three weeks." I pressed a hand to my belly, coaxing it to stop its sudden churning at this unexpected kink in the works. I cleared my throat, which was tightening more each second. "Exactly what kind of dietary restrictions are we talking about?"

"Let's see." I heard the rustling of papers as Jan checked her notes. "He requires English breakfast tea only, absolutely no Earl Grey. He's on a low-salt diet on account of his high blood pressure, and he has an intense dislike for whipped cream. Oh, and absolutely no strawberries. He's allergic to them."

"I see." My response was all of two syllables, and neither one of them came out sounding remotely calm, and for good reason. A quick scan of the currant scones ingredients list left me hollow inside. Tons of salted butter and generous dollops of both strawberry jam and homemade whipped cream. Not to mention the note that they were best served with a steaming cup of Earl Grey, because of course they were. "Jan, have you actually seen the menu for the authors' tea? This isn't a tweak you're talking about. It's an entire reworking."

"Is it?" She said it a nervous way that suggested she'd known all along how much work she was asking me to do but was hoping I'd be too polite to call her out on it. "But you can do it, right?"

I wanted to shout no, but I couldn't let Aunt Gwen

down. Fighting back panic, I ran my thumb along the pages of the grimoire. I had no idea how to pull it off, but with its centuries of family wisdom, there had to be a useful recipe or two in there somewhere, right? I was going to have to take a leap of faith. "I think I can manage something. Just as long as there aren't any other changes."

"Nothing else, I promise. It'll be thirty people, max, and James Thorne will set up the tables in the back room of his bookshop, the same as he does every year. It should be a piece of cake."

Yeah, a piece of whole wheat, gluten-free, organic cake. Would my old-fashioned family grimoire even know what to make of such a newfangled request? "Okay, I'll do my best. I should have a revised menu for you by Thursday morning."

"Great. Thanks, Tamsyn." I was just about to hang up when Jan's voice rang out again. "Oh, one more thing. Do you have a room available for Mr. Grenville and his fiancée?"

"We're booked solid on account of the festival." A strangled sound coming through the phone immediately made me worry the woman had swallowed her own tongue in a fit, so I rushed to add, "But with Aunt Gwen out of town, I guess I could sleep in her room and make mine available."

"Does the inn have an executive suite?"

I snorted into the phone as I did a quick mental

inventory of the inn's charmingly folksy accommodations. "Uh, no."

"Oh, dear. Mr. Grenville specifically requested an executive suite."

I hadn't met the man yet, but I'd already had just about enough of Mr. Grenville and his requests. "This is Summerhaven Island. I know you're new to the festival and might not know a lot about the area, so let me just tell you now that I doubt you're going to find anything like that. Perhaps he'd be better off renting a house for his visit."

"I've already tried, but everything's full. Isn't there anything you can do?"

I blew out a breath, sending a loose strand of flaming red hair flying from my forehead. No matter how badly I wanted to tell her to go jump in the bay, I was a Bassett. While I had little hope of not screwing up the new tea menu, the least I could do was uphold my family's reputation for hospitality. "I can't promise an executive suite, whatever that is, but I do have two rooms with an adjoining door. The smaller one's just a storage room at the moment, but I think I can clear out the boxes and turn it into a sitting area with a desk, if you think that will work." I'd still have to give up my bedroom to one of the other guests, but it's not like Jan seemed troubled by those types of details, so I didn't mention it.

"That would be perfect," Jan assured me, the relief in her voice taking some of the sting out of the inconvenience that my VIP guest was posing. "You're a real lifesaver."

I ended the call and set the phone on the counter. At some point during my conversation, Lillian and Gus had disappeared to wherever it was they went when not tormenting me, but when I turned to face the grimoire, I found that both had rematerialized. Lillian leaned casually against the stove while Gus, much to my dismay, was prancing across the open cookbook, leaving a trail of paw-shaped smudges on the pages as he went. Though he could sometimes be every bit as incorporeal as his ghostly companion, other times he was very much a regular, flesh-and-blood cat. Everything about Gus was a mystery to me, but between the dirt and the fur, perhaps the hardest thing to figure out was how he managed to make such a mess wherever he went.

"Gus!" I scolded, although I'm not sure why I bothered. The only effect it had was to make him stop in his tracks and sit his ample, fluffy rear end down in the middle of my magical book. "Lillian, can you do something about your cat?"

"Ah, lighten up. He's only trying to help."

"Help?" I spluttered, swatting the air just above his tail in an effort to make him move. "That's the last thing I need."

Eventually, he stood and stretched before moving so slowly from his spot that I was certain he was deliberately trying to provoke me. When I was finally able to see what his fur had obscured, it turned out to be a lemon layer cake recipe that somehow met every single one of Sebastian Grenville's dietary preferences. All I had to do was leave the salt out of the frosting, and I was set. So, fine. The darn cat had been trying to help after all. But did he have to be so obnoxious about it? Now I had to be grateful to the little cuss, which annoyed me to no end.

I rubbed my temples as I studied the untested recipe. It was Wednesday, meaning I had three days to get it right, with no Aunt Gwen to ask for help. Any halfway competent kitchen witch would be able to master it in a fraction of that time. I, on the other hand, was fairly certain I'd just been pushed from the proverbial frying pan right into the flames.

CHAPTER TWO

The Owl and Quill Bookshop occupied a prime location at the edge of Summerhaven's Main Street, overlooking the village green from the front and scenic Turner Pond from the rear, where an airy sunroom doubled as a gathering place for special events. When I arrived at the shop on Thursday morning, I found the space was already equipped with several round tables, and as soon as they were draped with white linens and topped with crystal vases of fresh-cut roses, the room would be a lovely venue for the annual authors' tea. Lucky for me, the festival committee was responsible for the lion's share of the details. All I had to do was provide the treats and avoid any major disasters. Considering my track record where cooking was concerned, even *that* small feat would probably turn out to be easier said than done.

The shop's owner, James Thorne, was something of a local celebrity. He was a colorfully quirky figure, a dapper gentleman of nearly forty who was never without a pair of suspenders and a tweed newsboy cap. He'd written a series of travel memoirs several years back that still sold well with the outdoorsy adventurers who often made day trips to the island for swimming and hiking. Every so often, he would give an interview for the public radio station on the mainland or attend a book signing in Portland, and framed photos of him at such events were proudly displayed on the wall behind the register.

Though the shelves were brimming with an impressive selection of titles, the purpose for my visit that day was not to buy a book but a jar of preserves. That might seem like a strange thing to find in a bookstore, but James had a sister who ran a home canning business and he'd given her some space near the front of the shop to display her wares. Aunt Gwen had placed an order for a dozen jars of strawberry jam for the authors' tea, but with the new dietary guidelines, I was a woman in search of a plan B. I studied the rack of *Pam's Jams* intently, grabbing a jar of deep crimson raspberry and adding it to the apricot I already held in my hand. I was debating whether to get the black chokeberry, too, when James Thorne slid into place behind the counter.

"Well, hello there, Ms. Bassett." A jovial smile accompanied his formal greeting, the corners of his mouth disappearing beneath his impeccably groomed handlebar mustache. "You here to pick up your aunt's order?"

"Actually, I hope it isn't too much of an inconvenience, but I need to make a slight change. I'm afraid the keynote speaker has a strawberry allergy."

The smile faded from James's face, replaced by a look of confusion. "Keynote speaker? But, I'm the keynote speaker."

I tensed, wondering whether I'd gotten something wrong. I cleared my throat and proceeded with the utmost caution. "Have you spoken with Jan recently?"

"As a matter of fact, I was going to call her today because I haven't heard from her yet about the particulars of my speech, but," his voice trembled, "I've been the festival's keynote speaker for almost ten years."

"You know, I wouldn't worry too much," I said, projecting more reassurance than I felt. "It's just I thought Jan told me yesterday that Sebastian Grenville would be giving the keynote address, but I may not have all my facts straight."

"Sebastian Grenville?" James's expression turned to stone, causing me to shift my weight uncomfortably from one foot to the other. He most definitely did not consider this welcome news.

"Yes. I assume you've heard of him?"

"You could say that," he replied stiffly. He stood in brooding silence for a moment before giving his head a slight shake. He attempted to plaster a cordial smile on his face. The effort fell far short of succeeding, but I pretended not to notice as he gathered up the jars of jam I'd placed on the counter. "Will this be all for you today?"

"Yes. I'll be back for more as soon as I decide which flavor I need." I handed over my money once he'd totaled the sale, then stuffed my change into the front pocket of my jean shorts, the September air still being warm enough to get away with summer clothing for a few more weeks. Before turning to leave, I hesitated, struck by the hurt and disappointment that still lingered on the shopkeeper's face. "You know, James, I probably got something wrong. You should give Jan a call. Maybe it wasn't the keynote address she meant, after all."

He brightened a little at that. "Maybe you're right. It's probably just a misunderstanding. I can't imagine ol' Bash Grenville's too keen to show his face on the island again after all these years."

I mulled over his comment on the short ride back to the inn. Did he mean to imply that the famous Sebastian Grenville had a connection to Summerhaven Island? Given the way islanders were about things, I would've expected his picture to be splashed all over town if he were one of our own. On the other hand, the nickname James had used suggested he knew the man personally. There had to be more to the story.

I was two-thirds of the way down the inn's crushed-seashell driveway when I spotted Noah sitting in one of the rocking chairs on the front porch. A burst of adrenaline sent my heart into overdrive, and for a moment, I considered turning the wheel of my bicycle toward the thick brush and diving in headfirst so he wouldn't see me. I had no good excuse for why I'd been ignoring his calls, so the wisest course of action, naturally, was to avoid him in person, too. Alas, he lifted a hand in greeting, and I had no option but to continue up to the house.

"Hey there," he called out as I leaned the bike against the side of the house. "I was starting to worry I had the wrong number for you, so I thought I'd swing by on my way home."

"Have you been trying to call? I'm afraid I get terrible reception out here." As if to prove me wrong, a jaunty jingle began to play from deep inside my pocket. Cheeks aflame, I shoved my hand in and shut the phone off without checking to see who it was.

Noah gave me a quizzical look but refrained from shouting *liar, liar, pants on fire*, which was nice of him under the circumstances. "I've been trying to get a hold of you because I was hoping to ask…"

Here it comes. I held my breath, knowing there was no way I'd be able to say no to a date directly to his face.

"See, the thing is, I was hoping to get your help."

"My help?" I'd never heard a date referred to in quite that way before, but okay.

"Yes." He shifted nervously in the rocking chair, an

adorable look of surprise on his face as the seat started to wobble on its runners. I'll be honest. It made me a little giddy that I was going to have to say yes to dinner after all, just as soon as he worked up the courage to ask. "You see, I'm coordinating a fundraiser for the island's flu clinic."

"I see." Was it a fundraising dinner, and if so, would I need a formal dress? I might need Sybil's help on that one.

"In the past we've held a bake sale, which has been very successful, only my receptionist, Ros, is out for the next few weeks and won't be able to head it up, so I guess I was hoping…"

I sank my front teeth into my bottom lip. This was not sounding very much like a date, after all. "You need me to bake something?"

"Would you?" His smile radiated relief. "And if you could possibly check in with some of the volunteers from last year, it would really help."

"Well, I mean, I guess I…" *He wants me to coordinate it, too?* I was beginning to think an invitation to dinner was the least he could offer in exchange.

"If we could raise enough to make sure all the children on the island get free flu shots this year, it would mean so much." He fixed his deep brown, hope-filled eyes on me, and I melted inside like whipped cream frosting under the noon sun.

Well, poo.

"I'd be happy to coordinate the bake sale," I found

myself saying. *I mean, how do you say no to kids, not to mention that puppy dog face of his?* With the changes to the authors' tea, I was a little on edge, but as long as nothing else was added to my plate, I was fairly sure I could handle it.

Once Noah left, after promises to be in touch with all the details soon, I went inside and immediately checked around for my spectral roommate and her demon sidekick—I mean, cat. I'd expected them to be eavesdropping on my conversation with Noah, but I was in luck. Both had seemingly disappeared back into the ether, or wherever it was they went when I couldn't see them. With the house quiet at last, I opened the grimoire and set about studying my new recipes in earnest. First things first: an allergy-approved cake for the authors' tea. I'd located all of the ingredients for the lemon layer cake and was just about to begin measuring when an urgent knock at the front door broke my concentration. I opened it to find a harried, middle-aged woman with her fist raised to strike the door that was no longer in front of her.

"Tamsyn? Jan Prince." She blinked a few times, belatedly lowering her hand and holding it out to shake.

"Jan, what a surprise." What was this, national "drop in unannounced on Tamsyn" day? "What brings you here?"

"I tried calling, but you didn't answer. I was hoping we could talk."

Oops. That must've been the phone call I'd silenced while talking to Noah. My bad.

"Of course." I stood back, ushering her into the front room, but instead of stopping to chat, she paced to the far end of the room, muttering to herself as she went. When she reached the end, she shook her head, pivoted ninety-degrees, and started to pace again. At the next corner, Jan stopped, her shoulders slumping.

"This room won't hold very many people." Without explanation, Jan peered out the large picture window, gazing past the porch to the sprawling green lawn. "What if we did it out there?"

"What exactly are we talking about?" I looked at the grass, but whatever she was envisioning remained a mystery to me.

"There's a problem with the authors' tea."

"Another problem?" I asked, although what I really wanted to ask her was why this was *my* problem. All I was supposed to do was make the food.

"James Thorne has just informed me that the back-room at the Owl and Quill is unavailable this Saturday."

"He did?" I swallowed nervously, feeling suddenly parched. "Why would he do that?"

"Apparently, the news made its way to him about this year's surprise keynote speaker before I had a chance to tell him myself. He *claimed* he'd accidentally double-booked, but..." She tilted her head to one side in a way that said she wasn't buying his excuse.

"Oh, I see." I pressed my lips together firmly and did not elaborate. *Shoot. This might sort of be my problem after all.*

"He's sometimes given the speech himself, from what I hear, and I guess he assumed…"

I nodded, and while I held out hope she hadn't figured out I was the source of the leak, I felt a tickle of guilt, just the same, and was inclined to help her out as much as I could. "And now I take it you'd like to host the tea here? I know the front room isn't huge, especially with all the furniture, but the dining room is quite a bit larger and the table has several extra leaves. We could easily accommodate twenty-five to thirty guests. We seat almost that many for breakfast some mornings."

Jan ran a hand through her cropped, gray hair, which only succeeded in making her appear more frazzled. "Actually, it's a bit higher than that now."

"How much higher?" I squeaked. "The menu I've been working on is for twenty-five people, thirty at the most, like you said on the phone. I can't stretch it much further."

Jan's hand flew to cover her mouth. "Oh my gosh, did I forget to tell you? I've been running around like a crazy person since I checked the registration numbers this morning. Ever since I updated the festival website yesterday to say that Sebastian Grenville would be giving the keynote address at the tea, registrations have been pouring in."

"You know, I don't think The Owl and Quill's space is much bigger than mine, even if James *were* willing to host." I shot her a look that I hope conveyed how very much this situation was *not* my fault. And, was I understanding correctly that she'd had the time to update the website before getting around to telling James he'd been replaced? No wonder he was upset. "Exactly what are you planning to do about this?"

She must have caught onto my lack of sympathy for her because Jan's demeanor did a one-eighty, from barking commands to full-on pleading, in about the time it took for me to blink. "Is there any way you could possibly be so gracious as to host the event on your lawn? I have access to a tent, one of those big ones like you use for weddings. I can get it shipped from the mainland on the first ferry tomorrow. Tables, chairs, and linens, too, enough for let's say a hundred and fifty, since tickets are still on sale through tomorrow night."

"A hundred and…fifty?" I sucked in my breath. Even as a worst-case scenario, that number was much higher than I'd expected. I didn't even know that many people, and I certainly had never cooked for a crowd of that size. "I can't possibly prepare and serve afternoon tea for a hundred and fifty people by myself."

Jan stared at me blankly as the seconds ticked past, until all at once it was like the light switch had gone back on in her brain. "I'll increase your fee, naturally.

Not just for the extra food but enough to hire more help. Plus, a bonus."

At the word *bonus*, my ears perked up immediately. Thanks to Aunt Gwen's thoughtfulness, my finances may not have been quite as dire as they were in June when I'd left Cleveland to move to the island, but it wasn't like I was in a position to turn up my nose at a little extra cash, either. "Okay. Let me make a few calls so I know for certain I can find enough helpers, but assuming I can, I guess I can do it."

"The tent and everything?" Jan asked, as if suspecting my sudden cooperation was a little too good to be true.

I nodded with my eyes shut, already regretting it. "You can put it out front, but I'll need you to take care of all the setup and cleanup, including the tables, chairs, and all the dishes, same as it would've been at the Owl and Quill."

"Absolutely." Jan's grin shone with pure relief. "The crew will be here in the morning, and all the work will be done well before Mr. Grenville and his fiancée check-in that afternoon."

Right. Somehow it had managed to slip my mind for a moment that, in addition to learning new recipes and preparing a spread that was five times bigger than what I'd been expecting, I had about twenty-four hours to transform a humble storage room into a space worthy of the title *executive suite*. And had I honestly agreed to coordinate a bake sale, too? It was like I'd forgotten how to use the word no. I had no idea how it was all going to happen, but at least, thanks to my newfound status as an honest-to-goodness witch, I knew the first call I was planning to make. After all, what was a coven for if not to come to the rescue at times like this?

SYBIL STUDIED THE STORAGE ROOM WITH AN expert eye as I held my breath, waiting for her assessment of the space. My fellow coven member was the most creative and capable woman I'd ever met, but as I took in the dusty boxes and shabby bits of furniture that filled the unused room, I feared the task of converting it into a workspace worthy of a famous author was beyond even her abilities. I, for one, hadn't the foggiest idea what an executive suite was even meant to look like.

I held my breath for so long I started to see little black speckles in the corners of my eyes, until finally, she spoke. "I can work with this." My spirits soared as my friend flashed a smile nearly as shiny as her platinum hair. For all her assurances that her inherited talent for glamour magic had nothing to do with her perfectly coiffed appearance, I secretly had my doubts.

"You're sure?" My heart had already begun to beat faster as I anticipated disappointment, and now I was nearly shaking from the good news. "I know it's an awful mess."

"This is nothing. You should have seen the state of my shop when I first started," she replied. "It was a hundred times worse than this."

"That's hard to imagine." I pictured the chic yet cozy vintage clothing store my friend had opened over the summer. It had only been in business two months, but somehow, in that short timespan, it had earned a full page spread in the Style section of *The New York Times*. My own new career endeavors hadn't met with quite the same level of success, but I consoled myself with the knowledge that I hadn't blown anything up in a good, long time. Weeks, at least. "So, you think this will be able to pass muster with our fussy guest?"

"Darling, when I've finished, it won't just be an executive suite. It'll be a *presidential* suite, at the very least. You can count on it."

I laughed at the utter confidence she portrayed, but I didn't doubt she was right. Sybil was just that type of person who you knew could get the job done. If it weren't for her charm, she would be annoying as heck. "I can't thank you enough. I never could have done this on my own."

"Don't be silly," she said with a wave of her hand. "That's what covens are for. Besides, this is my kind of project. I don't envy you one bit having to cook all that food for so many people. Then again, you're a kitchen witch, so that type of thing is pretty much your specialty, lucky for you."

"Yeah. Lucky me." I croaked out a nervous laugh. Though I hadn't hidden my disasters where kitchen magic was concerned, I hadn't exactly been forthcoming about just how deeply I doubted my heritage, either. How could I be? Aunt Gwen had made it clear that the entire magical future of Pinecroft Cove pretty much rested on my ability to take her place. If anyone knew how much of a fraud I was, I'd probably be kicked out of the coven on the spot, if not booted from the island for good. Then what?

"I guess I'd better get to it." I squared my shoulders, attempting to summon even a small fraction of my friend's natural confidence. I might not have been born with the skills the women in my family were expected to possess, but I was determined to learn what I could.

Cassandra had been quiet, perhaps as overwhelmed by the untidy space as I had been, but at this point, she turned to me, her deep brown eyes filled with an eager earnestness. "What can I do to help? Anything you need, just ask. I have the house to myself with Mom and Grandma gone, and frankly, I could use a distraction."

What I'd come to love about Cass was that, while she lacked Sybil's take-charge attitude, she was a champ at pitching in and getting work done. This was lucky for me, because work was something I had plenty of to go around.

She followed me downstairs to the kitchen, where a towering pile of ingredients eclipsed the counter. The grimoire sat open to the next recipe on my list, taking up the last remaining inches of space. "Is *this* enough of a distraction for you, do you think?" I asked.

She blinked several times before responding, managing to keep any trace of whatever panic she might have been experiencing out of her voice. "When is this tea again?"

"Saturday. I've whipped up a few test batches and it all tastes okay, but the magic isn't setting quite right." My cheeks tingled as I confessed the worst of it in a near-whisper. "No matter what I do, fifteen minutes after eating, I start burping soap bubbles."

I could see Cass's mental wheels spinning as she pondered this detail, and the empathy in her expression was reassuring. I would've died from embarrassment confessing it to Sybil, who seemed to learn new spells just by looking at them, but Cass had been upfront about her own struggles with magic, so I felt we were kindred spirits.

"Do you think it's supposed to do that?" When I shook my head, Cass's expression grew grim. "Right. Probably not. Have you considered, like, skipping the magic part, and just baking a cake?"

My eyes widened. "You mean, not work the spells? Just...cook?"

"Exactly. We can't all be as talented as Sybil, and I, for one, know exactly how hard it is to get these things right, especially under pressure. So, maybe put that special spoon of yours away." She gestured toward the intricately carved, magical spoon my aunt had presented to me to help me hone my craft. "Close up the grimoire, and see if your aunt has an old Betty Crocker cookbook hiding around here somewhere."

"I couldn't do that," I argued, the words tapering off as I realized what a brilliant plan it was. Just because I was supposed to be able to work magic in the kitchen didn't necessarily mean it was required... did it? "Is that allowed?"

Cass shrugged. "My family runs a tearoom. We bake stuff all the time, and none of it has any of that kitchen witch stuff going on. It just tastes good. Is there really a rule that says you have to make it magical just because you're a witch?"

I considered for a moment and couldn't remember any time I'd been told for a fact I had to do spells when I baked. I'd just assumed. "Well, I guess not. It sure would help with getting things done. I'm up to my eyeballs in work as it is, and I still have no idea how I'm going to serve a hundred and fifty people all by myself."

"You haven't hired help yet?"

"I made a couple calls, but I haven't had any luck. Sheila at the diner thought she might have a few wait-resses to spare, but it turns out two of her summer girls left earlier than usual for the mainland this year and she's short-staffed. At least that's what she claimed. Or maybe she's still upset with me about landing her sister in jail." It was one of the downsides I hadn't considered when I'd launched headfirst into my short stint as a crime solver. Things get a little awkward when your meddling puts someone's loved one behind bars, no matter how deserving of it they may have been. It really was a good thing I was done sticking my nose into other peoples' business. Summerhaven was a small island, and the way I'd started out, I might end up with no friends if I kept it up.

"Have you tried Happy Helpers?"

I frowned. "What's that?"

"It's a new temporary staffing agency on the island. We used them a few times this summer when we had sold-out teas, and the people they sent were very good." Cass pulled her phone from her pocket. "I'll text you the number. I'm sure they can find you some help."

As I dialed the Happy Helpers agency, I let out a breath, feeling as though a weight had been lifted from my chest. Thanks to Cassandra's genius, I had no more magical baking headaches looming over me, and no more staffing worries, either. And as soon as Sybil finished decorating the room upstairs, I would be free to enjoy a visit from a world-renowned author under my very own roof. When I'd moved to Summerhaven

Island, I'd felt like I was under a curse, but it seemed clear to me at that moment that the tide was finally turning. I was so busy congratulating myself on the return of my good fortune that I didn't pause for a moment to consider what could possibly go wrong.

Such a classic rookie mistake.

CHAPTER THREE

"It's..." My mouth gaped as I took in what had, just the day before, been little more than a threadbare bedroom and dingy storage closet. It was now Friday morning, and the space was unrecognizable. Sybil eyed me expectantly while I struggled to find the right words to describe the upscale, art-deco-inspired oasis in front of me. "It's amazing. When Sebastian Grenville and his fiancée arrive later today, there's no way they won't be impressed. But, I have no idea how you managed it."

She pressed her fingers to her lips to suppress a giggle. "I'll admit I even surprised myself this time. It's not at all what I pictured going in, but once I started working, it just came to me like—"

"Let me guess, like magic?" I lifted an eyebrow wryly at my word choice, but we were, after all, witches, and there was absolutely no way this transformation had occurred without some major supernatural intervention.

Sybil laughed heartily. "Exactly."

My eyes shifted from the gleaming wood of the antique bed, past the gold velvet draperies that hung in thick folds from the windows, and settled on the sturdy yet feminine desk and upholstered chaise lounge that turned the former storage room into an inviting space for work or relaxation. I was certain I'd never seen either of them before. "Where on earth did you even get this stuff?"

"Here and there throughout the house, and a few things from the attic," Sybil said with a shrug. "Now that you've let me see what you have hiding up there, you might never get rid of me."

"Now that I've seen how much better you are at finding treasure, I might never let you leave." I bit my lower lip, suddenly realizing that, with the room done hours ahead of schedule, there was another task I would love to pawn off on my extroverted friend. "Except, I was kinda hoping I could get you to run over to Owl and Quill for me."

"You're having a book emergency?" she asked with a healthy dose of skepticism.

"No, a jam emergency. I need a dozen jars of Pam's raspberry jam for tomorrow, but now that the entire island knows I'm hosting the tea, I'm too chicken to show my face in the shop. James Thorne is fuming over it, and I'm afraid I've made myself an enemy for life."

"Oh, James is a teddy bear," she replied with a laugh. "Besides, he's always had a crush on me, so I'm probably safe from his wrath."

"A crush?" My ears perked up immediately. "Please, go on."

"It's nothing." Sybil gave her head a dismissive shake, but there was no mistaking the sudden blush of pink that had flooded her cheeks. I was pretty sure James wasn't the only one who was smitten.

"Well, since you're on such *friendly* terms with dear Mr. Thorne," I teased, "maybe you could extend an invitation to him for tomorrow? I'd rather there weren't any hard feelings about this whole festival speaker snafu, at least not where the Pinecroft Inn is concerned. Aunt Gwen loves *Pam's Jams* and would kill me if we had to find a new supplier."

"Not a problem. I'll take care of—" Sybil's eyes doubled in size as a loud clattering followed by a noise like the sound of a dentist's drill set to maximum volume pierced the morning quiet. "What was that?"

"I think the tent crew has arrived," I said with a groan. A quick glance out the window confirmed my suspicion. A large truck had pulled onto the front lawn, and I could just make out Jan's head behind a pile of shiny silver poles as she instructed a group of men on where to set it up. "This is going to be a long day."

"I'd stay and chat, but..." Sybil ducked out of the room without finishing her thought, and I heard the front door click closed just as another burst from the dentist's drill sent a shiver down my spine.

Seconds ticked by, but instead of returning to normal, my quaking intensified as the air around me grew increasingly colder, until I had to wrap my arms across my chest to soothe the gooseflesh that had erupted on my bare arms. At the same time, the space around me shifted slightly, almost imperceptibly, like the room had become trapped inside a bowl of clear Jello that someone had given a good shake. When the jiggling stopped, Lillian stood, Gus curled in a ball at her feet, in the middle of a delicately patterned, oval rug that had definitely not been in the room the day before, and to be honest, I couldn't even swear it had existed at all prior to that very moment. It wasn't the only change, either. As the room came more into focus, I noticed the phone was missing from the night-stand, and the sound of workmen outside had been replaced by the chatter of birds.

Lillian caught my eye and grinned, spreading her arms out wide. "How do you like it?"

"What exactly is this?" I asked warily, suddenly feeling oddly out of place in my own home.

"My bedroom, of course." She let out a contented sigh as she sank into the quilt on the bed. "Oh, how I've missed it."

"You mean your bedroom, as in the one you had in

the 1920s?" Realization struck me with the force of a physical blow. "You're the one behind Sybil's sudden burst of inspiration."

Lillian shot me a saucy look from beneath her smoky eyelids. Though it was not yet noon, she was, I couldn't help but notice, dressed in a gown and full vamp makeup as if ready for a night on the town. "But, of course."

The room around me wobbled, bringing about an instant return of the Jello sensation, and with it an unsteadiness in my legs so unexpected and pronounced that my arm shot out toward the night-stand so I could steady myself. My fingers stung as they made contact with the phone that hadn't been there moments before. All at once, the birdsong was replaced by the ringing of hammers, and the wide pine floorboards shone brightly, now lacking both the floral-print rug and the napping cat.

"What just happened?" I asked, bringing my smarting fingers gingerly to my lips as if to kiss away the pain. "I feel strange, sort of dizzy."

"Sorry about that, but we couldn't hang around 1929 forever."

Somehow, the revelation I'd just been an unwitting time traveler didn't surprise me nearly as much as it probably should have. I simply looked at the bare floor and shook my head. "Pity. That was a nice rug."

"Oh, it's around here somewhere," Lillian said with a dismissive wave of the hand.

"I doubt it," I replied, not because I knew for sure this was true, but more because I was annoyed and felt like being disagreeable. She really thought it was okay to drag me almost a hundred years into the past without so much as a word of warning?

"Try the attic." She was still seated on the bed, studying her fingernails nonchalantly and not even bothering to make eye contact. She was such a rude ghost sometimes.

"I've been all through the attic already and never saw it. Plus, even if it were here, it would be almost a hundred years old. It would probably be ruined." My voice trailed off as I took a closer look at my surroundings, which sparkled with a newness the items couldn't have possessed after a century in storage. The velvet drapes were plush and luxurious, without so much as a single crease or moth hole. The bedding was crisp and fresh, though it was identical to what I'd just seen in 1929, and the bed itself, along with the nightstand and dresser, lacked so much as a single scratch. "Lillian, where exactly did all of this stuff come from?"

"The house, of course."

"*Where* in the house?" I demanded, frustrated by her evasiveness. "Because I've never seen any of it."

"Not where, Tamsyn," she replied with a patronizing tone that managed to kick my annoyance up another notch. "The question is *when*."

"You're telling me you time-traveled Sybil back to

the Jazz Age and made her move your stuff to the present?"

"Of course not. Mortals are terrible at time travel. Such an energy drain." The observation that I was mortal and yet had just hopped through time with relative ease niggled at the back of my mind, but I kept it to myself, figuring if I raised the question, I might not like the answer.

"So, how did this get here?" I asked instead, gesturing around me.

"I simply showed her a quick glimpse of what the room had looked like and then moved the pieces here myself for her to find."

"Really?" My eyes narrowed. "It was as simple as that?"

"Well, no," she admitted. "It's not simple at all. It's hard to control and very draining. But I wanted my things."

"Can't you just slip back in time on your own and see them whenever you want?" Honestly, I'd assumed that's where she went whenever I couldn't see her, but as Lillian shook her head sadly, I realized that wasn't the case.

"I can see it, but I'm not really there. I miss it."

The greater portion of my annoyance fizzled away at this admission, as I saw Lillian for the bewildered and homesick girl she was behind her brash bravado and heavy makeup. It occurred to me that she was probably no more comfortable with being a disembodied spirit than I was with being a witch. "So, what's happened to the rug?"

"Try the hall closet."

Now, normally I don't like being bossed around by a ghost, but the vulnerability in her tone was too much to ignore. With a resigned slump of my shoulders, I turned and headed down the stairs. Sure enough, when I opened the closet door off the front entryway, I was greeted by the sight of a rolled-up rug, with a furry black cat snoozing alongside. The closet hinge squeaked, and Gus opened one emerald eye.

"Hey there, buddy," I said. "I see you made it in one piece."

He closed his eye in response, very much unfazed by his recent jaunt through time and space. I couldn't help but wonder whether it was Lillian's power that made the journeys possible or if it could possibly be Gus who was calling the shots. He was a sneaky sort of cat, and I wouldn't put it past him.

I'd no sooner gotten the rug in place upstairs than the sound of the doorbell sent me scurrying down again. The closet was empty now, Gus having gone wherever it was he went when I wasn't looking, and I shut that door and opened the front one simultaneously. On the front porch stood a woman dressed in a sensible pair of khaki pants and a navy blue polo shirt with *Happy Helpers* stitched across the left chest. She was no more than five feet tall, if that, with a mousy brown pixie cut and no makeup, and I might have mistaken her for a young boy had it not been for the flecks of gray in her hair and the cheerful, feminine voice that greeted me.

"Ms. Bassett? I'm Vera Stone from the Happy Helpers agency." She stuck out her hand, and as I shook it, I was surprised by her strength, and the doubts that had been forming as to whether she was up to the task of waiting tables for the large crowd we were expecting quickly dissipated.

"It's nice to meet you, Vera. Please come in." A particularly deafening clatter arose from the workmen on the lawn, making me cringe and shut the door as soon as she was inside. "Sorry about that. They're setting up for tomorrow."

She nodded, seemingly unbothered by the melee. "It looks like you're getting a big crowd."

"A lot bigger than I know what to do with," I admitted. "Do you have serving experience?"

She pulled her shoulders back, maximizing what little height she had. "Absolutely. I've been a waitress in two restaurants on the island, plus spent several summers working weddings for a caterer, and I've also cleaned houses and have some light administrative experience."

"Wow. I think you might be more qualified for this gig than I am. These weddings you did, were they big ones?"

"The largest had over three hundred guests. It was

a cousin of one of the Kennedys," she added with a meaningful look.

"You mean *those* Kennedys?" If Vera had managed to serve twice as many guests while working for relatives of a president of the United States, I had every ounce of confidence she could handle a simple authors' tea. "I think you're my new best friend."

Vera laughed and opened her mouth to reply, but before she could speak, we were both jolted by a violent pounding on the front door.

"It must be one of the workers," I guessed.

"Why don't I just see myself into the kitchen and start to get acquainted with everything?" she suggested, and I nodded gratefully, thanking my lucky stars for having been sent such a proficient and reliable helper.

The pounding repeated, and I flung the door open, prepared to give a piece of my mind to the member of the crew whose impatience was threatening to put a crack in the inn's solid oak door, but the scolding words died in my throat at the sight of a well-dressed man of around forty and a woman who appeared to be a decade or so his junior, standing amidst a towering pile of expensive looking luggage. The man was red in the face, but for some reason I got the impression it was the woman who had done most of the lifting and carrying.

"What the hell is all this racket?" the man said, his flush cheeks intensifying to an alarming shade of scarlet. At first, I thought he was yelling at me, but then he turned to face his companion, who withered visibly at the attention. "I specifically said I needed peace and quiet."

"Can I help you?" I choked, as much in exasperation over this stranger's behavior as in confusion over who these people were.

"Sebastian Grenville," he announced with the air of someone who was used to his name being introduction enough. I waited a beat for him to introduce his companion, but when he failed to do so, I raised my eyebrows and gave her a pointed look, at which he added, "And Jacqueline Cortez."

"His fiancée," she mumbled without enthusiasm.

Yikes. "I apologize for the chaos outside," I told him, not bothering to thaw the ice from my tone, "but our usual check-in time isn't until after three."

"I assume our suite is ready now," he stated, one foot already over the threshold without invitation. It hadn't been phrased as a question, and somehow, I wasn't surprised. I wanted to snap at him that no, it was not, but the look of weary mortification on his fiancée's face made me think better of it.

"It's just up the stairs, to your right," I directed, since Sebastian Grenville had already made it several steps into the living room and there was no way I could get ahead of him to lead the way. I looked in sympathy at his companion, who had been left to gather up the bags. "You can leave those there, Ms. Cortez. I'll make sure they get up to the room."

"He's nervous about the book launch," she explained with a weak smile. This was certainly not the first time in her life she'd apologized on this man's behalf. Heck, it probably wasn't even the first time that day. With a fuse as short as his, was it any wonder he had high blood pressure?

"Can I bring you some tea?" I offered, not certain why except that her defeated demeanor inspired me to help, and it was the first thing that came to mind.

"That would be so nice," she responded with a contented sigh. "Thank you."

"Who was that?" Vera asked when I entered the kitchen. She held an open notebook in one hand and a pencil in the other. She appeared to have been in the middle of making an inventory of Aunt Gwen's serving platters before being interrupted.

"Our guests of honor," I said, biting back any additional commentary. I grabbed the teakettle from the stove and crossed to the sink to fill it. "I hate to ask, but would you mind helping me get their luggage upstairs? I'll be there in a second, as soon as I get some water going for tea."

"Don't be silly," Vera responded pleasantly. "I'll take care of the bags. You focus on the tea."

"Are you sure? There's quite a bit sitting on the front porch, and some of it looks heavy."

"I'll be fine. I can lift and carry anything, but between you and me, I'm a terrible cook."

You and me both, sister, I said inside my head, while all I said aloud was, "Thanks."

I grabbed a plain white porcelain pot off the shelf and searched the cupboard for a fresh tin of English Breakfast tea, which I found beside a bottle of dried chamomile flowers. As I took them both into my hands, I recalled a page from the grimoire with herbs for common ailments. Chamomile promised sleep and healing, I knew, and after a quick look at the page to refresh my memory, I returned to find lavender, St. John's wort, and celandine. The first two were for Ms. Cortez, to reduce anxiety and elevate mood, while the third I'd chosen especially for Mr. Grenville. Technically, it was a treatment for hemorrhoids, but I figured the man had already made himself a big enough pain in my rear end that it couldn't hurt to try. I brewed enough tea for two, giving the special ingredients a quick stir with my magic spoon while hoping for a quiet evening and better behavior from my cantankerous author once the rest of the guests had arrived.

CHAPTER FOUR

By the time evening came, the Pinecroft Inn once again had a full house, and then some. The tent and tables were set up outside, and once the workers had departed in the afternoon, I'd taken advantage of a few quiet moments to move my personal belongings out of my bedroom and into Aunt Gwen's room. I then set about whipping up some platters of cheese, crackers, and fruit, along with uncorking several bottles of wine to welcome the arrivals for the literary festival.

This was a favorite food ritual I'd devised, which had the advantage of looking impressive while not requiring me to actually cook anything or perform any magic spells to put the room in a good mood. It was one of the many little tricks I'd learned to hide my shortcomings as a kitchen witch, and that evening, I was greatly relieved to see it was working exactly as planned. All of the inn's guests had gathered in a circle in the living room, with Sebastian Grenville occupying a place of honor in the armchair next to the fireplace. Though it was still technically summer, there was a chill in the air that evening, and a small fire crackled cozily in the hearth. There were several older couples, plus about a dozen single women who were members of the same book club on the mainland—one, I was assured, where they actually read the books along with their wine and gossip. The one thing that every guest had in common was the surprised facial expressions that grew dreamier with every surreptitious glance at the famous author. Finally, one silver-haired lady gathered up enough courage to hold out a tattered copy of *Magnolia Sunset* with a pen on top.

"Mr. Grenville," she asked haltingly, "would you mind autographing this for me?"

Now, even though the man had emerged from his room a good seventy percent more human than when he'd arrived, I still braced myself for a fresh onslaught of bombastic ego. I prepared to leave my post in the dining room, where I usually hovered silently until I was needed, being absolutely certain I would need to provide a distraction before things got ugly. Instead, I was shocked to see Sebastian take the book and pen and graciously scribble his name across the title page. Even more surprising, instead of handing it back, he took his reading glasses from his pocket and cracked the book open to a carefully chosen spot in the middle.

He looked mildly around the room at the audience that waited in rapt silence. "Would anyone mind if I read a few of my favorite passages aloud?"

Eyes widened, and here and there a jaw outright dropped as the guests did their best imitation of what it would look like to tell a roomful of people they'd just won the lottery. I simply stared, unable to believe this was the same man who had fumed in the entryway and berated his fiancée just a few hours before. Had my magical tea really had that great an effect on such a seemingly rotten disposition? If so, I'd need to make a note of the recipe in the family grimoire before I forgot.

Just as the author cleared his throat to begin, I felt Vera come up behind me. "What's he doing?" she whispered.

Immediately, I turned and placed a finger to my lips, then shot an apologetic glance at Sebastian, who smiled indulgently and began to read. Both Vera and I remained rooted in place for several minutes as he read, until finally I heard her retreat to the kitchen, but not before I detected some quiet sniffling. She was hardly alone in this. My own eyes were misty from the beauty of his prose, and a few of the guests were openly weeping.

The clock on the mantle had just struck nine when Sebastian finally closed the book and handed it back to its owner. "Time for bed," he announced, standing and giving a big stretch. As if a spell had been broken, the guests stood and stretched, too, after which the gathering quickly dispersed as they all headed to their rooms for the night. I was turning toward the kitchen when Jacqueline approached.

"I wanted to thank you," she said, "for the tea earlier. I'm not sure what kind it was, but it really hit the spot. I haven't seen Bash this calm in weeks."

"It's a specialty of the house," I said, figuring it was best to leave it at that. It was probably not good business practice to let guests know you'd been using magic on them without their consent, even if it was for their own good.

"I don't suppose we could get another pot, could we?"

"Of course," I replied with my best hostess smile. "I'll bring it right up."

When I entered the kitchen, I saw Vera standing by the sink beside a pile of clean dishes glittering on the rack. She was just polishing the last plate dry with a cotton towel when she paused, probably hearing my footsteps, and discreetly raised the cloth to her face before turning to greet me. Despite her efforts, the puffiness of her lids and faint sheen of moisture on her cheeks gave away how deeply she'd been moved by the reading.

"You could've stayed longer," I told her gently. "The dishes can wait."

"I'd heard all I wanted." Vera sniffed, and for a moment, I thought the conversation was over, but after some time she added, "Do you think, if a man could write words like that, you'd call him a genius?"

I thought about her question as I scooped herbs and tea into a fresh pot. "I suppose I would, yes."

The teakettle whistled, and I went to fetch it from the stove.

"Is this for him?" Vera asked.

"Yes. Jacqueline said it did wonders for him."

"It did seem that way." She watched as I poured the hot water into the pot. "I can take it up, if you'd like."

"Thank you, Vera." I let out a breath as I took in the spotless kitchen and the carefully wrapped platters of baked goods we'd spent the day preparing. "You've been a godsend today. I couldn't have done it without you."

As she put the pot and a teacup on a small silver tray, she smiled but said nothing before heading up the back stairs. Alone in the kitchen, I thumbed through the grimoire as an idea formed in my head. Sebastian Grenville might well be a genius, but he had a terrible temper and I had no desire to encounter it again anytime soon. If I'd had enough herbs in the pantry, I'd be tempted to spike every pot of tea the next day, just to make sure he stayed mellow. Unfortunately, I barely had enough ingredients left for another pot. But what I *did* have was just enough time and expertise to bake up one last treat for the authors' tea. I'd sworn off enchantments in the interest of saving time and my sanity, but everything for the menu was made, and it seemed worthwhile to work just one spell if it was guaranteed to keep a particular author in line.

As if by magic, the pages fell open to the luscious lemon layer cake I'd eyed before. I say *as if* by magic and not actually *by* magic, because the real culprit for it opening where it did was the way Gus had bent the pages when he'd walked across them. Even so, I smiled as my eyes landed on the nearly forgotten recipe. It would be the perfect vehicle for the simple spell I had in mind, and I'd practiced it several times already while preparing the tea, so I knew I was likely to get it right. I might not have had all of Aunt Gwen's finesse when it came to cooking, but the success of my calming tea concoction gave me just enough confidence to give it a try. Knowing what a bear Sebastian Grenville could be if left to his own devices, I was certain the one hundred and fifty guests who had paid for an elegant authors' tea would be grateful for my efforts to tame the beast.

I'd awoken to a beautiful Saturday morning, and as I smoothed my fingers over the gossamer fabric of the floral tea dress Sybil had lent me from her shop for the day's festivities, I breathed a sigh of relief. Under the sprawling white tent, fifteen round tables were perfectly set, with vases of pink roses in profusion thanks to the local garden club, each with a sparkling jar of fresh raspberry preserves and its own three-tiered serving stand laden with a dainty assortment of teatime treats compliments of yours truly. I still couldn't believe I'd pulled it off, and if it hadn't been for Vera's help, I knew it wouldn't have happened.

Across the tent, my tireless helper was busy adding a small square of lemon cake on a tiny china plate to each place setting. Somehow that, too, had come together without a hitch. Frankly, I was shocked. I'd been baking well past midnight—casting an untested spell, no less—and yet not a single item in the kitchen had burst into flames. Not even a puff of smoke! The final cake was edible, and even pretty to look at, with swirls of rich, yellow buttercream on top. Whether the magic I'd imbued it with turned out to be effective or not, I was still going to call it a win.

The tables slowly filled as guests made their way from the sun-drenched lawn to the cooling shade beneath the tent. Most everyone was dressed to impress, with some of the women wearing gargantuan hats laden with ribbons and flowers. There was no doubt the authors' tea was the social event of the season on Summerhaven Island this year. As more people filed through, I was elated to see my coven members make their way beneath the tent and to my side.

"It's perfect," effused Sybil, who was dressed in a classic Chanel suit of periwinkle blue topped with a pillbox hat. Coming from her, the compliment meant a lot, as Sybil wasn't always able to hide it when things didn't meet with her exact standards.

"Amazing," agreed Cass, whose own hard work had contributed greatly to the success of the event. She wore a dress of sage green lace and gold hoop earrings with a certain fortune-teller's quality to them that managed to lend just the right amount of witchiness to her ensemble. "Speaking of amazing, have you seen the garden club?"

I frowned, looking around the crowded space. "They're here somewhere. They delivered the center-pieces an hour ago, when I was still inside getting the last of the food ready."

"No," she corrected, "I meant, have you *seen* them?"

My frown deepened as I scanned the sea of faces more closely, my gaze finally landing on Mildred Banning, the club president, who was seated with nine other ladies at a VIP table near the podium. Nothing seemed amiss. "I see them. What exactly are you getting at?"

"Just keep watching," Sybil said pointedly. "You'll see."

It took me a moment to catch on, but once I had, I saw it all right, and it was something I couldn't unsee. Though the women talked and laughed like normal, their faces were frozen stiff except for the occasional eye blink. "They look like those comedy skits on TV where they superimpose moving lips on a photo of a celebrity," I remarked. "What happened?"

"Rumor is it's Botox," Cass said with a snicker. "A whole lot of it."

"Every year over Labor Day weekend," Sybil added, "Mildred hosts an exclusive spa retreat at her house for all of the garden club ladies. This year, someone heard one of the members bragging about how they were going to have a Botox party."

"A Botox party?" I frowned, and as I did so, I became unusually aware of the creases that formed on my own forehead from the action. I ran my fingers across the shallow lines and wondered if a party like that would sound more appealing in twenty years. "I had no idea that was a thing. Don't you need a doctor for that?"

Cass shook her head. "Apparently, you can hire a spa service to do it. It's cheaper than a doctor."

"Based on the results, I think you get what you pay for," Sybil observed. "It's times like these I'm grateful to be a glamour witch. I'll never have to poke needles into my skin to make it look good."

"These parties are all the rage in Los Angeles, from what I've heard," Cass added. "That's where Mildred spends her winters."

Sybil rolled her eyes. "And she'll never let anyone forget it, either. It's all she talks about. So pretentious." Since Sybil's family had multiple homes themselves, I knew it wasn't Mildred's wealth that bothered her, but her lack of good taste in bragging about it.

"Remind me to avoid talking to her, then," I said. "If she can even talk with her face like that."

"Speaking of people you've been avoiding," Sybil said with a sly smile, "there's Noah."

My heart slammed into my ribcage as I turned to see the handsome doctor, who was wearing a sharp navy blazer with khaki pants like some sort of ad for an ivy league college. He looked magnificent, but all I could think of was how my dinner date expectations had fizzled last time we'd spoken, and even though I was on top of my game that day—dressed well and in the middle of pulling off a particularly impressive tea party—I had a sudden irrational fear that talking to him would send it all rolling downhill. That seemed to be our thing.

"I'm not avoiding him," I corrected. "But now really isn't a good time—"

"Noah!" Ignoring my protestations, Sybil waved her hand frantically above her head to capture his attention. "Noah!"

"Why did you do that?" I hissed. Noah waved in return, then motioned for us to come over. "Now look what you've done."

"I thought you weren't avoiding him," she observed in an exasperatingly bland tone.

"I...that's..." I spluttered. As the crowd shifted, I got a better look at the person standing beside him and groaned. It was none other than Sheriff Grady, the one man on Summerhaven Island whom I knew for an absolute fact hated my guts. "Ugh. Not him, too. I promise I'll talk to Noah all you want, but don't make me say hello to Joe Grady."

"Put on your big girl pants, Tamsyn," Sybil scolded, dragging me by the elbow through the crowded tent. I thought Cass was still standing beside me, but she'd slipped away at some point without my noticing, and a frantic search of the crowd revealed she was busy showing Vera something about the table settings for the tea and was, therefore, no use at all in springing me from Sybil's grasp. "You've got to get past whatever this thing is with the sheriff if you're going to make it through the winter on this island."

"It's not my fault," I whined, scuffing the heels of my shoes through the clipped grass to slow our progress. "Ever since the investigation into Douglas Strong's murder ended, he's gone out of his way to be snippy to me, and I have no idea why. I helped him solve the case!"

Sybil paused in her tracks and gave me a pointed look. "Maybe that's the reason. You know everyone on the island's been saying he couldn't have caught the killer without you."

I lifted my chin. "I doubt he could have."

"See, it's that attitude that gets you in trouble. You need to learn that a little bit of sugar goes a long way."

"But you're so much better at it than I am. Can't you just smooth things over with him on my behalf?"

"Like I did with James Thorne yesterday?" Sybil cocked her head, propping a hand on each hip. "Sorry to say, but you're on your own."

"Fine," I muttered under my breath, not putting up a fight as she prodded me the last few yards. She wasn't kidding about leaving me alone. No sooner had I reached my destination than Sybil melted away into the crowd, leaving me to stand directly in front of Noah. He was deep in conversation with the sheriff, who I was surprised to see was jotting down notes in a small tablet.

"And that's when you noticed the keys were missing?" Sheriff Grady asked, in an especially deep and official-sounding tone that I was pretty certain was put on for my benefit.

"Exactly," Noah replied, then turned to me with a lopsided smile that seemed to betray just how harried his day had been. "Hey there, Tamsyn."

"Hi, Noah," I said, shooting a worried glance from the shiny sheriff's badge on Joe Grady's shirt to the notebook in his hand. "I hope I'm not interrupting."

"Of course not," Noah began, but the sheriff cut him off.

"Actually, I was just taking an official statement about an incident at the clinic. So, if you don't mind waiting."

It wasn't what he said, but how he said it that lit a

fire in my belly. My eyes narrowed and a thick syrup of sugary-sweet sarcasm coated my next words. "Maybe you should give me all the details. I have an excellent track record at solving crimes."

Did I intend for Sheriff Grady's cheeks and neck to turn the shade of an overripe tomato? Yes. Yes, I did. Did it feel good to actually witness it happening like I'd envisioned? I mean, I'd like to be able to say that it didn't, and that I regretted my pettiness, but that would be a lie.

"Police reports are no joking matter," the sheriff growled.

"Now, Joe," Noah hastened to soothe, "I honestly don't think there's a need to file a report right now. It's just a missing key. I only mentioned it because there's a chance someone found it and used it to open the supply cupboard. That's all."

"Opened the cupboard? That sounds like larceny to me." The sheriff's eyes lit up like a kid on Christmas morning, and I could tell he was super excited for the chance to show off one of his big boy police words in front of me. "What'd they take? Drugs? Needles?"

"No." Noah shook his head. "I don't think so, anyway. I won't know for sure until I get a locksmith out to get me a new key. It's just, when I looked through the glass, it seemed like something might've been moved around, but I could be wrong. Ros has been out on vacation, so maybe the temporary receptionist I hired put some things back in the wrong place. For that matter, she might've just put the key back in the wrong spot, too."

"Oh." The sheriff's face crumpled a bit as he snapped his notebook shut.

"I shouldn't have troubled you with this until after I thought it all the way through," Noah told him.

"Can't be too cautious." With obvious reluctance, he returned the notebook to his pocket. "Keep me informed of any new developments."

"Of course," Noah assured him. Once the sheriff was gone, he turned his full attention to me, flashing those sheepish grins of his that accentuated the dimple in his cheek and made me go all wobbly from the knees down. "Sorry about that. I didn't realize when I told him about the missing key that he'd take it so seriously."

"Larceny is no joking matter," I replied in my best Sheriff Grady impersonation, eliciting chuckles from both of us that trailed off into awkward silence.

Noah cleared his throat a bit more vigorously than was probably necessary. "Thanks again for agreeing to help with the bake sale. Maybe we could meet up for dinner and work out the details."

"Um…" So, now a dinner date was back on the table? I was getting so confused. Before I could say anything else, the microphone on the podium made one of those high-pitched squealing sounds, saving us both from whatever inane response I'd been about to deliver. I really don't know what I'd been about to say, but let's face it, whatever it was wouldn't have been suave or sophisticated, and I was grateful for the reprieve. "Looks like we're about to start. I guess we'll have to come back to that another time."

I made a beeline for my seat, which one might have expected to be up with the festival VIPs, given the fact I was technically hosting the event and all that. But, apparently, my generosity hadn't held much sway with the festival committee when it had come to seat assignments, so I found myself bobbing around some-where in the middle of the vast sea of tables, chairs, and oversized hats. A quick glance around showed me Cass was three tables to my right, while both Noah and Sybil had been seated at adjacent tables much closer to the front, where I also recognized the members of the garden club. As I settled into my chair and poured a cup of tea, I wondered whether any of them would be able to drink their tea through their stiff lips without dribbling.

The microphone squeaked again, and this time it was closely followed by the sound of Jan Prince's voice, which was met with a polite smattering of applause. "Ladies and gentlemen, the Summerhaven Island Literary Festival is honored to introduce our keynote speaker this afternoon, Mr. Sebastian Grenville."

The applause that followed was significantly more enthusiastic than before, but above the din came a hissing noise. My head whipped around in the direction of the lone heckler. I didn't catch him in the act, but I was positive the sound had come from the table in the very back where James Thorne was sitting. The last thing I needed was for my first solo gig managing the Pinecroft Inn to turn into a disaster. Though I'd intended my lemon cake spell to calm Sebastian, I crossed my fingers beneath the tablecloth, fervently hoping the magic it contained would prove strong enough to mellow James's mood, too. Mercifully, when I turned around again a moment later, James was gone.

As Jan's introduction ended, I turned my attention back to the front of the tent. Sebastian Grenville strolled to the podium, well-dressed in a beige linen suit, crisply starched white shirt, and muted tie. He held a book in one hand and a plate of lemon cake in the other. He set the plate down and popped the last bite of cake into his mouth. From James's table, a loud cough made me cross my fingers tighter. The only thing worse than being banned from buying the island's best jam would be to have a brawl break out between two authors on the front lawn of the inn. With all these witnesses, I'd never live it down.

"Greetings, Summerha—" The author stopped mid-word, placing a hand to his throat. Perhaps the cake hadn't gone down smoothly. He took a sip of water and began again. "It's a dream come true to be back in Summer—"

This time, the man gripped the podium tightly with both hands, and even from the middle of the tent, I could see the sheen of sweat on his brow. He squeezed his eyes shut, then opened them again, the expression on his face as he stared at the open book suggesting he was having trouble seeing. Finally, he straightened up, but instead of beginning his speech once more, he stiffened, rocked back on his heels, and tipped over backward, landing on the grass with a thud. There were gasps all around me, and I watched, heart racing, as Noah dashed to his side.

"Sheriff Grady," Noah's voice boomed from behind the podium, and the sheriff joined him beside the fallen author. They did CPR for an eternity. Not a single person moved, spoke, or even breathed. After a span of time that might have lasted minutes, or possibly years, the roar of an approaching helicopter sounded overhead. A chopper landed in the middle of the lawn, and a team of paramedics loaded Sebastian Grenville onboard.

With a whir of its blades, the helicopter was airborne once more, and with a sinking feeling inside, I realized homemade jam and authors engaging in fisticuffs were now the very least of my concerns. My magic may have poisoned Sebastian Grenville.

CHAPTER FIVE

he phone was cold against my ear, the buzzing ring hollow and distant as I counted. *One. Two. Three. Four.* I burrowed my head into the nest of pillows on Aunt Gwen's bed, resting with eyes closed as I waited for my aunt's voicemail greeting to end. I breathed in the scent of my aunt's favorite potpourri, and a tear pooled in the corner of my eye. I'd made a real mess of things this time. Why did the one witch who would know how to fix it have to be so far away?

"Uh, hi Aunt Gwen," I said when at last I heard the beep. "I was just calling to ask…that is, um, hypothetically, if I was a little overly enthusiastic with a relaxation and calming spell, and let's say a famous author just happened to take a bite and pass out, how exactly…?" Another beep sounded, telling me I had run out of time, and a recorded voice asked if I wished to send the message. I pressed option two for delete and ended the call. This was a conversation best had live.

As I left the bedroom and paced the hall, my footsteps echoed through the empty house. Sheriff Grady had insisted on having all one hundred and forty-eight tea attendees accompany him to the station downtown for questioning. He'd allowed me to remain behind to keep a watch on the inn, but only after an ominous warning that my turn would come. I'd never seen a man look so thoroughly in his element as when he'd led his procession of well-dressed witnesses down the driveway and onto Cove Road. I expected my overnight guests would be returned to me at some point, but I had no idea when. I could only assume the rest of the people who'd sat beneath the tent on the lawn earlier that day were gone for good.

I came to a stop outside the art deco suite that had been occupied by Sebastian Grenville and his fiancée. I wondered what exactly was the protocol for entering a guest's room when said guest was currently in a hospital on the mainland and you might have been the one who put him there. I inched into the room, eyes darting to the rumpled bed. Vera was meant to come up during the tea and do the housekeeping, but understandably in the ensuing chaos, she'd let it slip. I tugged at the covers, pulling them straight and smoothing them as best as I could. It would do for now. I spun from the bed toward the window and screamed.

"Geez, Louise!" Lillian exclaimed. She stood no more than an inch away from me, her sudden materialization into that space being the source of my outcry.

"Do you mind?" I panted, pressing my hand to my chest. "You nearly gave me a heart attack."

"Well, that caterwauling you made was loud enough to wake the dead." She paused a beat, then broke into a grin. "Get it? Wake the dead?"

I rolled my eyes, in no mood for childish humor. "You can't just go around sneaking up on me like that. I might've walked right into you. Or, wait. Would it be *through* you?"

Lillian cocked her head to one side. "You know, I'm not sure. Wanna give it a try and see?"

"Absolutely not!"

"Listen, bluenose, I was just trying to *liven* things up." There was a sly twinkle in her eye that faded as the seconds ticked by, and I once again failed to laugh at her ghost humor. "Say, why's it so quiet around here? Isn't today that author sockdollager?"

"If by that unpronounceable word you mean the tea, then yes." My breath came out as a whistling groan. "Right up to the point where I accidentally sent the guest of honor to the hospital."

Lillian's perfectly rouged lips fell open so wide I could see her tonsils. "How'd you manage that?"

"I tried a little spell, and I think I messed up. He took one bite of my enchanted cake and fell over backward, stiff as a board."

"That's not what the spell was supposed to do?"

"Of course, that's not what the spell was supposed to do," I snapped. "What kind of witch are you?"

I'd meant it as a dig, but a thoughtful expression crossed Lillian's face as she grew unusually quiet. "I'm not really sure. Back when I was alive, I just sorta did as I pleased."

Like she didn't do the same now. "Some help you are," I muttered.

"Is that author guy gonna be okay?"

I swallowed hard as I gave a slight shrug. "I don't know."

"I've got an idea. Let's ankle over to the police station and see what's going on."

"What exactly is ankle, other than what your foot's attached to?"

"To walk, silly."

"Walk? You're a ghost," I replied with a laugh. Now who was the silly one? "First, you don't actually have feet, and second, aren't you, like, stuck in the house you're haunting or something?"

Lillian pursed her lips, clearly not amused. "I'll have you know I'm not haunting anything, okay? That's just offensive. I was conjured. By you, in case you don't remember."

"By me?" I cringed as my voice crept up a full octave. "I had no part in this. I wouldn't know how to conjure a spirit if I tried. Which I didn't."

"Oh, but you did. I've been giving it some thought,

and remember that crystal pendulum you had, the amethyst one you were swinging around all willy-nilly over my old party dress? I think that's how you did it."

I opened my mouth to argue but snapped it shut when I realized that *no, I didn't* wasn't exactly going to earn me top prize for my debate skills. "Fine, but even if I did, I have no idea what that means."

"Well, I think it means *you* have control over where I'm allowed to go."

"Me?" Yikes. There was that high-pitched squeal again. "Well, I have no idea how that's supposed to work."

"I have a theory. Wanna hear it?" I really didn't, but the question was rhetorical. "Since I've been back, I've felt a strong pull from a couple of objects. One's that silver bracelet of mine you like to wear, and the other is that amethyst pendulum. Now, neither one seems strong enough on its own, but I've given this some thought, and just maybe, if you have the bracelet on *and* you carry that pendulum with you at the same time, I can go where you go. So, let's go!"

"Not so fast. I've got a guest in the hospital and a police station full of witnesses giving statements. This is hardly the time to test out taking my pet poltergeist for a walk."

Lillian straightened her back and gave her head a haughty toss over her shoulder that sent her perfectly bobbed hair momentarily into disarray. Instead of looking back in my direction as I'd expected, if only to see what effect her little outburst had had, she remained frozen in place, her head twisted at an unnatural angle as she stared into the suite's adjoining room. "Uh, Tamsyn?"

My belly tightened, and I sucked in a quick breath. "Yes?"

"There's someone—"

I jumped as the doorbell rang, followed by a hard knock that echoed up the stairs. "At the front door? Yeah, got it."

I raced down the steps and was gasping for breath as the bell sounded again. I wrenched the door open to find Noah wearing the face of a pallbearer. My heart plummeted even before I heard the news.

"He didn't make it. I just got the call from the hospital. Sebastian Grenville is dead."

"But he was just..." Every muscle in my body began to shake. "What happened?"

"It's too soon to know for certain, but my initial assessment at the tea was that he was in anaphylactic shock." Some of Noah's tragic look seeped away as he found himself in the more comfortable territory of discussing medical diagnoses. "Do you know if he had any allergies?"

"Strawberries." My voice sounded hollow in my ears, lifeless and robotic. I shook my head to snap myself out of my trance. "He was allergic to strawberries and had some other dietary concerns, but I was very careful."

"Of course. I'm sure your aunt Gwen trained you well." He paused, chewing reflectively on his lower lip. "Have you had other food training? Or certification. The kitchen's licensed for catering, right?"

"Um..." I fumbled for an answer. "I mean, I *think*..."

Whatever else I had planned to say was lost to the sound of the sheriff's car crunching its way along the driveway. When it reached the end, the engine shut off, and Sheriff Grady got out, followed by one of his deputies.

"You've heard?" the sheriff asked as he approached the porch. Meanwhile, the deputy made his way toward the tent, pulling out a large roll of yellow crime scene tape.

"About Mr. Grenville?" I gulped as the deputy secured one end of the tape to a tent pole and began a slow circle around the structure as he allowed the spool to unwind. "Noah just told me the sad news."

"Tragic," he agreed, but without a hint of emotion coming through. "Obviously, with a victim as high profile as Sebastian Grenville, we'll be launching a thorough investigation."

"Yes, of cour—wait." Belatedly, my brain emerged from its fog to fully engage. "Did you say victim? I thought Noah said this was an allergic reaction. Is victim really the right word?"

Ignoring me, Sheriff Grady took out his notebook, the same one I'd seen earlier in the day when he was taking notes on the possible break-in at the clinic. Only this time, it was a much larger case. "Ms. Bassett, I'm going to need all your food service and health and safety files."

"I'm sure I can get those for you." If Aunt Gwen ever answered her phone. To think I'd actually looked forward to her going away for a while. I should've known better.

"And we'll need to close the kitchen, effective immediately, until we can complete an inspection of the premises." He handed me a stack of half a dozen large, red signs that read *closed until further notice*. "If you could just post those on all the entrances to the crime scene, I'd appreciate it. Nobody in or out of the kitchen, period."

Crime scene? "But, I have twenty-eight guests expecting breakfast in the morning. Surely—"

"That's twenty-seven guests now," he reminded me. "Noah, could you come with me to the station? There's some paperwork."

Noah shot me an apologetic look, but I waved it aside, assuring him, "I'll be fine."

When all three men had left, I retreated inside, closing the door behind me and leaning against it as if in a stupor. One guest was dead, my kitchen was closed until further notice, and deep inside was the growing dread that it was all my fault. I should never have tried to work a spell I didn't know backward and forward. Heck, I probably should avoid ever working a spell of any kind ever again, because this pretty much settled it. In the entire history of kitchen witches, I was the absolute worst.

"Tamsyn?" Lillian materialized in the entryway, a respectful distance away this time, with Gus at her feet.

"Sebastian Grenville's dead," I informed her in a flat tone, studying a scuff mark on the floor and letting out my breath as if all the air had gone out of my words.

"I know."

"You do?" My head shot up. "Were you eavesdropping just now? You know I hate it when you do that. It gives me the creeps."

"I wasn't eavesdropping. I swear." She glanced behind her, up the wide mahogany staircase. "He's sitting on the chaise lounge upstairs."

My entire body tingled. "He's *what?*"

"That's what I was trying to tell you before the doorbell rang." Her matter-of-fact reply sent my blood pressure skyward.

"The ghost of Sebastian Grenville is haunting the Pinecroft Inn?" I bellowed.

Lillian simply shrugged as though nothing on earth were amiss, while Gus responded with his characteristically self-satisfied meow. Whatever was going on with Grenville's ghost, I blamed them both first and foremost.

"Come on, Aunt Gwen," I muttered as the third ring sounded in my ear. "Pick up the phone. Pick. Up."

But for the third time that morning, she did not answer, and having already left her several messages, I disconnected the call as soon as I heard the familiar refrain of her voicemail greeting.

Sunday morning at Pinecroft Cove was famous for its decadence. There would be eggs and thick slices of bacon in silver chafing dishes on the sideboard, towers of fresh fruit, and the aroma of cinnamon and vanilla hanging heavily in the air from homemade waffles and muffins. No online guest review was complete without a mention of our brunch, which is why it was no surprise that the muttering complaints of the inn's guests the day after the fateful authors' tea could be heard from several rooms away.

Disgust twisted the corners of my lips as I set an assortment of half-finished cereal boxes on the dining room table. Even those had been in the forbidden zone, but I'd been able to stretch past the yellow police tape blocking the entrance to the kitchen just far enough to retrieve them without technically stepping foot in the quarantined space. Milk was another story. The guests would have to make do with dry flakes, and I found myself hoping Aunt Gwen wouldn't call back until all evidence of this culinary travesty had been eradicated. As for coffee? I shuddered. It was going to be a very long day.

I swiveled my head as a light tapping came from the back door. I could just make out the edge of Noah's face in the window, and as we made eye contact, he held up a large paper sack. I recognized the logo of the island's best donut shop instantly and grinned.

"Is that what I think it is?" I called out as loudly as possible, hoping he could hear me through the open window.

"Four dozen donuts," he confirmed. "And two gallons of hot coffee."

"I'll be right there!"

The obedient citizen in me told me I needed to use the front door and walk all the way around to the back. The rebel in me gave the tape barrier a long, hard look. The deputy had outdone himself, tracing multiple Xs across each doorway, but they weren't exactly laser beams. With a little flexibility and some blatant disregard for the law, I shimmied my way under and dashed across the room with the speed and care of a thief in the middle of a museum heist.

"Kitchen's still closed, I see," Noah remarked as he took in the tape. "I thought it might be, and I know how cranky people get without breakfast."

"You're a lifesaver." I took the bag from him, my eyes growing wide at the huge cardboard container he still held, a plastic pot spout sticking out from its side. "You weren't kidding about the coffee."

"The Gallon of Joe is one of Holey Moley's specialties. It even comes with paper cups and all the fixings."

"I might have to run out for another one, just for me."

I led Noah into the dining room, lifting up the police barrier for him to pass under, then smoothing it back into place to erase all signs of our trespassing. "We speak of this to no one."

"My lips are sealed."

His lips twitched with humor, and as he came up close beside me to set the two Gallons of Joe on the table, my pulse quickened, bringing me to a state of alertness that no mere cup of coffee ever could. My hands shook ever so slightly as I set the donuts on the table. *Get a hold of yourself, Tamsyn,* I urged myself, knowing his gallant actions had nothing to do with any romantic feelings for me. Noah was a do-gooder, plain and simple. He'd never let a houseful of people suffer a morning without coffee if it was in his power to help.

Do you really want to be anyone's damsel in distress? I took a slow breath and put some distance between us under the pretext of grabbing a platter from the built-in china hutch in the far corner. I had enough history with fixer-upper boyfriends of my own to know I never wanted to be anyone's pity project. No sooner had the donuts hit the table than the guests descended on the dining room like hungry lions circling a wounded gazelle.

"Looks like I arrived just in time," Noah whispered, backing away from the table with a laugh.

As he turned toward the entryway, I stopped him, feeling guilty that he was leaving with an empty stomach. Aunt Gwen would never let me hear the end of that. "Do you want to stay for a bite?"

"No. Thanks, though. I'm on my way to the airfield. I have a meeting with the hospital, and then I have to give a statement to the medical examiner's office."

I glanced warily at my closed kitchen. "Do you really think it was something he ate? I don't know what I'll do if it turns out I'm responsible for Sebastian Grenville's death."

"I wouldn't worry too much about it yet," he assured me. "You were careful with the menu, and honestly, strawberry allergies aren't usually so severe they could cause instant death. I'm sure it will turn out to be something unrelated to anything you did. I've asked to have a copy of all the lab results sent to the clinic to review, so I'll keep you updated."

"Thank you, Noah." I appreciated his diligent efforts, but I wondered if lab results could ever truly clear me of guilt if it turned out the cause of death was faulty magic.

By now, both the living and dining rooms had filled with guests, who lounged in chairs munching donuts and sipping coffee in subdued silence. A quick scan told me only one person was missing: Jacqueline Cortez. The grieving fiancée had been whisked to the mainland shortly after the medevac helicopter had departed. I'd heard her return to the inn late in the night, I hadn't actually seen her since the tragedy had occurred. *I should take her a tray*, I thought, my hostess skills finally kicking in.

Fortunately, there was a blueberry donut left intact amidst the carnage on the table, and I placed this on the prettiest plate I could find, then poured steaming coffee into a cup and set a few sugar packets and two of those thimble-sized milk containers on the saucer. I had no idea how Jacqueline took her coffee, or even if she drank it at all, but the gesture of bringing it to her was the very least I could do.

I'd arranged the meager offerings on a tray, which I balanced in one hand as I tapped on the door to the suite. My stomach tightened at the sound of movement on the other side. Would the woman blame me for her fiancé's death? I stiffened as the doorknob turned, bracing myself for an onslaught of rage at the worst, or uncontrollable sobbing at best, but when the door opened, I was puzzled to be met with a face that radiated calm.

"Yes?" she said, her tone quiet, almost soothing.

I pressed my lips together and swallowed. "I brought you some breakfast. It's not much…"

"I appreciate it." She took the tray from my outstretched hands and set it on the bed.

I hovered in the doorway, uncertain what to do or say. As the silence dragged on, I finally opted for the timeworn, "I'm so sorry for your loss."

"Thank you," she replied, her eyes remaining dry.

"If there's...uh...anything you need," I stumbled, confused by her lack of emotion. She might as well have been thanking me for bringing her an extra towel or telling her the time of day. Was she in shock?

She nodded. "If you'll excuse me, I have a lot of work to do."

She turned her back and walked to the desk in the adjoining office, but before the door closed all the way, I could just make out a hazy figure on the chaise lounge. It was unidentifiable in its features, no more solid than a wisp of smoke or a smudge on your glasses, but deep down I knew I was seeing Sebastian Grenville's ghost.

My throat was dry and my breathing shallow as I stood in the deserted hallway on the second floor. I'd had encounters with ghosts before, of course, but not like this. Douglas Strong, the murdered real estate developer, had only come to me in dreams, or else in the guise of a large, black raven. And Lillian...well, she was a witch, and besides, she'd accidentally been summoned by some combination of my aunt Gwen's and my spells and actions, so it was no wonder she was almost as solid as a flesh and blood human. This foggy apparition in the bedroom was something new, and I didn't know what it might mean. Were my powers growing stronger, allowing me to see more clearly into the spirit world? Or could I only see the shade of Sebastian Grenville because I was the one responsible for his demise?

CHAPTER SIX

The last crumbs of donut had been consumed and the coffee finished. Since the rest of the literary festival had been cancelled and folks had little reason to stick around, the house emptied out completely right after breakfast, with the exception of Jacqueline. Thanks to the festival, her room had been paid in advance for a two-week stay, and she showed as little sign of checking out as she did of emerging from her bedroom, where she'd been holed up all morning.

Downstairs, Cass, Sybil, and I clustered together, peering into the kitchen and hoping for inspiration to strike. From outside, there came an immense racket as the team of workers from the rental company dismantled the tent. The sheriff's department had called to say their investigators were on their way, which was why it was of the utmost importance that we come up with a plan, and quickly.

"A potion?" Cass suggested, which made sense because that was her specialty.

"What would we do with it?" I asked, surveying the space dubiously. "If we had someone in mind, we might be able to make him or her drink it to reveal what happened, but the closest thing to a suspect we have is the kitchen itself. I don't think you can get a potion to work by spritzing it around like air freshener."

"What about a glamour to show us the kitchen the way it looked yesterday?" But Sybil's lackluster tone told me she had little faith in her own idea.

"No, and I don't think I can whip up a magical bunt cake, either." I bit my lip and let out a huff. "None of us has quite the right skill set to figure this out."

"But isn't that what covens are for?" asked Cass. As the youngest in the group, she often had that hopeful optimism that, at least for me, grew more jaded the closer I got to thirty. Still, I didn't want to discourage her, so I waited patiently for her to go on. "What we need, I think, is a spell that combines all of our energies to create a new set of skills."

"But how, and what do you think we'd find?" Sybil asked, cautiously intrigued.

"Tamsyn, didn't you say you were worried you'd forgotten one of the ingredients in the lemon cake?" Cass asked.

I nodded. "I was cutting back on the salt because of Mr. Grenville's hypertension, so I left it out of the frosting, but later on I remembered there was a note about it being important."

"What if we join hands and ask the kitchen to reveal what, if anything, was out of place or wrong?" Cass suggested. Sybil and I hesitated a moment, then nodded. It was worth a try.

As the three of us formed a circle, a jolt of electricity traveled through my fingertips and up my arms. It was the same magical current I'd experienced for the first time on the night the three of us had met. That evening, there had been a violent storm brewing, and at first, I'd blamed the curious sensation on the static in the air, but since then, I'd learned to recognize the feel of magic flowing through me, and it always intensified when the three of us joined hands. Cass was right. We were stronger together.

We stood like that, hands joined and eyes closed, for several seconds. Sybil chanted unintelligibly under her breath, magical words I had yet to learn. When it came to magical studies, she was by far the most advanced of our little group. Cass and I remained quiet, focused on our goal, until there was a shift in the current running through us that told me the spell was beginning to work. I cracked one eye open and saw a bright crimson glow coming from the counter.

I opened both eyes and whispered, "Do you see that?" The others looked, too, and nodded.

"Should we take a look?" Sybil asked.

"We can't," Cass said, pointing to the yellow tape. As much as she wanted to help, I could tell she didn't relish the idea of breaking any laws. I, however, had no such compunction.

"Wait here," I said, smirking as I ducked beneath the obstacle for the second time that day. I dashed across the room and grabbed the glowing object. I was back on the proper side of the barrier in seconds, but the creak of floorboards in the adjacent room warned me it may not have been fast enough. I tensed and called out, "Hello?"

"We're here to inspect the kitchen," a man's voice replied. "The door was unlocked, so the sheriff said we should just go on in."

"Yes, fine." My heart pounded as the unfamiliar man rounded the corner and came into view, certain he'd watched my every move and was about to arrest me, but he proceeded to remove the tape without so much as a second glance in my direction. "We'll get out of your way." I tucked my contraband under one arm and hustled my friends out the front door onto the inn's wide, shady porch. Only then did I bother to inspect what I had retrieved.

"A jar of jam?" I held it out for the other two to see.

"Raspberry," Sybil offered, taking the jar and holding it up for a closer inspection. "It looks like one of the ones I picked up from the Owl and Quill."

"Let me see it again," I said. I studied the label,

which had a watercolor illustration of raspberries on it. I twisted the lid, and there was a pop as the pressure was released.

"It hadn't been opened," Cass observed.

"This was an extra. All the others were put out on the tables yesterday by Jan's staff," I explained. I held the jar to my nose and frowned. "Get a whiff of this."

Sybil took the jar, inhaled, and passed it to Cass. Their confused expressions mirrored my own.

"Did either of you try the jam during the tea?" I asked.

They shook their heads.

"Neither did I. Does it smell like raspberry to you?" I asked.

"Definitely not," Sybil confirmed. "I know the scent of strawberries when I smell them."

"But it's clearly labeled," Cass said.

I held the jar up and turned it slowly in my hand. "This label's crooked, don't you think?" The others murmured their agreement. "Pam's a stickler for her labels. We buy a lot of jam, and I've never seen one that wasn't completely perfect."

"Were the others like that, too?" Cass asked.

Sybil's face scrunched, and she blew out her breath. "I just can't remember. Where are the rest of the jars now?"

"Thrown away," I said. "Vera and I cleared all the tables as soon as the helicopter left and all the guests had gone to the station. We didn't want the food to attract bugs."

"So, we have no way of knowing if all the jars were like this," Sybil concluded.

"There's one person who would know. Looks like I need to go visit James Thorne and have a chat." I let out a heavy sigh. He'd know, all right, but would he have any interest in telling me?

The Owl and Quill was closed on Sundays, but as I cycled past the shop, I detected activity coming from the rear, from the room where the authors' tea was originally to be held. I felt a stab of regret as I walked up the steps to the back door. If only there had been no last-minute change of venue, I wouldn't be living with a potential crime scene in my front yard. The door was a French variety, and I could see James clearly through it. I rapped my knuckles against the glass and waited for him to acknowledge me. And acknowledge me, he did, turning around and pulling a scowl, the likes of which I'd never seen.

"Ms. Bassett," he said, standing at the door and shouting, but not bothering to crack it as much as an inch. "I'm very busy."

"We need to talk," I yelled back. I pulled the jar of jam from my satchel and held it up for him to see. "About this."

The scowl morphed into a look of chagrin. There was no doubt in my mind that James Thorne was my man. The guy looked guilty as sin. He opened the door and stood aside so I could enter, then let it shut with a click. The room was set up with tables, just as it had been the last time I'd been there, only now they were draped with rumpled cloths of purple and gold.

"Looks like someone had a party."

"Yes, like I explained to Jan the other day, I'd accidentally double-booked the room." He bustled around, straightening the tablecloths nervously. "Silly of me, really. Who forgets their own high school reunion, right?"

"High school reunion?" I knew the island's school was small, but even so, the space would surely never hold that type of crowd.

"Class of 1999," he said in a monotone. "Proud purple and gold. Go panthers."

It *did* explain the color scheme, but still, I was suspicious. "The reunion was last night?"

"No, no. It's next week." He wore an anxious expression, as though eager to convince me I had not caught him in a lie. "This was a private party for the old student council. They're in charge of the reunion plans, you see. I'd completely forgotten I offered to hold it here until I got an email from the class president, asking me what time. Like I said to Jan, it was no hard feelings. They'd just booked it first."

"Uh-huh." It's not that I totally believed his story, but I had more pressing concerns and needed to move on. "Look, it doesn't matter to me. What I actually came to discuss was this."

"What's that?" As soon as he saw the jar of jam, James's face went through a fascinating contortion before settling back into place, but he proceeded to talk as though nothing had happened. "Oh, one of Pam's things. Was the order to your satisfaction?"

"The jam was fine, but, funny thing, it was actually strawberry."

He blinked. "Didn't you order strawberry?"

"I think we both know I changed that order, and then I sent Sybil in here to buy a dozen jars of raspberry."

He pinched the corner of his mustache between his fingers, coaxing it to curl. "Oh, yes. Now I remember. So, what's the issue?"

"My raspberry jam was strawberry. That's the issue." I shot him a hard look through narrowed lids. "A fact I'm positive you are well aware of."

"Me?" A bit of the color seemed to drain from his face. "That's my sister's department. I just sell the stuff."

I shoved the jar closer to his face. "I'm familiar enough with your sister's products to know there's no way she would allow a crooked label like this one out the door."

"Well...I..." The color he'd lost from his face pooled in a bright red band around his collar, which he tugged at as if it had suddenly become two sizes too small.

"Admit it. You peeled the labels off the strawberry

jam I ordered and pasted on raspberry labels instead. Why, James? You knew the speaker had an allergy."

"I was supposed to be the speaker!" The red had returned to his face with a vengeance. "Bash Grenville's a pompous jerk."

"So you killed him?"

"Huh?"

"Haven't you heard the news? Sebastian Grenville's dead."

"What? But, how?"

"How? Come on. You were there at the tea yourself. I heard you heckle him during Jan's introduction. You saw what happened."

"But," he spluttered, "but I didn't! I left before he got up to speak, right after you saw me, in fact. I just couldn't bear to listen to him talk. I came straight here to set up the space. You're telling me...he died?"

"He keeled over right at the podium. Anaphylactic shock. They airlifted him to the mainland, but he didn't make it."

As far as I could tell, James Thorne stopped breathing the instant he processed my words. He stood stiff as a statue in front of me, and at this point, the red in his face didn't know whether it was coming or going and had turned into a blotchy mess that looked like he'd developed a plague.

The statue blinked, returning to life. "I hadn't heard. I was at the shop all day, and, well, honestly, I had no desire to hear how it had gone."

"How did you think it was going to go. You were jealous that Sebastian Grenville replaced you as keynote speaker, so you sent me the wrong jam. And now he's dead."

"No!" James shook from head to toe. "I mean, yes, I'll admit, I was jealous. And yes, I swapped the labels on the jam. But not to kill him, I swear. I knew Bash from school, knew all about his allergy. One time at a party, the punch had strawberries in it, and he got itchy welts all over his body. He scratched himself so much it looked like he was doing a jig, and I figured if that happened in front of the whole literary festival crowd, it would serve him right for taking my place."

"I thought you said you went to Summerhaven High. Didn't Sebastian Grenville go to that other school on Northport Island?"

He nodded. "Northport Prep, yeah. We graduated the same year, him from Northport and me from Summerhaven."

"I thought Northport Prep was some fancy private school. You're telling me he went slumming to Summerhaven for parties?"

"They all did. Have you ever been to Northport?"

I shook my head.

"Other than the campus, there's nothing much there. Besides, we're the only two schools around, with miles of ocean to the mainland. Our teams would practice together, and we had a joint band program and the like. It makes sense that sometimes we pooled resources, right?"

"I guess so." The gears in my head were whirling. "Look, it doesn't matter if it was just a prank. You're the one who switched the jam, and I'm the one about to get blamed. You need to tell Sheriff Grady what happened."

He rocked back and forth on his heels. "I'll go to jail."

"Not if you confess now, James. Now, before they figure it out, which they will." Let's face it, the sheriff might not be the brightest bulb, but it wouldn't take a genius for someone to figure out that a guy with a strawberry allergy died from eating strawberries.

"Okay." His shoulders slumped, but there was a look of honest resignation on his face that assured me he would do the right thing. Mystery solved, I sighed in relief as I retrieved my bike and headed home with the hope that Sebastian's ghost would soon be on its merry way to the great beyond.

All was quiet when I returned home. The tent had been packed up, and the workers were gone, taking with them all signs of the ill-fated tea. The same could not be said indoors. Opening the door to find Gus pacing the entryway and meowing his fool head off, his legs covered up to the haunches in a layer of white powder, was my first clue that all was not right with the Pinecroft Inn world. He'd tracked the stuff everywhere, leaving behind a trail of appropriately ghostly white paw prints across the hardwood floors.

"Hey, Buddy," I greeted him, kicking off my shoes and placing them in their usual spot beneath the antique hall tree. As soon as I did, Gus pounced, nipping my bare toes. "Ouch! What's got you so riled up, huh?"

As if in response, he turned and pranced toward the kitchen, his fluffy tail held aloft, twitching and bearing an uncanny resemblance to an oversized dust mop. He stopped at the edge of the dining room, sat in the kitchen doorway, and let out a plaintive yowl. The Xs of yellow tape had multiplied, woven like a plastic tapestry to seal the space completely. In addition to this, a sign had been added, reading, "These premises are closed until further notice, by order of the Summerhaven Sheriff's Department."

Stifling a groan, I peeled back a loose edge of tape and peered into the room beyond. My heart sank. Every drawer had been emptied and every cabinet opened. A twenty-five-pound bag of flour, the source of Gus's footprints, had been overturned in the pantry and spread across the floor like freshly fallen snow. My stifled groan morphed into a full-throated moan. "What's going on here?"

"The coppers had a real beef with your kitchen. That's what."

I whirled around, but no one was there. "Lillian, you've got to stop doing that." I swear, if I lived another hundred years, I would never get used to the sound of a disembodied voice talking to me from the middle of an empty room.

"Doing what?" She came into view beside the dining room table, smoothing a hand over a smart 1920s' frock in a pale shade of lilac. She twirled one way and then the other, beaming with pride as the hem flared out around her calves.

"Is that new?"

"What, this old thing?" Her laughter chimed, then faded as her face took on a hint of confusion. "Actually, I guess it *is* an old thing now. It was new that last summer, but now it would be ancient."

"Did you find it in the house?" I'll admit my head spun just a little trying to figure out all the inner workings of time. Then again, when asking yourself the question of how a ghost could be wearing a new dress and have it be sitting in a century-old trunk at the same time, where does one even begin figuring out which part of that question is the most insane?

"No, it's more of a memory, I suppose." Lillian shrugged, seemingly as confounded by the whole thing as I was. "I can't explain it, except to say that I wanted to wear it, and there it was."

"That's handy," I quipped. "Even better than next-day shipping. But what am I going to do about the inn? I've never seen such a mess as that kitchen is right now. Aunt Gwen is going to kill me when she finds out."

Lillian's eyes brightened. "You know what we need? A nice walk. We could take in a Vaudeville show at the Orpheum downtown."

I shook my head. "I told you before I'm not taking you for a walk."

"Oh, come on!" Lillian slumped onto a dining room chair, and even though she had no actual weight or physical form, I could almost hear the thud. Gus jumped into her lap, and she ruffled the fur behind his ears. "I'm so bored. There aren't even any guests to keep me entertained anymore."

"They *all* left? Like, every single one?"

"All but that one who was with the writer."

"Jacqueline?"

"Yes. She told that sheriff's deputy who was here that she had some work to do, and she's been up there in the room ever since." Lillian wrinkled her nose. "Kind of a cold fish, if you ask me. Boyfriend's been dead for all of a day and she's thinking about work."

"Everyone grieves in their own way," I chided, though deep down, I had to agree. Jacqueline Cortez was not exactly the picture of a grieving almost-widow. *Oh well,* I thought, remembering that even as I stood there, James Thorne was busy making a full confession to the authorities concerning his role in the man's death. *Not my problem now.* "At least I don't have to worry about Sebastian Grenville's ghost anymore."

"Why do you say that?" Lillian asked without looking up from tickling Gus's ears.

"I figured it all out," I replied cheerily. "Found out how he died, confronted the culprit, and convinced him to turn himself in."

"You did all that?" Lillian sounded impressed.

"I did. Second murder I've solved since I got here. Sheriff Grady really should have me on retainer. But anyway, Sebastian Grenville's free to move along now."

"Well, he's not."

"He's not what?"

"Moving along. He's not."

I squinted at her, not understanding. "He's not?"

Lillian shook her head, the ginger curls of her bob bouncing around her chin. "Nope. He's still upstairs, right where you left him."

Did she really mean to tell me after all I'd done for him, my ghostly houseguest was refusing to leave? What an ungrateful... "Mothersmucker," I muttered, coming closer to saying an actual curse word than I had since college as I stomped toward the door. "I'm going out for some fresh air."

"Can I come, too?"

It was the last thing I wanted, but Lillian had jumped up and followed me like an eager puppy, and I simply lacked the heart to tell her no. I glanced down at the silver bracelet around my wrist. "Sorry, but I have no idea where that pendulum-thingy is."

Just as I said it, Gus sauntered out from behind a corner, the amethyst crystal dangling from the chain clasped between his teeth. He dropped it at my feet like he might a dead mouse, then continued on his way with a flick of his bushy tail.

"Oh, look," Lillian said. "There it is."

"Fine," I said through gritted teeth. "Let's go for a walk."

I snatched the pendulum from the floor as Lillian clapped her hands soundlessly, since, of course, her hands were just an illusion. It was truly unnerving how she got that cat to do her bidding, or maybe it was the other way around. I had no idea who was in control anymore, except that it sure as heck wasn't me.

CHAPTER SEVEN

J shuffled my feet through the dirt path on the side of the road, kicking up a cloud of dust as I went. The chaotic swirl of it reflected my mood and, in an odd way, made me feel better. Lillian's hunch about the bracelet and amethyst pendulum combination had been correct. I'd clasped the silver chain around my neck, and as soon as my feet had left the property of the inn, a subtle warmth had started to emanate from the crystal, echoed by a band of mild heat around my wrist. As soon as she'd realized her new freedom, Lillian had all but skipped down the middle of the street and was now marveling at every leaf and twig as if she hadn't been outside in a hundred years. She began to whistle, and I opened my mouth to snap at her, irrationally incensed by her cheerfulness, but thought better of it. The truth was, Lillian really hadn't been outside in a century. Just because I was in a foul mood didn't mean I had the right to spoil her fun.

"What do you think went wrong?" I asked instead. "Maybe James decided not to confess after all. I should go by the sheriff's office, just to make sure."

Lillian ignored me and continued to frolic in the road.

"What else could I have missed?" Again, she didn't respond, and this time it irritated me from the inside out, like I'd swallowed an itchy wool sweater. "Lillian!"

She stopped in place and turned, startled. "What?"

"I need your help; that's what. I've got to figure out what else I need to do to get Sebastian Grenville to walk off into the light."

She wrinkled her nose, scratching the side of her head. "Well, how should I know?"

"You're a ghost," I told her, stating the obvious.

"Yes, but it's not like I've crossed over into the light, now have I?" Lillian responded, equally adept at stating the obvious. "I've never even seen the light. I know absolutely nothing about it."

I pressed my lips into a thin line as I mulled this over. It was becoming clear that neither one of us knew the first thing about the spirit world, which, for someone whose house was now being haunted by two spirits, was not a comfortable thought. "Come on. First stop, Sheriff Grady."

Main Street was mostly deserted when we arrived,

something I'd never witnessed firsthand but apparently wasn't unusual for a Sunday after Labor Day. Summerhaven was a tourist destination, but as its name implied, once the lazy days of summer were gone, so were the vast majority of visitors. A few of the shops had already closed for the season, their front windows boarded up in anticipation of ravaging winter storms. Other businesses would remain open until after Halloween, while a few would continue to operate year-round to accommodate the island's small population of permanent residents. In any case, nearly everything was closed on Sundays beginning in September. It was something that, having spent my formative years in Boston and then Cleveland, would take some getting used to.

"Oh, the Orpheum hasn't changed at all!" Lillian clapped her hands as we passed the island's movie theater, which in my childhood had seen better days, but whose original lighted sign had been painstakingly restored to what it must have been in my companion's time. "I saw Charlie Chaplin in a comedy review there when I was young."

"Live?"

"Yes, of course, I was alive. I haven't always been a ghost, you know."

"I meant, was *he* live, or was it a mov—?"

The gunning of a car engine made us both jump, and I put out my hand to stop her as a sports car zipped by like a one-man drag race. Of course, I'm not sure what good my hand was supposed to do, since she could have walked right through it, and the car would've gone right through her, but that's not the type of detail that runs through your head at a time like that.

"A lot has changed in the past ninety years," she remarked, looking disapprovingly at the trail of exhaust the car had left behind.

"I'm sure it has," I said and wondered what things I would find shocking if I could suddenly see almost a century into the future. "Are you going to be okay, or should we turn around and go back?"

"No, not yet. I see the Island Market's still here." Lillian pointed across the street to the white clapboard building with the green striped awning where the grocery store was housed. "What about the ice cream counter in the back? Please tell me that hasn't gone away."

"Going strong," I told her, and as if to confirm this, a customer exited carrying a shopping bag in one hand and holding a cone in the other.

My answer seemed to cheer her up. "Can we go in? I remember my last summer, they served an ice cream unlike anything you could get anywhere else. It was chocolate, but with nuts and marshmallows in it. Incredible!"

"You mean rocky road?"

"Yes! Have you ever tried it?"

"Once or twice," I said, wondering what she would

think if I told her you could now get that rare flavor in every supermarket in America.

"Can we get some?"

"Not today."

The grocery store was just about the only exception to the *closed on Sundays* rule, as they were open from noon to two, but it was nearly that now and I knew Mr. Brisby, the owner, would not appreciate it one bit if I went traipsing into his shop at five minutes 'til closing with no intention of buying anything. It's not like Lillian could actually eat an ice cream, no matter how good she thought it was, but considering her enthusiasm for the stuff, it seemed cruel to point that out.

"There's my friend Sybil's shop."

She looked in the direction of my hand. "That used to be a restaurant."

A chill traveled down my spine as I recalled the time I'd stood in Sybil's shop, trying on one of Lillian's dresses from the attic. In an instant, I'd found myself in the middle of a crowded restaurant, the sounds and smells so real that even when, just moments later, I was back in the shop, the scent of onions lingered and the distinctive horn of a Model T car still rang in my ears. "I know it was."

She gave me a funny look but didn't press for an explanation. Instead, her eyes lit up with a mischievous gleam that made my belly do a flip-flop. "Wanna see something?"

Probably not, I thought, but decided it would be rude to rain on her walk down memory lane, so instead I gave a noncommittal shrug and followed her down the narrow alley alongside Sybil's shop. As we neared a plain wooden door, a strange lightheaded feeling came over me. She raised her fist to give the door a sound rapping, and as her knuckles made contact with a solid thud instead of passing through the surface as I'd expected, the hairs on the back of my neck stood up. How could a spirit do that? In the distance, the unmistakable *awooga* of a Model T's horn broke the stillness and set my heart racing.

"Where are we?" I whispered, my mouth and throat suddenly so parched that I struggled to pry my tongue from the roof of my mouth.

"You'll see. This is one of my very favorite places."

She pounded her fist against the door again, and this time I made out a distinct pattern to the tapping, two slow raps followed by three short ones, like a secret code. A tiny slot slid open in the door, about eyeball height, revealing nothing beyond it but shadow. A moment later, a pair of eyes emerged from the blackness and blinked. There was the scraping of metal as a latch on the other side was undone. Then the door swung open, allowing strains of jazz music to escape into the alleyway along with the odor of cigar smoke and perfume.

I'd pretty much caught on at this point that Lillian's idea of reminiscing was to transport me through time to visit her favorite speakeasy. Was I freaked out? Yes. But I was also intrigued. Who wouldn't want to witness the Roaring Twenties first hand? With Lillian as my personal tour guide, the prospect seemed less scary than when I'd found myself there all alone.

Naturally, having seen my fair share of movies, I expected the eyes behind the door would belong to some cartoonish brute of a bouncer. Instead, I was mystified when I got a good look at the sandy-haired young man who stood guard at the door.

"That's Tony," she said.

It's not that I didn't know staring was rude, but I couldn't help it. I stared at poor Tony so hard my eyeballs started to get dry, because while his name was in keeping with my expectations, Tony was shorter than I was, even while standing on a stack of wooden crates. The man could've had a promising career as a racing jockey or gone to Hollywood to play the role of a hobbit. In fact, as I took in his tousled hair and rumpled clothing, I found myself wondering if the scuffed shoes he wore covered hairy hobbit feet. Fortunately, when I opened my mouth, I didn't ask him that, but simply said, "Nice to meet you." He didn't respond, or make eye contact, and it occurred to me to wonder whether he could see me, or if perhaps I was as much like a ghost here in Lillian's time as she was in mine.

The door shut quickly behind us as I followed

Lillian down a narrow, dark hallway which had to be navigated more by feel than by sight. By the time we reached the main room, the dimly glowing lamps and a dozen or so votive candles scattered on tabletops provided ample illumination and a welcome relief from utter darkness.

I'd watched enough movies to have a pretty good idea of what a speakeasy should look like. I pictured a room full of gangsters carrying Tommy guns and women wearing short fringed dresses with feathers in their hair, all doing the Charleston while bathtub gin flowed freely from barrels marked XXX in black stencils. I could not have been more wrong.

The room itself was not very large, maybe the size of a private banquet room in a restaurant or hotel. There was no bar in sight. Instead, along the back wall was a bookcase that gave the place the appearance of a library. On the other end of the room, a jazz quartet played on a raised platform. In between were numerous small tables, maybe fifteen or twenty in all, with groupings of two or four people at each. The patrons who occupied them were well dressed, with men in three-piece suits and women in silk gowns, the expensive embroidery and beadwork sparkling in the candlelight. Everyone drank from fine china teacups balanced primly on saucers, while several waiters in crisp uniforms circled the room holding teapots and doling out refills. If it hadn't been for the secrecy involved in gaining admission, I would have sworn we'd wandered in on a church tea party.

"What is this place?" I whispered to Lillian.

"This?" She looked at me as if bewildered I didn't know, then said in a tone that suggested she were introducing a national monument, "This is Davenport's. Surely you've heard of it?"

"No, never," I said, my brain churning. "You don't mean, as in, *the* Davenports who founded Summerhaven Island?"

"Those are the ones." Lillian's laugh tinkled like a wind chime in a light breeze. "You sound surprised."

Surprised wasn't the half of it. The Davenports were revered on the island, with their names gracing municipal buildings and their statues keeping watch in the town square. Let's just say that running a speakeasy didn't exactly fit the history book version of the founding family. "I thought they made their money in lumber or something."

"Oh, back in his grandfather's day, maybe, but Teddy's a thoroughly modern man with an entrepreneurial spirit and an adventurous streak." Even in the dim lighting, there was no mistaking the sudden flush of color in her cheeks or the dreamy quality to her tone.

"Sounds to me like you have a little crush on this Teddy Davenport," I teased.

"Oh, he's a sheik all right, and a real egg, too. If it weren't for my mother—" Whatever she'd been about to say was swallowed as she pointed to a man in a sleek black tuxedo who was speaking in a hushed tone to the man playing piano. "There he is, right over there."

The man shifted, bringing him closer to the stage lights, and my breath caught. Ignoring for a moment his slick-backed hair and pencil-thin mustache, Teddy Davenport was a dead-ringer for Noah Caldwell. "Him?"

"Edward Angus Davenport, the third."

"But, he's—"

Before I could complete my thought, the band abruptly shifted tempo from sensual blues to a ragtime tune that was jarringly upbeat.

Lillian gasped. "It's a raid. Let's blouse."

"Let's what?"

"Let's get outta here!"

All at once, spurred by the band's musical signal, waitstaff scurried toward the bookcases as patrons guzzled the contents of their teacups and set them clattering onto saucers. Lillian darted toward the back wall, but my feet were glued to the floor. I watched, astounded, as one of the servers yanked at the books on a top shelf, which instead of tumbling to the floor, swung open to reveal a hidden cabinet jammed full of liquor bottles. He stowed his cocktail filled teapot inside and shut the compartment, while other servers repeated the process all along the library wall.

One bookcase had slid away from the wall entirely.

It was toward this opening that a crush of people now swarmed, disappearing into the blackness like rats fleeing a ship. The shrillness of a police whistle pierced the air, and I heard someone call out, "Tamsyn!"

Lillian's pale white face shown in the secret passageway, and the urgency reflected on it spurred me to action. I raced across the now empty club, zigzagging around chairs that had been strewn haphazardly. As I reached the entrance to what I could now see was a narrow tunnel, my foot caught on a chair leg, and I stumbled forward. Heat surged from my wrist through my arm as Lillian reached for me, and in the dim light, the pendulum around my neck glowed like a red-hot coal. Though thankfully not as hot as that, it did sting uncomfortably. I winced, navigating the first several yards of the escape route with my eyes squeezed tightly shut. When I opened them, I could see nothing but unrelenting blackness. My ears strained for the sound of footsteps or whispers, but I heard nothing.

I progressed as best I could, crouching as I ran my fingers along the rough walls of the corridor. There was a downward slope to the passage, which was filled with a salty, fishy smell that grew stronger the more I walked. Finally, a faint light shone not too far in the distance, and soon I stepped out of the tunnel and found myself in a rocky outcropping near the shore. Lobster traps were piled high in front of the mouth of the tunnel, but other than that, the area was deserted. I blinked, looking frantically around me for any sign of

Lillian or the others from the speak easy, but it was clear I'd been left behind, alone.

I hiked up a steep bank to the road. It, too, was deserted. I looked back to find stacks of lobster traps obscured the entrance to the tunnel entirely. No one would ever know it was there. At least the view from higher up told me I was not far from Main Street, while the sudden blaring of rock music from an approaching car radio let me know I was no longer in the 1920s. But how was it possible, when Lillian and I had been running from a police raid just moments before?

Lillian. A quick glance revealed my bracelet was still in place. I put a hand to my throat, my fingers searching for the pendulum but coming up empty. Frantically, I felt around my shirt and pockets, but no luck. With a sinking feeling, it dawned on me why my companion had disappeared. Our magical connection must have been severed when the chain had come undone, and now she was—where? Trapped in the past, perhaps, or lost in some sort of ghostly limbo, all because of my carelessness. Guilt washed over me, and I clasped my hands together to stop them from shaking. I needed to get that pendulum back right away.

Warily, I eyed the rocky path leading back to the tunnel. Climbing up had been a challenge, but the way down seemed even more treacherous. One wrong step would send me tumbling, with no one in sight to come to my rescue. I sighed. The safer option was to return to the alley and see if I could locate the entrance to the speakeasy's old escape route in the present day. I shivered as it crossed my mind that the tunnel had probably been abandoned for decades and was likely filled with all sorts of nasty creepy crawlies. I wanted nothing more than to turn toward home and keep walking, but I forced my feet in the right direction and set off. That amethyst crystal was too important to leave behind, so what choice did I have?

Downtown Summerhaven felt even more deserted than before, and the closer I came to Sybil's shop, the more halting were my steps. The late-afternoon sun cast long shadows that shrouded the alleyway as if it were night. Though the temperature was still pleasant enough outside, I hugged my arms close to my chest for warmth as I slipped into the darkness.

It wasn't long before I'd reached the wooden door, or at least it was *a* wooden door, though it must have been a replacement from the one in Lillian's time, as it was solid now and lacked the sliding peephole. I gave the rough surface a timid push, tensing as the squeak of rusty hinges reverberated all around me. I slipped through into the tight space behind the opening and paused to switch on my phone's flashlight function before proceeding, though I soon regretted the action. Being able to see the dingy, cobweb-covered area clearly did little to boost my morale.

The passage widened, and I entered the room where I'd been with Lillian not an hour before, but it bore no resemblance to Davenport's swank speakeasy now. The cleverly disguised bookcases were gone, leaving behind a blank cinder block wall lined with boxes and debris. I propped my phone up on a discarded crate so as to illuminate as much of the area as possible, then got to work moving whatever I could in an attempt to locate the tunnel's entrance. I worked until a dribble of sweat ran down my forehead and into my eye. When I straightened up to rub away the sting, I froze. Against the wall was a person's silhouette, deep black and holding a gun that was most definitely aimed directly at me.

CHAPTER EIGHT

My heart pounded with urgency, but my feet seemed frozen to the ground. The shadow of a gun remained fixed at my head, unwavering, and I knew this was where I would die. *Run*, a voice in my head cried out. *Escape!* It was no use. My brain spun, but my limbs did nothing in response. When they found my bullet-ridden body, would I have one of those spinning discs in the middle of my face, the kind my phone got when it was trying to reboot?

The next sound I heard was not the gunshot I'd expected but a familiar voice echoing across the room. "Tamsyn?"

Though it was too dark to see, I knew who it had to be. "Sybil?"

"Yes. It's me, and Cass, too." The silhouette on the wall lowered its weapon, much to my relief. "What are you doing here?"

"I was..." *Looking for the magical amethyst pendulum that binds me across space and time to my new roommate from the spirit world.* Yeah, no. Even to witches, that would sound way too ridiculous and lead to personal questions I had no desire to answer. I was going to need a cover story. "I was following a stray cat. I thought I saw it run down here and didn't want it to be trapped."

"Oh," replied Cass, shifting out of the shadows so I could just make out the look of confusion on her face. "Summerhaven's full of strays, but that was nice of you, I guess."

"Anyway, what are you both doing here?" I asked. I led the way back down the corridor toward the alleyway, trying to put some distance between us and the old speakeasy. "And what are you doing with a gun?"

"We heard a noise and thought someone might be up to no good. As for this," Sybil held up the weapon, and I flinched as she brandished it in front of my face, a bit too carelessly for my taste, "it's not real. It's a vintage cigarette lighter. I had it at the shop and grabbed it in case we ran into trouble back here.

"On a Sunday afternoon?" I cocked an eyebrow as I stared down the pearl-handled pistol. Whether real or not, I wasn't a fan. "It's not like downtown Summerhaven's a hotbed of criminal activity."

"There was a break-in at the tearoom," Cass said. "I was just heading over to fill out a police report, and Sybil volunteered to come along."

"Oh no!" As the three of us emerged from the alley and onto the sunlit sidewalk on Main Street, I could see the tension etched on Cass's face. "Was anything valuable taken?"

"Several bags of herbs we'd just finished drying for teas and potions."

I frowned. "That's odd. Why take those? Unless maybe it was a prank."

"Or if they thought it was a different type of herb. Like, the recreational kind." Sybil gave me a significant look as she lifted two fingers to her lips and took an imaginary puff.

My jaw dropped as I spun to face Cass. "You haven't been dealing drugs in the shop, have you?"

Her eyes widened. "Of course not. I would never break the law. But Sybil has a point. It's an easy mistake to make, and there are plenty of young troublemakers looking for something to do now that summer's over."

"Still," I shot a dubious look at the entrance to the station, "do you really think the sheriff is your best bet for dealing with this? He won't take it seriously, or if you're really unlucky, he'll arrest you as some sort of drug mule or something."

"It was herbs!" She let out a huff of breath. "The sheriff's not my first choice, either, but what else can I do? I need to figure out who broke into the shop and put everything right, preferably before my mother and grandmother get back from the cruise."

"We should all go together," I suggested.

When we walked through the front door at the sheriff's office, the scowl on Joe Grady's face assured me the interaction would be full of the usual charm I'd come to expect in my short time on the island. Of course, he had good reason to scowl. It was a Sunday, usually one of his days off, but the suspicious death of a world-famous author was the type of thing you couldn't just delegate to underlings.

"Oh, look. If it isn't Charlie's Angels." The sheriff laughed heartily, clearly impressed by his own wit, and several of the deputies around him joined in, though considering he was their boss, I decided not to hold it against them too much. I could only imagine the daily torture of having to endure that man's subpar sense of humor. To spend your weekends doing it, too? Forget about it.

"We'd like to report a break-in," I announced, ignoring the jibe. It technically wasn't my crime to report, but I'd dealt with him so many times since moving that I felt like I should take the lead.

"All three of you?"

"Just me," Cass answered sweetly, always the peacemaker. I was too busy glaring at him to respond, hating that every so often he was able to get the better of me, even if it was only to correct my wording. "There's some stock missing from the tearoom."

"Fill out a form, and leave it at the front desk," he

advised in a dull monotone. "I'll get to it on Monday, during regular business hours.

I rolled my eyes. "That inspires confidence."

Sybil and I followed Cass as she went to collect the required forms, though I had little reason to think her report would be taken seriously. This feeling was reinforced when Grady took the finished form and plopped it into the inbox without so much as giving it a second glance.

"You're not even going to read it?" I asked.

"I've got better things to do right now."

I leveled my gaze at Grady. He'd plunked himself down on a chair and steadfastly refused to look up from what appeared to be a glossy magazine with some type of sport on the cover. Better things to do? Yeah, right. "Has James Thorne been in to see you today?"

"Yep."

Don't get me wrong, I was relieved to hear the case was closed, but I was annoyed, too. Being falsely suspected of someone's death will do that to a person. I crossed my arms. "You know, your boys left me quite a mess in the kitchen. Now that you're done with this high-priority investigation of yours, when can I expect you to send someone by to clean it up?"

"We're a law enforcement operation here, Ms. Bassett, not a housekeeping service." He looked up from his magazine, and I couldn't tell if the look in his eyes was one of humor or taunting. "Besides, who said

anything about closing the investigation? If I'd closed
the investigation, do you think I'd still be here on a
Sunday?"

"I guess I just assumed, since you had a
confession—"

"You mean that whole jam thing? It was a stupid
prank, but irrelevant, since the lab reports came back a
big negative on the allergy front."

My eyes widened. Had I come to the wrong conclusion? Maybe that was why Sebastian's ghost was still
hanging around. "If it wasn't allergies, what was it?"

"Possible food-borne neurotoxin. Which means
you're free to clean up that kitchen of yours if you
want, but you won't be cooking anything in it anytime
soon. Not until every sample my boys collected has
been thoroughly analyzed."

The news left me reeling, in part because I had
been left in charge of a bed and breakfast and could no
longer serve breakfast—literally half my job!—and also
because Grady's revelation meant I wasn't off the hook
for Sebastian Greenville's death, either. I still felt
shaky inside when Cass, Sybil, and I reconvened on the
sidewalk outside the station. "What am I going to do?"

Sybil placed a hand on my shoulder. "Don't you
mean what are *we* going to do?"

"I appreciate the gesture," I said, "but I'm the one
who got myself into this pickle. If I hadn't been so
keen to work an untested relaxation spell on an unwit-

ting guest, we might not be standing here. You two have plenty of your own responsibilities to deal with."

"Nonsense," Cass argued, her hand coming to rest on my other shoulder. As always seemed to happen when the three of us made contact, a gentle electric hum began to tickle my toes. "What's the point of a coven if we're not here for one another?"

"Cass is right." The determination in Sybil's eyes was formidable, and I was thankful to have her on my side. Coming up against a witch like her as an opponent would be most unpleasant. "Ladies, up until now, we've taken a pretty informal approach to our witchcraft. I think it's time we up our game."

"How do you mean?" I asked.

"We need to be more disciplined," she answered. "We need regular meetings and a place to gather, not to mention the right clothes."

I cocked one eyebrow at this last bit. "Did you say clothes?" I looked down at what I was wearing, which was basically more of the same casual style I'd rocked 24/7 since arriving on the island. As far as I was concerned, Thoreau had hit the nail on the head when he warned against enterprises that required new clothing. But the enthusiasm on my friend's face was completely unbridled.

"Ceremonial garments." Her eyes twinkled. "Of course, not all covens opt for that. Some wear regular clothes."

"Or go skyclad," Cass added, to which Sybil nodded her agreement.

I just looked from one to the other, completely without a clue. "What is skyclad?"

They exchanged a look. Then Sybil's grip on my shoulder tightened ever so slightly as if lending me support. I soon found out why. "You see, some witches feel that clothing inhibits the natural connection between our world and the divine, and so they opt to perform their rituals and spells, well..."

"Naked?" My eyes were practically bugging out, my head swiveling back and forth on my neck so fast I was in danger of whiplash. "Oh, no. That's not happening."

"Of course not," Cass was quick to assure me. "It's totally optional."

"Absolutely," Sybil concurred. "Besides, I think robes are much more stylish."

I tried to form a mental picture but came up short. "Are we talking bathrobes or, like, something you'd wear at Hogwarts?"

Sybil removed her hand from my shoulder and tilted it back and forth. "Somewhere in between, maybe? We're getting off track here. The point is, with our elders away, we're currently the only three witches in Pinecroft Cove. If we're going to function as a real coven, we need to start acting like one."

"You're right," I said, her words like a rallying cry that stirred confidence deep within and made me forget temporarily that, in the past twenty-four hours, my bungled attempts at magic had possibly killed a famous author and gotten a ghost lost in a time warp. "We're witches. We can take care of our troubles on our own."

SOMETIME LATER, CLUTCHING A BROOM IN one hand and an old rag in the other, I stared at the disaster zone that had once been my aunt Gwen's pride and joy. "We're witches," I muttered under my breath, trying to reclaim the tenacious spirit Sybil had kindled with her speech but coming up short. Magic or not, I simply couldn't see how I would ever get this kitchen clean again.

"Wow, this is…" Sybil's voice trailed off as she stood beside me, surveying the damage and appearing to be similarly overwhelmed. After agreeing we should have an official meeting that night, Cass had gone back to her house to prepare the tower room, leaving Sybil to lend me whatever cleaning help she could. She'd stopped by her house first, donning a sweet pair of denim overalls and a red bandana tied around her head just so, further proof that Sybil saw no reason not to do even the smallest tasks with style. "Now would be a good time for your aunt's famous cleaning spell."

"It truly would be, if only I'd managed to learn it." I plucked at the yellow tape, gingerly at first and then more vigorously, until it tore away from the doorway in strips and chunks. I kicked at an overturned basket on the floor with my toe, leaving a trail in the powdery white flour that coated every tile. I went to the sink and turned on the faucet, letting the water run until steam rose up from deep within the basin. "I guess I'll just have to do this the old-fashioned way."

We both got to work, putting stray items back in place and scrubbing surfaces until slowly the room once more bore some resemblance to its usual self. Though I wasn't pleased with the sheriff's office in the least for the mess they'd made, and at least part of me suspected the excessiveness had been intentional because of Grady's dislike for me, there was something oddly therapeutic about doing such a simple task. As much as I appreciated the convenience of Aunt Gwen's cleaning spells, it occurred to me that using a little bit of elbow grease from time to time wasn't such a bad thing. It cleared my head and helped me think.

The problem was, I had two distinctly different ghost problems. The one who was supposed to be here —because I guess after all those weeks I'd finally gotten used to the idea of having Lillian around—was missing. And the one who had no business whatsoever hanging around the place showed no signs of leaving. But what to do? With the pendulum gone, I had no hope of reconnecting with Lillian. And if it turned out I was the one actually responsible for Sebastian Grenville's death? I gulped down a lump that blocked my throat. If that were the case, his spirit wouldn't be going anywhere, but that would probably be the least of my concerns.

I was on my knees, deeply engrossed in thought while cleaning grout between the floor tiles, when a voice other than Sybil's reminded me we weren't alone.

"Excuse me?" Looking up, I saw Jacqueline Cortez standing in the doorway to the kitchen. With all the other guests gone, I'd almost forgotten she was still in the house. Her face was pale and drawn, and her tone had an almost robotic quality, devoid of emotion. "I'm having trouble with the Wi-Fi. Is it down?"

"Not that I know of." I patted my pockets but couldn't locate my phone, so I turned to Sybil, who was busy wiping flour dust off the jars and cans in the pantry. "Can you check and see if you've got a Wi-Fi signal on your phone?"

Sybil pulled her phone from the top pocket of her overalls and squinted at the screen. "Looks fine to me. Would you like to borrow it?"

Sybil held the phone out toward Jacqueline, who shook her head. I was relieved to see some of the color had returned to her cheeks, and when she spoke, it was with a much more natural tone. "No. Thank you, though. It's really sweet of you to offer. I'm in the middle of doing some research, and I really need to be able to access it on my laptop so I can print."

"You might try the library." Sybil fumbled with the

phone in an uncharacteristically clumsy way, missing her pocket twice before finally stowing it safely away, then wiping her hands along the legs of her overalls before reaching out to shake Jacqueline's hand. "I'm Sybil, by the way. As it happens, I'm kind of in charge of the archives section right now, so I'd be happy to show you around and get you settled in. We've got computers there, and if you promise not to tell anyone, I'll let you print whatever you need for free."

The woman's face melted into a grateful smile. "I'm Jackie. Nice to meet you. And, yes, I would really appreciate that. I've got a terrible deadline looming, and I absolutely can't afford to miss it."

I gave her a sharp look, wondering once again how, with her fiancé so freshly departed from this mortal realm, her first thought could possibly be about work. Sure, people grieved in their own way, but was this normal? "Right, I'll just finish up here," I muttered as the two women left the kitchen together without so much as a backward glance, "and then go check on the upstairs router." There was no reply, and I could hear them chatting as the front door shut. Looked like I was on my own, although at least with Sybil keeping Jacqueline entertained, I didn't have my weird guest to worry about for a while.

Considering I wasn't allowed to cook in it, the kitchen seemed fine for the moment, so I put the cleaning supplies away, retrieved my phone from my bag, and headed upstairs. Though the router in the hall closet seemed fine, I reset it just to be sure, then poked my head into Jacqueline's room with the intention of checking the signal strength on my phone. There was no need. As soon as I looked into the room, I had a pretty good idea what the problem was.

The ghost of Sebastian Grenville sat on the chaise lounge in his usual spot, but his appearance had changed. He was no longer shadows and mist, nor was he in the nearly solid state Lillian usually manifested. Instead, he glowed. I could make out his form and features much more clearly than before, but the best way to describe it might be to say he was like plastic or glass through which a blue-green light shone. Energy radiated from him in waves, like ripples moving across an unseen pond in all directions, forming a sort of bubble that extended several yards beyond the core of his being. The desk, and Jacqueline's laptop, were fully engulfed by this luminous orb, and it didn't take an expert in ectoplasm to peg that as the source of the Wi-Fi interference.

"Look, Sebastian," I said, taking a step closer. The rippling vibrations seemed to change their frequency, which I took as a sign he heard me. "I don't know what you're doing here, but you need to tone down whatever you've got going on with the energy, okay? It's interfering with the internet connection."

There was no response, so I inched closer until I stood just at the edge of the blue-green sphere. I held up my hand and poked the periphery with a finger, not my index finger, but the pinky on my left hand. I figured if it was vaporized by Sebastian's energy orb, that was the finger I could most readily live without. Luckily, my digit remained intact as it passed across the boundary. A faint chill traveled up my arm as I allowed the rest of my hand to follow, though whether it was because of the supernatural vibrations or just my imagination, I wasn't certain. Feeling reassured it was safe, I stepped completely inside the bubble.

The first thing I noticed was a low hum all around me, and when I swiveled my head to take in my surroundings, there appeared to be an iridescent film separating me from the space beyond Sebastian's influence. As for the man himself, he remained on the chaise, looking a bit more human from this vantage point, but faded as if he'd been left out to bleach in the sun. I took several steps toward the desk, and he watched me but didn't react.

Jacqueline's laptop was open on the desk, with piles of papers all around. With one eye on my spectral guest, I took a closer look. The document on the screen was not his forthcoming novel, *Azalea Nightfall*, as I'd expected it to be, but something else, half-finished at best. The papers were scrawled with notes in various colors of ink and two distinct handwritings. As for the explanation, a theory had begun working its way through my brain, and I didn't like it one bit.

"Are you possessing her?" I turned to face Sebastian's spirit. "Is that what this is? You left a novel

COVENS, CAKES, AND BIG MISTAKES   125

unfinished when you died, and this is your plan to get it done?"

He didn't answer, but he didn't have to. It explained so much, especially Jacqueline's odd fixation on work ever since her fiancé's death. I'd assumed she was cold and unfeeling, but perhaps that wasn't the case. What if she was under the famous writer's influence, pressed into doing his bidding so that he could finish his book and move on to the next plane? Considering how quickly she'd warmed up once she was downstairs and away from the ghost's sphere of influence, it was the one explanation that made perfect sense. But it had to be dangerous for Jacqueline, being possessed like that. I felt duty bound to help Sebastian cross over to whatever lay ahead of him, but I couldn't allow him to resolve his unfinished business at the expense of a living being. The question remained, now that I knew what was going on, what was I going to do about it?

CHAPTER NINE

I'd been to the tower room at Cass's house a number of times, but as I approached the door of the gingerbread-trimmed Victorian that night, two things made it feel very different. First, her mother and grandmother were not at home. Whatever mishaps might occur, we were on our own. But perhaps even more unnerving, unlike other times we'd met to work magic, tonight would be the official consecration of our coven. After this, there would be no going back. As I reached for the brass ring of the old-fashioned knocker, I was grateful to have something solid to hold onto to keep my hand from shaking.

The door opened, and I would be lying if I said the sight of both Cass and Sybil standing, fully clothed, in the foyer didn't provide just a hint of relief. I hadn't forgotten about my earlier lesson on the meaning of the term "skyclad," nor had I changed my mind about exactly how much I did not want to be a part of anything that involved prancing around naked. My relief was somewhat short-lived. As soon as we climbed to the top of the tower and I got a look at how the big, round table in the middle had been set, my heart was thumping once more at double speed.

A velvet cloth of deep forest green had been draped over the table, heavily embroidered in gold thread with a pentacle in the middle, surrounded by a circle of mystical symbols, which my limited training led me to believe represented the wheel of the year. Candles had been positioned to form four corners, and the four spaces in between had been filled with a variety of magical objects. There was a heavy silver chalice filled with what appeared to be dark red wine beside a shallow dish containing bite-sized cakes. A stick of incense sat in mahogany holder that had a design traced in a mother-of-pearl inlay, and a brass dish sat nearby, holding a bundle of sage. A cut crystal dish contained salt, while the matching one beside it held water. Three sticks sat off to one side, burnished to a high sheen. All of these things were mysterious and exciting, but what struck fear in me was something else: a long knife placed atop a thick, leather bound book.

Every movie I'd ever seen about witches came back to me as I stared at the book, and at the wickedly sharp blade. My imagination ran wild. Would I be required to slice my palm and sign my name in blood, and if I did, would my soul belong to some evil horned beast? Or maybe, I thought, my eyes darting around the room, there was a chicken in a cage waiting to be sacrificed. Maybe it was both. I jumped as a hand landed on my back.

"Tamsyn?" Sybil searched my eyes, and I could see the concern in her creased brow. "Are you okay?"

"Just a little nervous," I admitted, not bothering to raise my fears about blood oaths and sacrifices, as already they seemed rather far-fetched. It's not like I hadn't learned enough from Aunt Gwen by now to know that Hollywood images of witches were dead wrong. I just wished that knife was not quite so pointy.

"I know it looks a little intimidating," Cass said, an apologetic expression on her face, "but I wanted to do something special to mark the occasion."

"No, it's amazing," I assured her. "I just don't know what it all means."

"Allow me." Sybil said, entering full schoolteacher mode. "Here, you have the four elements. Salt signifies the earth. The athame is a symbol of air. Candles are for fire, and there's water, of course."

"Wait, that's a symbol for air?" I gave the dagger-like implement a sidelong look.

"Yes," Sybil said, "along with feathers and incense."

I snorted. "The feathers and incense I get, but I didn't know air was so stabby."

"We don't use it to stab or cut. I promise," Sybil soothed.

"So, I won't have to sign my name in blood in that book in order to join the coven?" My voice was barely louder than a whisper, a combination of worry and embarrassment.

"Oh, you'll definitely have to do that. How else will the goat-god know you've been marked as one of his own. Right, Cass?" It was only when Cass started to giggle that I realized the joke was on me. Sybil broke into a grin. "I don't know what you were allowed to watch and read growing up, but we have got to find you some better, witch-positive, forms of entertainment."

"Okay, you got me," I said. "But at least you can tell me what the book is actually for."

"It's blank right now, but starting tonight, that will become our Book of Shadows." Sybil ran her hand along the cover. "It's where we'll record our spells and rituals, although tonight it's really more for writing down our coven rules."

"Covens have rules?" I frowned, having never considered this possibility. "Like what?"

"Paying your dues on time," Cass suggested, and Sybil nodded in agreement.

My eyes darted from one to the other, shocked. "We pay dues?"

"Candles aren't free, Tamsyn," Sybil pointed out. "It causes fewer problems if we all pitch in ahead of time instead of everyone owing or someone getting stuck with the bill. Which reminds me, I was kind of hoping you'd agree to be treasurer, since you used to be an accountant and all."

"Covens have treasurers?" I made my way to one of the chairs that had been pushed to the edge of the room and sat down. This was starting to sound less like a mystical gathering and more like my high school student council. I'd been treasurer then, too, naturally. It might not have been my life's calling, but before discovering I was a witch, I'd been a darn good accountant. "Is there a president and a secretary, too?"

"Not exactly, but we'll have to decide on a High Priestess," Sybil said.

"That should be you," Cass told Sybil without a moment's hesitation.

Sybil waved a hand dismissively, but she wasn't fooling anyone. I had no idea what the job entailed, but I could tell Sybil wanted it.

"What does a High Priestess do?" I asked.

"She's the one who is best at all the spells, and the most organized," Cass replied.

I looked at Sybil. "Well, that's definitely you."

"I wouldn't say that," Sybil demurred dutifully, though her heart wasn't in it. "We're all equally good."

"I just had half my potion herbs stolen from under my nose," Cass pointed out.

"And my kitchen has been quarantined by the police. So, yeah. Sybil's got my vote, for sure."

"Mine, too."

Sybil's cheeks flushed pink. "Well, thank you both. I'll accept the honor, but only with the understanding that we can revisit it later, when you've both had a chance to grow into your magical abilities some more. Practice makes perfect, and I've simply had more practice than you two."

It was exactly the kind of humble and diplomatic response that pretty much guaranteed Sybil would be High Priestess for life. Honestly, I had no designs on it myself. I just dreamed of the day when my powers came naturally enough to me that I didn't live in constant fear of my dinner exploding because I made some stray wish while stirring the pot.

Far from what I'd expected from the elaborate set up, the evening turned out to be mostly mundane. Cass, who had a flair for calligraphy, inscribed the Wiccan Rede and Rule of Three on the first page of the leather book. They were singsong poems, and while I'd never heard them before, both she and Sybil knew them by heart, nursery rhymes every witch child could recite at bedtime to remind them to harm no one with their magic and that what they sent out into the world would return to them threefold.

Then we each took turns signing our names at the bottom, but in regular black ink instead of blood, and without invoking any frightening beasts or removing articles of clothing. To say I was relieved would be an understatement. We'd been there for hours, and it was nearly time to leave when the conversation finally turned toward the initial reason we'd decided to gather.

"What are we going to do about Tamsyn's kitchen," Cass asked, "and about my missing herbs, too? I've been trying all day, but I just can't think of a magical solution to either problem."

Sybil sat for a while in serious thought. "We could cast a spell to bring the perpetrators to justice."

"That's all well and good for the thieves," I said, a knot forming in my belly as I silently recited the Rule of Three in my head, "but what about me? If we go asking for justice to rain down on Sebastian Grenville's killer, and it turns out I was responsible, isn't that just inviting trouble?"

Oh, who was I kidding? Even without knowing the rules, I'd been inviting trouble my way since the moment I'd stepped on the island.

"What about a finding spell for now?" Cass suggested. "As long as I get my ingredients back, I don't really care if I find out who's responsible."

"That could work," Sybil said, rising from her chair and going to the altar in the center of the room.

"What's a finding spell?" I asked.

"Pretty much what it sounds like, a lost and found for the universe," Cass said. "We cast a circle, then focus our energy through our wands as we recite the incantation, and the lost item we're trying to retrieve comes back to us."

"Great, except I don't know any incantations, and I don't have a wand." All I'd been given in that department was a magical wooden spoon, and let's just say, owing to our complicated relationship, that baby stays in the cupboard as much as possible.

"Oh, but you do." Sybil turned back to face us, the bowl of salt in one hand and the three sticks in the other.

Comprehension dawned. "Those are wands?"

"One for each of us," Sybil said. "They're made of three different trees from the sacred grove: oak, ash, and willow."

"There's a sacred grove?" I swear I was learning something new every second.

Sybil nodded. "In the heart of the woods just off the banks of Pinecroft Cove. It's been there since the first witches settled there over three hundred years ago."

She held out the wands, and I could see that they were, indeed, three different types of wood. One was a dark, rich brown, another almost pure white, and the third was light with a graceful curve. My fingers hovered above them, uncertain if I should touch. "Do I pick one, wave it around, and see if sparks come out?"

Sybil gave me a look. "That really doesn't work outside of wand shops in Diagon Alley. The real world is a little subtler."

I'll admit I was disappointed. For all the ways I had struggled with accepting my relationship with magic, this was one of the few times when I wouldn't have minded finding out that something from a movie was real. I mean, how cool would it be to pick up a stick and have flames or a laser beam fly from the tip?

"So, what do I do?" I asked, probably more sullenly than was appropriate considering I was still being offered a magic wand.

"Close your eyes, and let your hands drift over the choices. See if you can feel anything."

I was about to spout off some smart-aleck comment, except that as soon as my hand got within a few inches of the dark wand, I felt a distinctive pull, like I was being drawn toward it with an invisible force. "This one," I said, sucking in my breath as my fingers wrapped around the wood.

When I picked it up, no sparks flew out, but it didn't matter. Don't get me wrong. I gave it a quick flick of the wrist to see, just in case the others had been incorrect. Nothing dramatic happened, but it didn't matter. I knew I'd found the one. It felt like an extension of my arm, almost as though, if I closed my eyes, I could sense the tip of the wand in the same way I could feel my own fingertips. I looked to Sybil, surprised, but she just nodded as if she'd expected this all along.

"Oak is for strength," she told me. "Some say that

oak trees are immune to lightning strikes, and its wood is prized for its invulnerability."

"May I try?" Cass asked breathlessly, looking at the two remaining wands with eyes shining.

"Of course." Sybil held them out, and after a moment of deliberation, Cass took the one that was nearly white. Again, Sybil smiled knowingly. "Ash is for protection. When your skills with potions are properly honed, you'll be a powerful healer, so it makes sense you'd be drawn to that one."

"What about the third one?" I asked. "You didn't get to choose."

"Oh, I knew this one was mine all along." Sybil gave the remaining wand a playful swish. "It's willow, representing intuition and femininity."

She was right. The description of the willow wand fit Sybil perfectly. As I held mine, getting accustomed to the feel and weight, I wondered if I would live up to the wand I had chosen. Strength and invulnerability were hardly characteristics I would have attributed to myself. I didn't have any particularly notable physical abilities, and both mentally and emotionally since coming to live in Pinecroft Cove, I frequently found myself on the verge of falling apart. I hadn't even been strong enough to keep Lillian from getting lost somewhere in the void.

Finding spell. The words echoed in my head as I watched Sybil begin casting the circle by sprinkling salt around the room. When she'd finished, I asked the question that had suddenly presented itself as a possibly brilliant solution. "Can you use the finding spell to locate anything that's lost, including people?"

"That's a good question." Sybil twisted her lips as if giving it some thought. "I've only ever had luck with smaller items."

"It's great for keys," Cass chimed in, "and cell phones, and the like."

"I used it to locate a particularly rare Fortuny dress once, but my grandmother helped, and they're very light weight."

I stifled a sigh. The idea of getting Lillian back via a simple finding spell had been too good to be true, anyway. "But it'll work on the herbs?"

"Only one way to find out," Sybil said.

With the circle cast, Sybil and I stood together while Cass wrote out the words to the incantation on a fresh sheet of paper, our first spell entered in our coven's Book of Shadows. When she'd finished, she stepped aside so we could read.

"What once was lost, now is found,
The wheel of time circles round.
Whether hidden far or near,
We bid you now to come back here."

"That's it?" My confidence increased a bit. It was a simple spell, as easy to remember as a nursery rhyme. Just a few times through and I knew it by heart.

"If we're ready," Sybil directed, "wands together. Stand close, and point the tips to the floor. Then close your eyes, and focus all your energy on the missing ingredients, until I begin the incantation. Then you can all join in."

We did as she said, repeating the words until they flowed together and seemed to lose all meaning. It was impossible to say how long we stood like that, intoning the magic spell, and while I could feel something happening, I couldn't have described it, or even put my finger on exactly what it was. Eventually, though, Sybil raised her wand as a signal to stop, and we did the same. Whatever the spell was meant to do, it appeared it was done.

"Now we wait," Sybil said.

After a ritual of wine and cakes, we closed the circle and departed for home. The inn was dark when I arrived, as I'd left without turning on a lamp for my return. There was no sign of Jacqueline, though a faint glow from the bottom of her closed door as I passed it on my way to the third floor made me wonder if she was still up working. Was the glow from a light, or was it coming from Sebastian's ghostly energy? I worried he might be growing more powerful and regretted not having raised the issue at the coven meeting, but I still wasn't able to bring myself to admit, even to the witches closest to me, that I could see spirits the way I did.

Speaking of spirits, I looked around hopefully when I reached my room, which I had moved back into since all the guests had left, but was disappointed to find that, though Gus was snoozing on my comforter and spreading liberal amounts of fur all over it in the process, Lillian had not returned. "Still no sign of her?" I asked the sleeping cat, who did not respond, as was usual for him.

A fresh wave of guilt washed over me as, in the process of putting on my pajamas, I spied the bracelet on my wrist and the bare spot on my chest where the amethyst pendulum had rested on its chain. Why had I not noticed when it had fallen off? The tunnel was difficult to access, and even if I could get in, it was a long shot I'd ever find—

The finding spell.

I reached for my bag, pulling out the dark oak wand I'd stowed there inside a velvet pouch Sybil had provided for that purpose. I ran my finger over the smooth, shiny wood, wondering if I could work the spell on my own. Given my track record, the odds of it being a success weren't great. All I knew was I needed to try.

I pointed the wand to the floor, clearing my mind until all I could see was the pendulum. Then I began to recite the spell, over and over, until I no longer was aware of my surroundings or anything at all except the rhythm of the words as they slid in a whisper over my lips.

What was lost…time circles round…come back here…

I have no idea how long I was at it, only that eventually I stopped and slid beneath the covers, too exhausted to go on. I must have spent a restless night because the sheets and blankets were strewn everywhere when I awoke, but I had no memory of it. All I was aware of, when the first rays of light flickered in through the window, were claws in my chest and something hard and cold whacking me in the nose.

I opened my eyes. Gus stood on top of me, a silver chain clutched in his mouth, the amethyst pendulum at the end swinging back and forth, and occasionally making contact with my face. I had no idea where the rascal had found it, but I didn't really need to. The important thing was, the pendulum was back and my finding spell had worked. It might not be Lillian, but at least it was a start.

onsidering my job was to run a bed and breakfast, only pretty much all of my guests had checked out and my kitchen had been closed by order of the Board of Health, it turned out that Monday morning lacked the urgency it once had held when I was a regular working stiff with a nine-to-five job. After checking on Jacqueline, only to be met by a grunt from the other side of a closed door that indicated she did not need anything, my biggest concern was what to do with the pendulum. Should I wear it in hopes Lillian would be drawn to it and return, or should I opt to put it somewhere safe until I could do some research on whether there was a stronger finding spell that might bring her home? Given my poor track record, I was tempted to tuck the object away in the top drawer of my dresser for safe keeping, but at the last second, I clasped it around my neck instead. There was a better chance she'd come home that way.

Had I just referred to the inn as Lillian's home? When had I developed such a sentimental streak? I still wasn't entirely certain why I wanted Lillian to come back. It had been awfully quiet in the hours since she'd disappeared, which was a welcome relief to my ears after weeks of nonstop chitchat. On the other hand, I'd gotten used to the feisty flapper and her unintelligible slang. The house seemed rather empty without her. And, of course, there was the issue that the house was, in fact, not empty at all. I had an uninvited and unwelcome spirit hanging out, and possibly possessing my one and only guest, which surely couldn't be a good thing. For all her foibles, Lillian was my window to the spirit world. Without her, I had no idea how I would ever get Mr. Grenville to move along.

When I was dressed and ready for the day, I stopped in the kitchen, intent on making myself a cup of tea, but I found myself standing in the middle of the room instead, wondering what to do. Thanks to Sybil and my efforts the day before, the space was clean and sparkling, but technically, it was still off-limits. The problem was when the sheriff had delivered the news, I'd failed to clarify what that meant. If I boiled water, could I be hauled off to jail? Normally, this wouldn't have been a concern, but I swear the man had it in for me and I seriously didn't put it past him to be waiting for the opportunity. With nothing else on my agenda that day, I decided to make a trip into town and get breakfast at the Dockside Diner.

The weather was crisp but pleasant, so I hopped on my bicycle and pedaled off. By the time I reached the diner, my stomach was rumbling, and the smell of bacon and biscuits that wafted through the parking lot made my mouth water. I opened the door and was met with dozens of pairs of staring eyes, coupled with deathly silence. I felt itchy all over and totally self-conscious, like I was wearing a wool sweater that I'd also suddenly discovered was see-through. Perhaps it was because I'd delivered a batch of truth-laced magical pies to the restaurant, which had started a brawl, or maybe it was because my meddling had led to the owner's sister going to prison for murder, but whatever the reason, some of the townsfolk looked at me a little differently these days. A little less friendly. I'll be honest; I wasn't enjoying it.

There are drawbacks to being a witch on a small island.

Just as I was about to leave, I heard someone call out, "Tamsyn, over here!"

It was Noah, and seated across from him at the table was Sybil, who turned around long enough to flash a friendly smile. After the chilly reception, I'd lost all desire to stay, but the rest of the diners had gone back to eating, and I couldn't very well turn around and leave now that I'd been spotted by people I knew. Instead, I made my way to their table as unobtrusively as possible. My eyes darted from Noah to Sybil, trying to figure out the exact nature of their cozy seating arrangement at this table for two tucked away in the back. A pang of something I was absolutely not going to refer to as jealousy bit into me, which I immediately banished to the furthest corner of my mind. It's not like it was any of my business, but had I missed something of a romantic nature building between them? Monday morning breakfast strongly suggested more than casual friendship.

"I was just coming in for some tea and a quick bite," I said as I got close enough to speak without shouting so that the whole room could hear me. "Sorry to interrupt. I don't want to butt in on your breakfast."

"Don't be silly," Noah said. "You're not interrupting at all."

"I just popped in for a cinnamon roll to go," Sybil added, "but they're not out of the oven yet, so I sat here to wait." It was at this point I saw, while Noah had a full breakfast in front of him, Sybil's place was conspicuously empty. I prayed my cheeks weren't turning bright red as I realized the error of my earlier assumptions.

"Shirley's making cinnamon rolls?" I asked, taking a seat in the chair Noah had procured for me from a nearby table. "I hope she won't mind selling me one."

"Why would she mind?" Noah asked.

"I couldn't help but notice I got a chilly reception

when I walked in the door," I said with a shrug. "I have a feeling some people around here don't like me much."

"I don't think it's anything personal," Noah assured me. "It takes folks here a while to truly warm up to newcomers, even if you have ties to the island like you do. They don't mean anything by it."

"Your Pinecroft Cove connection doesn't help," Sybil said. "People can be a bit superstitious."

Noah laughed. "Oh, now, I wouldn't worry about that. I don't think anyone around here really believes in witches anymore."

I uttered a faint laugh, but inside, I'd gone cold. What exactly did people in Summerhaven think about the residents of Pinecroft Cove, and more importantly, what did Noah think? I was already biting my nails to the quick over the secrets I was hiding from my aunt and my coven. Did I need to hide from Noah, too?

I was saved from falling down this particular rabbit hole when Shirley brought over a paper sack for Sybil and, much to my relief, greeted me with a kind smile. "Tamsyn, I haven't seen you around in a while. How've you been?"

"I've been okay, thanks." I scuffed the toe of one shoe against the floor beneath the table but managed not to look away. "I trust you got your blueberry pies each week?" As we'd agreed, I'd continued to bake the pies she'd ordered for the diner through the end of the summer season, but I'd asked Aunt Gwen to take care of delivering them.

"Like clockwork, right up through Labor Day. But I've missed seeing you."

I dug the tip of my shoe deeper into the hard, checkered tile. "I wasn't sure how you'd feel, considering."

"You were worried about me?" Shirley's eyes widened, and she pressed her hand to her chest. "My sister tried to kill you. If anything, I assumed that was what kept you away. Can I get you a cinnamon roll?"

I nodded eagerly, relieved to have put the awkward incident behind me for good. "That takes care of one meal, anyway. Now to figure out lunch and dinner without a kitchen. I think the Pizza Shack's still open. Sybil, you up for grabbing a slice with me tonight?"

"I would," she answered, not meeting my eyes, "but I kind of have a date."

I glanced sharply at Noah, my earlier suspicions returning. But instead of fessing up, he tilted his head a fraction of an inch to one side. "You know, we need to talk through the bake sale details, and that dinner offer I made still stands."

"You don't have plans?"

"Nope."

"Oh." For some reason, my insides knotted up at that news. "But, considering my kitchen woes, aren't you afraid I'll screw up the bake sale? I know you're counting on it for the island kids, and I don't want to be the reason it fails."

"Don't be silly. I believe in you." His assurance was delivered with such genuine feeling that it made my eyes mist. "Pick you up at seven?"

I swallowed and nodded, the lump in my stomach dissipating once I'd sealed the deal. I had no idea why I had been so nervous about having dinner with him in the first place. It wasn't like it was a date, just pizza between friends, and a little bit of shop talk as we ironed out the details of the fundraiser. As Noah said his goodbyes and left the diner, I couldn't help but think I'd been a real idiot about the whole thing.

I turned my attention back to Sybil, who had grabbed her cinnamon roll and was just about to stand. "Not so fast. You think you can just say you have a date and then skedaddle? I don't think so."

Sybil's cheeks burned hot. "It's not a big deal."

"Is it James?" I narrowed my eyes in suspicion. "It is, isn't it? James Thorne finally acted on that crush of his and asked you out. This is all my fault."

Sybil gave me a dubious look. "How do you figure that?"

"If I hadn't sent you to his shop to get the jam, he never would've had the chance. He's ten years older than you, and that prank he pulled at the tea was just mean."

"Then why do you think I would go out with him?"

"You were probably afraid to hurt his feelings."

"Says the woman who sent me to his shop in the first place because she was too chicken to go herself."

"He's completely wrong for you," I argued.

"Fate works in mysterious ways. You shouldn't be so quick to judge." She took her bag and headed to the door without looking back.

My regret was immediate. I'd made her angry, which was the last thing I'd intended. "I'm sorry, Sybil," I called after her. "Enjoy your date tonight."

"You too, dear," she answered, leaving me to squirm in my chair as I fretted over exactly what everyone in the diner thought of *that* response.

I WAS STANDING ON THE PORCH AT PRECISELY seven o'clock when Noah pulled into the drive. The moment he got out of the car, I suspected something was amiss. While I'd dressed in jeans and a hoodie, he wore a button-down shirt and a tie. However, I was able to put my misgivings aside until he whizzed past the six empty parking spaces in front of the pizza place and pulled into the parking lot for the Salt and Sea, instead.

The Salt and Sea restaurant was the finest eating establishment on Summerhaven Island, hands down. The chef, Andrew Bacon, had trained in New York and Paris before marrying a woman who'd grown up spending her summers on the island, and they'd

decided to open a restaurant from May through
October to make the most of their part-time home.
The food was locally sourced, the menu filled with
unique variations of every type of seafood, caught
fresh from the bay. There was always something new
to try, and the only guarantee was the lobster would
never be boiled. There were half a dozen places to get
that, and lobster rolls, too, but only one Salt and Sea.

"Uh, aren't we just grabbing a slice?" I asked when
Noah circled the car and opened my door.

"Pizza?" He gave me a look like I'd grown a third
eyeball in the middle of my forehead. "I told you
weeks ago I was going to take you here."

True. He had. I just hadn't believed him. I glanced
self-consciously at my casual attire and wished I hadn't
done such a thorough job of convincing myself the
evening wasn't a big deal. *He must think I'm such a disaster.* Without admitting to any romantic interest in
Noah, I could safely say he was exactly the type of guy
I'd always *said* I wanted, successful and confident. The
only thing was, I had no real-world experience with a
guy like that. My previous boyfriends were more what
I liked to call fixer-uppers. Now *I* was the fixer-upper,
and I didn't like the feeling one bit.

The restaurant's deep navy blue storefront over-
looked a particularly scenic part of Main Street, which
offered views of both Penobscot Bay and Turner's Pond
from a lovely outside deck where drinks were served
while patrons waited for tables, which were always at a

premium no matter the time of year. Noah and I went to the deck first, and I stayed while he went to fetch me a drink from the bar inside.

Though the summer tourist season was over, the warm weather had not quite departed. The sun shone brightly as I made my way through the well-dressed patrons on the deck and tried to pretend I didn't notice the raised eyebrows my ensemble was generating. As I took a step toward the deck rail, I spotted the back of a head sporting a familiar platinum blonde bob. On the one hand, I didn't want to intrude on her date, but there was no sign of James. He was probably inside like Noah was, ordering something from the bar, so I figured it would be safe to chat for a minute or two. There were dozens of people on the deck, and it was only when I'd pushed my way quite close that I noticed Sybil was conversing with another familiar face, the sole guest of the Pinecroft Inn.

Coming up from behind, I placed a hand on Sybil's shoulder and was rewarded with a nasty look from Jacqueline. Unlike the other looks I'd been receiving, this one seemed less related to my clothing and more like I was interrupting or something. What an odd woman. "We just keep running into each other today," I said with a laugh.

"Oh, you scared me." Sybil had jumped at the sound of my voice, sending the drink in her hand sloshing dangerously close to the rim. I glanced around. If she already had a glass of wine, then James wasn't at the bar after all, and I wondered where he'd gone.

I looked to Jacqueline with genuine concern. Though she was dressed nicely and had put on a touch of makeup, her complexion still had an unhealthiness to it from too many hours spent indoors. "It's good to see you're taking a break from all that work of yours."

An image of her workspace flashed into my mind, deep within the bubble of Sebastian's ghostly influence. I remembered the document containing the unfinished manuscript on her laptop screen and the stacks of notes, which had left me puzzled. "What is it you're working on, exactly?"

"Oh, just some press releases." Jacqueline's eyes shifted downward as she took a sip of her wine. "Despite the sad turn of events, the launch of Sebastian's book is going forward full speed, so I have a lot of work on my plate."

Now, I knew that was a lie, and before I took a moment to think better of it, I said so to her face. "Sure didn't look like press releases to me."

Jacqueline's eyes shot back up. "Excuse me?"

Her tone sent up some red flags, but by this point, my heart was racing and I was too worked up to pay them any attention. "What I saw on your desk looked a lot like an unfinished Sebastian Grenville manuscript."

"You were snooping around my desk?"

My brain was really humming by this point, going

so loud and fast I barely registered what Jacqueline had said as a chilling possibility presented itself. "You're trying to pass it off as your own, aren't you? I'll bet you killed him for it!"

"Tamsyn!" Sybil cried out, sounding oddly reproachful. Considering the astonishing discovery I'd just made, I would've thought she'd have been proud.

"Think about it, all those brilliant manuscripts on his hard drive, just waiting to be plagiarized."

"Do you hear yourself right now?" Jacqueline said, her volume increasing with each word.

"You had easy access to his food," I said, pointing a finger at Jacqueline's chest, "and knew all of his dietary issues. Then you waited until you were on a remote island with no hospital nearby. What could be easier?" Truly, I was amazed I hadn't thought of it before. She'd been so cold toward her fiancé's death. Besides, Sebastian Grenville's ghost was haunting her room, so it had to be for a good reason.

Jacqueline turned to Sybil. "I think we should go."

"You can go if you'd like," I told her, "but the sheriff will be coming for you soon enough. In the meantime, I'm sure Sybil would appreciate it if you left so she can enjoy her date."

Sybil's face had turned bright red, and when she spoke, it was quietly, with her jaw clenched. "She is my date."

I stared blankly. "What?"

"Jackie *is* my date."

There was a whirring sensation between my ears, throwing me off balance. "But you said you were going on a date with James."

Sybil breathed in deeply. "No, you said I was going with James. I simply didn't say otherwise."

Jacqueline put a hand on her hip. "Gee, thanks."

Sybil turned to her, apologetic. "I just didn't want to get into a long explanation."

Jacqueline's eyes narrowed. "I don't see what's so complicated—"

"Stop it!" I bellowed, my voice reverberating in my nasal passages. I faced Jacqueline, fists clenched. "All that matters is you murdered Sebastian Grenville!"

All conversation on the deck had fallen silent, and for the second time in the day, I found myself the center of attention in a hushed crowd. It was at this point I realized Noah had reappeared from inside the restaurant. I wasn't sure how long he'd been watching, but the look on his face said it was long enough to have heard me accuse Jacqueline of murder.

"They've found us a table," he said quietly, looking directly at me and proceeding with all the caution of a man about to diffuse a bomb on a crowded subway platform. "It happens to seat four. Maybe we should sort this out inside."

In fact, all three of them were looking at me that way, and I had no idea why. I was not the one in the wrong here, other than making a public spectacle of myself, which, let's face it, was a personal talent. The evidence was stacked against Jacqueline as high as the Empire State Building. She was in possession of Sebastian Grenville's documents, which she seemed to be altering for her own gain. She hadn't shed a single tear for the man as far as I had seen, and now I'd found out she was on a date—and with one of my best friends—just two days after her fiancé had died. That wasn't normal. She was definitely up to no good.

But Noah and Sybil kept staring, and the more they did, the more my righteous indignation gave way to a tightness in my chest, until, somewhat meekly, I followed Noah inside, wondering exactly what I could possibly have missed, since my friends certainly seemed convinced I'd gotten something very wrong.

CHAPTER ELEVEN

The interior of the Salt and Sea was a combination of rich wood paneling like on an old ship and freshly painted white plaster. The ceiling was covered with heavily embossed tin tiles, from which hung pendant lights that looked like lanterns. One full wall was covered with dozens of small apothecary drawers from some previous incarnation of the space. Long wooden oars were mounted above this, and in front of the wide picture window hung a model of a shark. It was a fun and elegant setting for a meal, but I was too worried over the confrontation that was surely coming to get much enjoyment from it. Honestly, I was only paying such close attention to the decor to avoid noticing whether the people inside were already as aware of my outburst on the deck as those outside had been.

"What is this all about?" Noah whispered as we

took our seats inside the restaurant. "You accused a woman of murder in front of the entire restaurant."

"I may have leaped hastily to a few conclusions," I hedged, not wanting to come right out and admit to mistakes until I'd established that I had actually made any.

"By which you mean accusing Sybil's date of murder?"

I cringed. I'd been hoping he'd arrived on the scene late enough that he'd missed that part. "You knew Jacqueline was Sybil's date?"

"Of course. Couldn't you tell by the way they were standing so close to each other out there? I knew it the second we arrived."

In retrospect, they'd seemed kind of cozy, but honestly, I guess I hadn't given it a lot of thought. I'd just been so convinced that she was having dinner with James, I'd let that color my observations. "But, isn't that weird?" I argued.

Noah's expression turned more severe than it already had been. "I really didn't peg you as one to judge like that. People can't help who they're attracted to."

"I didn't mean it like that! The fact they're on a date isn't what's bothering me," I corrected. "It's that Jacqueline's fiancé just died—like, two days ago! I've heard of getting back out there, but come on. Even you have to admit that's a little fast. And why would Sybil agree to it?"

"What did I agree to?" Sybil asked as she and Jacqueline finally made it to the table.

Noah and I were seated on one side, with two empty chairs across from us. There had been a delay of close to a minute between us sitting and their arrival, during which I could only imagine one of the women encouraging and cajoling the other to hear me out, though I wasn't sure which one would be more inclined to argue on my behalf. I didn't have high hopes that either one of them would like what I had to say, but I planned to say it anyway.

"Thank you for deciding to join us," I began, starting with a conciliatory tone in hopes it would improve the outcome. "And Sybil, I owe you an apology. I shouldn't have assumed you were here with James."

Sybil lifted an eyebrow. "And what about owing Jackie an apology?"

"You're right. I shouldn't have voiced my suspicions out loud for half the island to hear."

"You shouldn't have had those suspicions at all," Sybil scolded. "Look, I understand about the thing with James. That's partially my fault, as I should've corrected you this morning. But how could you think Jackie would kill Sebastian?"

"Try to see it from my point of view. I already knew she was lying about working on press releases because I'd seen the papers on her desk. And she was obviously lying about being in love with her fiancé, too. Did it not bother you how quickly she moved on?"

"Why do you think she couldn't have been in love with Sebastian?" Sybil challenged.

"Well, because it's been two days and she's already on a date with you, for starters."

Sybil did seem to squirm a little at this, before sitting up straight and jutting out her chin. "She promised me an explanation about that, which was half the reason I agreed to go out with her tonight."

"That's another thing. If she's attracted to women, then she must not have been..." My voice trailed off as I saw the look on Sybil's face and realized my error. "Okay, I see where I may have made a false assumption."

"Yes. A big one." Sybil glanced toward Jacqueline, as if to confirm it was okay before speaking on her behalf. "As it happens, we were discussing yesterday on the way to the library how, given that humans have been reincarnated so many times, and given that souls are not male or female, gender isn't all that important when it comes to finding love."

"Oh." I mulled this over, then turned to Jacqueline. "You believe in reincarnation?"

She nodded. "Yes, I do."

"How do you feel about ghosts?" I was suddenly curious whether she'd felt any hint of the presence in her room, but before I could ask, I withered beneath the stern stare Sybil sent my way. "Never mind. The question still remains, how do you move on only two days after the loss of a fiancé?"

"You're right," Jacqueline said, her voice low and her eyes downcast. My pulse sped up. Maybe she was going to confess. But she was quick to add, "Not about everything. But the relationship between Bash and myself was not what it appeared. I wasn't really his fiancée."

"You weren't?" It was a shocking revelation in itself, but it didn't really clarify the situation for me.

"No. I was his student and then an employee. I was Sebastian Grenville's ghostwriter."

Silence engulfed the table as Noah, Sybil, and I digested this news. Noah recovered the ability to speak first. "You mean you helped him with his new book?"

"I mean I wrote his new book," she corrected. "Start to finish, although with plenty of direction from him, so the tone would be in keeping with the first. In fact, I was well into what would be his third book when he died, which is what Tamsyn saw on my desk yesterday."

"So, you weren't trying to steal his manuscript," I said.

Jacqueline gave a small, tired laugh. "No. Plagiarism was Bash's specialty, not mine."

"I don't understand," I replied. The looks on Noah's and Sybil's faces hinted they felt the same way.

The waiter came by to take our orders, and since none of us had so much as glanced at the menu, Noah saved the day by asking for the night's special. It was lobster bisque and pan-seared sea scallops. We ordered four and sent the waiter on his way, then turned our attention back to Jacqueline.

She let out a long sigh. "I wasn't planning to go into all this, but I don't think I have much choice. Two years ago, I enrolled in one of Sebastian's writing courses at the university. He didn't pay me much attention until after the second or third assignment, at which point he asked me to stay after class. He told me my writing showed great promise, and he wanted to know if I would be interested in private instruction."

"That sounds suspicious," Sybil muttered, her eyes narrow and sharp. "Men love to pretend that sort of thing, just to get a pretty girl alone."

Jacqueline nodded. "I was cautious, but it soon became clear he had no romantic interest in me. He was sincere about helping me with my writing. He gave me several exercises to do, and after each one, he became more and more excited. Finally, he told me he had a project for me, that it was top secret, but if I could agree to his terms, I would become very rich."

"I'm with Sybil," I said. "This all sounds extremely suspicious."

"Oh, I pressed for details; trust me. Sebastian admitted he had suffered from writers block ever since *Magnolia Sunset* was published. His agent and publisher had both been hounding him for years to write another book, but every time he tried, he couldn't do it. He said he'd toyed with the idea of working with a ghost-writer before, but he'd never met anyone with the right kind of natural voice that would make it believable. After all, his first book is so well-known that hundreds of experts would be scouring every word."

"That's a lot of pressure," Noah said.

"It is," Jacqueline agreed. "And the secrecy involved would have to be immense. That's why he insisted on getting married. We both knew it wasn't a real relationship, but for some of the legal protections we'd need, it was the only way. We were going to make it official and tie the knot right after the trip here, before *Azalea Nightfall* was released."

"Which is the book that you wrote," I said, not as a question but as a statement.

"Yes, I wrote that and was almost through the first draft of a third, when he died."

I took a moment to sort all the new puzzle pieces into place, then hazarded a guess. "You were hoping to get it finished quickly so you could submit it to the publisher without them realizing it wasn't his?"

Jacqueline's laughter was short and shallow. "Oh, they already knew. Who do you think encouraged him to find a ghostwriter in the first place?"

Our meals arrived, and we ate for some time without talking. Though she'd had the opportunity to slip something into his food, try as I might, I couldn't figure out a motive for why Jackie—the less I suspected her of murder, the more inclined I was to think of her by this name—would want Sebastian dead. From her perspective, everything would've been immensely easier if he'd remained alive. That brought me back around to question whether the death was a murder after all.

"So, if what you're saying is true," I began slowly, after I'd finished my bisque and made a good dent on the butter-and-garlic-covered scallops, "you had no reason to want Sebastian dead, nor did his agent or publisher. In fact, it seems that no one benefits from him being gone." Perhaps it had been a toxin in his food, just as the sheriff had said. If that were true, it meant I still couldn't rule out the possibility that I, whether through mishandling of the food or an accident of magic, was to blame.

But instead of confirming what I'd said, Jackie hesitated, dabbing the corner of her mouth with her napkin. "I don't know about that."

My breath caught as I saw the look in her eyes, the one that told me there were a few secrets she was holding back. "What do you know?"

"If his death had happened anywhere else, I wouldn't have thought anything of it, but Bash was funny about coming back to Summerhaven."

"Funny how?" I asked. Though Noah and Sybil were listening intently, the dinner conversation had, for all intents and purposes, become a question-and-answer session between Jackie and me.

"He didn't like the island. Not one bit. Said he had bad memories from his school days."

"From when he went to Northport?"

Jackie nodded. "He only ever said this once, and it was when he was very, very drunk, but about three months ago, when we first heard about the possibility of coming here for the literary festival, Sebastian admitted something to me about his first book."

"What?" I whispered, as all three of us waited breathlessly for her to continue.

Jackie's eyes darted quickly around the room. Then she leaned in a little closer to the table and said in a hushed voice, "He didn't write that one, either. It was written by one of his fellow students, someone who went to the public high school on Summerhaven Island."

"But, who wrote it," I asked, "and why would Sebastian claim it as his own?"

"He never said who the real author was, but as for why, it was pretty simple. Sebastian's father, Wallace Grenville, is a pretty big name in New York literary circles. The family's swimming in money, of course, and his father has been writing intellectual think pieces for several posh magazines in New York City for decades. Growing up, all anyone ever asked him was when Sebastian was going to publish his first book. They expected him to be a genius."

"And when he couldn't deliver a work of his own," I mused, "he took it from someone else."

Everyone at the table understood what that meant. Sebastian Grenville had been a thief and a liar, and someone on the island had every reason to want him dead. But who?

Perhaps because it had been such an unconventional evening, it was only after I was home and in my own bed that night that it hit me what a monumental mess I'd made. Accusing a guest of murder, ruining a friend's date—for that matter, possibly ruining my own date, because I seriously had no idea what Noah was expecting of the evening before I turned it on its ear—I'd been in particularly bad form that night, even for me.

It was only after vowing to make amends the next day that I was finally able to get some sleep, but even that was fitful and short. I was starting to learn that when there was a mystery to be solved, I couldn't stop until I got to the bottom of it. The problem was, I had yet to figure out what to do when I went in with a steam shovel full of suspicion only to discover that the truth was sitting right at the surface the whole time. If I wasn't careful, one of these days I was going to cause damage I couldn't undo.

MY FIRST STOP WHEN I LEFT THE HOUSE ON Tuesday morning to embark on the "Tamsyn world apology tour" was the clinic, but my efforts were thwarted when I got to the front door only to discover it was locked. A note in the window informed me Noah had gone to the mainland for a few days, which meant I was out of luck. Our heart-to-heart was going to have to wait for another day.

My next stop was the library. With her grandmother away, Sybil had been filling in at the library archives desk, which gave me two reasons to go there. The first, of course, was to patch things up with Sybil. Though we'd left the Salt and Sea in a much better place than when we'd arrived, I owed her a huge apology. Beyond valuing our friendship, I couldn't let a misunderstanding come between me and the High Priestess of my coven.

The other reason was that, following Jackie's revelation that Sebastian had plagiarized his award-winning novel from a student at the local high school, I needed to get a look at the yearbooks from his time on the island. It was possible I could figure out who the victim might have been. Was I risking digging in with a steam shovel again when I really only needed a teaspoon? Perhaps. But when it came to making changes to my personality, there was only so much I could handle in one day, and I thought saying I'm sorry was a higher priority, so keeping my nose out of places it didn't belong was just going to have to wait.

The library was nearly empty except for Sybil, who sat at the archives desk, too engrossed in something on her computer screen to notice me at first. I approached cautiously, a sheepish expression on my face that matched the embarrassment I felt inside. I hadn't handled myself very well at Salt and Sea the night before. Among other things, I'd managed to thoroughly ruin her date with what had turned out— once my suspicions of murder were assuaged—to be a really lovely woman. I felt terrible about it and hoped she didn't think I'd done it on purpose.

When Sybil looked up, my stomach tightened, but there was no use wishing I could turn back time to face this mess head-on. I lifted my hand and waggled my fingers. "Hi."

"What brings you in here at this hour?"

"I came to say how sorry I was about last night." I clutched the soft denim of my jeans with my hands, twisting the fabric as Sybil waited for me to continue. Her expression gave me little hint as to what she was thinking. "More than anything else, I want to make sure you don't think I'm a bigot or something, the way I reacted to Jackie being your date."

"I don't think that."

"But, why didn't you tell me at the diner?" This question had been bothering me all morning. Had Sybil not confided in me who her date was because she didn't trust me?

Sybil sighed. "I don't know. It's not like I have many secrets around here. Most people have watched me grow up, and they know I'm a free spirit. I do as I please, and I don't care who knows that. But it's been a long time since I made a new friend, or at least had a new friendship as important as ours. Out of the blue, I just found myself worried, I guess, that if you found out everything about me, you wouldn't like me anymore. Does that make sense?"

Boy, did it. Wasn't I hiding a secret from her and Cass for exactly the same reason? My fear to let on about my growing ability to see spirits came from the same source. If they found out I was a different kind of witch from what they assumed, maybe they'd decide not to like me anymore. Okay, so that wasn't the only reason. I was also afraid I would have to relinquish my powers if anyone found out how broken they were, but of the two, rejection by my coven probably carried the bigger weight. It was entirely unfounded based on my experience with them, and I could see that so clearly now. I opened my mouth, prepared to share everything, when Sybil's face lit up with a sudden remembrance.

"I almost forgot. I pulled the Summerhaven High yearbooks from the years Sebastian Grenville was associated with the island. I thought they might hold a clue as to who the real author of *Magnolia Sunset* could be. I'm afraid I don't have copies of Northport Prep's books, but it's a start, right?"

I reached for the stack of books, my eagerness to delve into the mystery in front of us pushing any other thoughts to the background. After thirty minutes of flipping through the pages and silently criticizing the turn-of-the-millennium hair styles—okay, sometimes not so silently—I made a discovery that got my blood pumping.

"Look. It says here that a joint group of students from Summerhaven High and Northport Prep started a literary magazine." I checked the date on the yearbook's cover. "It would've been Sebastian's senior year."

"Is there a membership list or a group photo?"

"A photo, but it's really fuzzy, and there aren't any names. But wouldn't there be copies of the magazine in the library archives?"

Sybil disappeared for several minutes, returning with a look of disappointment. "We have copies, but the oldest one only goes back to volume three."

My shoulders slumped. "Someone on the island must still have a copy. If only there was a way to locate it."

Sybil's face brightened. "What if I tried a glamour? That's what my grandmother would do."

"Do you know how?" I was all set to be really impressed with Sybil's magical prowess when her face scrunched into an expression that left me no doubt the answer was a big, fat no.

"We haven't gotten that far," she admitted.

"A finding spell, then?" I suggested.

"Let me check with Cass." Sybil dashed off a text, and a few seconds later, the device vibrated with a response. "She says she has a better idea."

Just as Sybil said it, my own phone rang. "Hello?"

Cass's voice sounded over the speakerphone. "Tam-syn, what do you have going on this Friday and Saturday night?"

"Pretty much nothing," I said, not even needing to check my calendar. Due to my ongoing kitchen situa-tion, I'd had to cancel all of the inn's bookings for the upcoming weekend, which left my schedule wide open. I'd considered teaching myself to knit, but frankly, I found yarn a little creepy, so I was glad for an alterna-tive. "What's going on?"

"I hope you won't think I'm crazy, but I was prac-ticing my divination today and I think I might have had a vision."

Crazy? The spirit of a murdered author had taken up residence in my guest room. I wasn't about to throw stones. "Continue."

"I saw the two of us wearing Happy Helpers uniforms."

This gave me pause. Was Cass implying my issues at the inn were going to drag on so long I would need to seek out temporary employment? That was not great news. "Any idea what it meant?"

"Well, I gave them a call, and it turns out they're absolutely desperate to recruit more help for the Summerhaven High School class reunion this weekend."

"The class reunion..." I had a flashback to the conversation with James Thorne. He'd mentioned the reunion for the class of 1999 was coming up. "That would be the same year Sebastian Grenville graduated."

"Yes, it would." I could hear the triumph in Cass's voice, and I had to admit that vision of hers might've been onto something. "If we need to know who in their class might have had a grudge against Grenville, why not ask at the source?"

"Do you need me, too?" Sybil asked.

"You're welcome to come, but I didn't see you in the vision. Only Tamsyn and me."

"I think I'll pass, then," she said. "I might have plans."

It didn't take a genius to figure out that, given the mess I'd made of her first date with Jackie, they might be tempted to try a do-over on Friday night. If that was the case, I was glad for them both.

"Sign me up," I told Cass. "It's a brilliant plan."

After ending the call, I piled up the yearbooks and headed home to study them in more detail. I doubted they would be of much use without a roster of the inaugural literary magazine club, but it gave me something to do while I waited for the reunion to arrive.

CHAPTER TWELVE

*W*hen I returned to the house, the blue-green glow from Jackie's room reminded me I hadn't yet raised my spirit-seeing issue with the coven. I didn't want to do it over text, and yet I also felt a pang of guilt at the thought of her continuing to sit there under Grenville's sphere. What if it was dangerous? I was no expert, but things that glowed like that often caused cancer. Until I found a better solution, my best bet was to keep her out of that room as much as possible.

"Hey, Jackie?" I called through the crack in the door, opening it all the way when I heard her say yes in response. Sure enough, the orb was still there, though I was relieved to see Jackie had spread her papers out on the bed, far from its edge. "Everything okay?"

"I needed a change of scenery. The desk was starting to feel...uncomfortable." She gave a wary glance directly at the spot where Sebastian Grenville's strangely translucent silhouette resided.

"I was about to suggest you might want to work at the library today. It's a beautiful day for a walk, and Sybil's pretty much by herself at the archives desk."

Jackie's face brightened at this news. "Maybe I will. Except for dinner last night, I've been working nonstop for days."

"You deserve a break," I encouraged and was rewarded by her gathering up her papers and putting them in her laptop bag. I followed her down the stairs and remained standing in the empty foyer after she'd left.

With Jackie gone, the house was emptier than I could ever remember it being. In all the years I had spent visiting the house, there had always been someone else there with me: my grandmother or mother when I was little, or more recently, my aunt Gwen or one of the inn's many guests. If nothing else, Lillian and Gus had always seemed to be lurking behind the next corner, but not right now. It was truly just me in the house, with the exception of an uncommunicative ghost on the second floor, whom I didn't count because he didn't seem inclined to acknowledge my existence. In fact, the only other time in my memory that I had been so completely alone in this house was the night my mother had disappeared.

An overwhelming sense of loneliness came over me. My body ached from the weight of it. I rested my hand on my chest, my fingers brushing the amethyst pendulum that dangled from its chain, just where I'd placed it the morning before. All I could feel in that moment was a chasm of emptiness inside me. I didn't want to be alone, stuck by myself in a house with an unhappy spirit I had no clue how to deal with. One thought came to my head and stuck there, repeating over and over: *I wish Lillian were here.*

"Well, it's about time. The rate you were goin', I thought I'd be trapped behind the eight ball for good."

I whirled around in a circle, but the source of the voice remained hidden. "Lillian! I told you not to sneak up on me." I'd meant to sound reproachful, but my wide grin and shaky laugh probably gave me away. In all my life, I don't know if I'd ever experienced a greater sense of elation and relief than when she slowly materialized in the middle of the braided rug in front of the door. "Where have you been?"

"Not sure," she answered, wrapping her arms around herself, "but it gave me the heebie-jeebies. Somewhere dark."

"You weren't in the tunnel this whole time, were you?" I would've felt terrible if that were the case, because maybe I would've been able to find her and rescue her if only I hadn't been interrupted by Sybil and Cass when I'd gone back to search for my pendulum.

"I don't know." Lillian scratched her chin. "I don't think so."

For the first time since she'd reappeared, I took a close look at Lillian's attire. She wore a dress I'd never seen before, made of white silk net over a pink sheath dress base, with a grillwork of variegated ribbon on which silk roses had been arranged like they were growing on a trellis. "You're all dressed up. Where'd that come from?"

"Paris," she said with a shrug. "It's where all my dresses come from."

"Oh, well. La-di-da." Sometimes Lillian could sound like a real snob, and it left me wondering exactly how any ancestor of mine, however distant, had been able to afford designer French gowns when I'd driven halfway across the country at the start of the summer with exactly three hundred and fourteen dollars in my checking account.

There was a flicker of something in Lillian's eyes that was hard to put a name to, but might have been sadness or even shame. "It wasn't my choice, you know."

I frowned. "What wasn't?"

Lillian took a deep breath. "The clothing. We couldn't afford it, but Mother insisted."

"I've seen some of your gowns in the trunks in the attic. They must've cost a fortune."

Lillian pressed her lips together, quiet for a moment. "Wanna know a secret? They cost less than you might think."

"What do you mean?"

"Mother had a connection at the fashion house of Jeanne Lanvin. Every year, after the wealthiest women in the world had placed their orders for new wardrobes, there would be items they didn't end up wanting. Maybe a style didn't fit, or the color wasn't what they thought. They were such good customers no one would argue, you know? They would just set the dresses aside. Later, Mother's friend would arrange for us to buy them at a fraction of the cost."

All at once, I remembered the dream I'd had shortly after arriving on the island. "They didn't fit. You had them altered by a local seamstress."

Surprise registered on Lillian's face. "That's right. Rose. Her brother Freddy played piano at Davenport's on Saturday nights. She's the one who introduced me to the place."

I nodded, more details flickering in the back of my mind as I recalled snippets of the dream. "There was something else. A man. Your mother wanted you to marry him."

Lillian gave me a long, hard stare. "How did you know that?"

"I saw it in a dream."

She looked spooked, which is a funny thing, really, if you think about it. My weird dreams spooked a spook. After several moments, she sighed. "Lord Rochester. It's all she talked about that summer. She was determined I should marry him, even though we'd never met."

"It wasn't uncommon, though, was it? I thought rich women did that all the time in your day."

"The Dollar Princesses, you mean? That was common enough. Rich American girls would marry into noble families in Europe, trading cabbage for crowns."

"Cabbage?" I asked.

"Yeah. You know, spinach. Sugar. Kale. Lettuce. Dough."

My ears perked up at this last option. "You mean money?"

"That's what I said. Only in our case, we didn't have the scratch and Rochester did."

"Your family was poor, but Lord Rochester was rich," I translated.

Lillian crossed her arms, clearly frustrated. "Is there a reason you keep repeating what I've already said?"

"Sorry," I replied, holding back a chuckle. Honestly, did she have no idea how thoroughly her generation had butchered the English language? "But, did your mother really expect you to go along with her plan? She must've known how unhappy it would make you."

She shook her head, her expression a blend of sorrow and anger. "It didn't matter. And I guess I would've done it, too, if I hadn't...well, if whatever happened to me to turn me into a ghost hadn't happened first. We were already struggling so much."

"What about your father?" I asked, trying to recall

if I knew anything about this generation of my family and coming up blank. "Was he in the picture at all?"

"My father?" Lillian smiled fondly. "Oh, yes. He was a kind and gentle man."

"And did he go along with your mother's plan to marry you off?" Frankly, if he'd been as great as Lillian seemed to think, I didn't see how he could've.

"Mother didn't ask his opinions on things of that nature, and Daddy's head was always in the clouds, so I'm not sure how much he noticed."

"A dreamer?" I guessed.

"An academic. He and mother were very different." It sounded like my own parents, in a way, polar opposites. Though my mother had been both the dreamer and the intellectual in their scenario, my father had been the practical one, who, for the short period of time they were together, took care of all the daily details.

"Why were they together?" Oh, how many times I'd asked that same question about my own family.

"Mother was born and raised on the island, and she saw my father as a real step up. He was a Harvard man, fiercely intellectual. I think she thought he'd travel the world and bring her along. She didn't count on him wanting to settle down here, nor did she realize how little professional ambition he had."

"What did he do for a living?"

"Not much, really. There was a bit of family money, which would've lasted much longer had my mother not set her sights on me marrying into a title. But every so often, Daddy did leave pure science aside long enough to come up with a number of clever inventions, which kept us afloat."

"Anything I've heard of?" I asked, captivated by the idea of having a famous inventor in my family tree.

"Oh, probably, but nothing he got credit for," she replied with a scowl.

"Why was that?"

"Because the guy he sold them to took all the credit." It had been nearly a century ago, but her bitterness was still fresh. "Those patents should've been Daddy's legacy, and instead, he's forgotten."

"Why didn't your father speak up?"

"We needed the money. People will put up with almost any indignity if there's enough jack on the line."

Assuming *jack* was yet another term for money, I nodded in sad agreement. But the story had started the wheels in my head turning. Things hadn't really changed in all these years. There were still a lot of poor families on the island, and a lot of rich summer folks with money beyond most people's wildest dreams. Sebastian Grenville had been one of them. What if the author he'd plagiarized had been a willing participant in the deception, like Lillian's father had been?

"Lillian, let's say someone had written a book, an

amazing book, one that was destined to be an instant classic."

"Okay." She was clearly humoring me, having no idea where my thoughts had led me. Also, I couldn't help but wonder how much, if any, of her father's intellectual curiosity Lillian had inherited. With her slang-riddled vocabulary and affinity for speakeasies, she didn't strike me as the reading type.

"So, maybe this gifted author is an islander whose family lives off tourist season and lobstering. If a rich kid from a private prep school offered them enough money, do you think they'd keep it a secret?"

"Sure. What would they care, as long as they got paid?"

It was as likely a scenario as any I could think of, but one thing bothered me. "What about when the rich kid got famous? Why not come forward and let everyone know it was really you?"

A sly half smile tugged at Lillian's lips. She rubbed her thumb against her fingers several times in a gesture meant to look like she was counting money. "Maybe it was worth more to the real author to keep his trap shut."

"Like bribery?"

"Sure. Or blackmail."

"You know what? I bet you're right." I laughed as it hit me how obvious the answer might be.

A new theory began to form in my brain, which

might not have been the only possibility, but it certainly made a lot of sense the more I looked at it.

Only, once Sebastian found Jackie and could publish something new, maybe he'd decided he didn't need to pay anymore. That would be a fine motive for murder. Finally, I had a sensible plan. When the reunion rolled around, I'd be keeping a sharp lookout for someone who'd been unusually successful in his or her life, with a tie to the literary magazine. I had a real shot at finding the culprit, and it was all thanks to Lillian. I never thought I'd be so grateful to have a ghost back in my life.

THE REUNION OF THE SUMMERHAVEN HIGH School class of 1999 was to be held on Saturday evening, in a gymnasium draped profusely in the same type of purple and gold bunting that had decorated the Owl and Quill the weekend before. Friday night was mandatory training for all temporary staff. I'd just received a briefing by the Happy Helpers' on-site coordinator, while Cass had been sent to a different group for a similar orientation. Much to my dismay, uniforms had been distributed, so I was busy tugging at the hem of my polo shirt when I saw a familiar face enter the room.

"Vera!" I waved at the woman who had been such a

help to me during my preparation for the ill-fated tea. She waved back and walked toward me.

"Tamsyn, how have you been? I haven't seen you since that terrible day at the authors' tea. What a shock that was." As she took in my uniform, her eyes grew wide. "You're working with us?"

"My friend Cass convinced me to apply at Happy Helpers since I can't run the inn right now."

"I heard a rumor, but I thought it would've all been straightened out already."

"You and me both," I said, offering a good-natured laugh, perhaps to convince myself as much as her that I wasn't letting it get me down. If it hadn't been for the private investigation I was conducting, I would've been taking the whole thing pretty hard. Of course, I couldn't let on that I was working that night with an ulterior motive. "Frankly, I was surprised they hired me for this gig, considering my kitchen's in quarantine and I'm under investigation for Sebastian Grenville's death."

"Maybe they don't know about that."

"Yeah, maybe," I replied, but I knew Summerhaven well enough by then to know that wasn't how things worked. You couldn't sneeze in a place like this without a dozen people calling out *bless you*. They knew. Everyone knew. Everyone, that is, except Aunt Gwen, who was blissfully cruising the Caribbean with a ship full of witches without the slightest idea that her niece was busy running her livelihood into the ground in her absence. Though I'd called several times, she'd still not picked up, and I hadn't worked up the courage to leave a message.

"The sheriff can't really think you had anything to do with all that, can he? I heard it was a food allergy."

Interesting. If that was still the word on the street, it meant Grady's office was taking pains not to release the latest lab results that ruled out an allergic reaction and pointed to a food-borne neurotoxin instead. This raised a number of questions in my mind, but Vera was hardly the person to discuss them with, so I merely shrugged. "I'm sure they'll clear it up soon. In the meantime, looks like I have a new occupation to learn."

"Do you know anyone else on the team?" Vera asked.

"Just Cass, but this is her first time, too."

"I'll talk to Becky, the supervisor, and get you put on my team." Vera gave my shoulder a friendly pat. "You just stick with me, and I'll show you the ropes."

After clearing it with Becky, I followed Vera down a tile-lined corridor that ran from the gymnasium to the school's cafeteria. There, boxes of refreshment supplies had been stacked along one wall in the kitchen. Vera pointed them out. "That's everything we'll need for the punch tomorrow. Equal parts juice and ginger ale, just pour it into the punch bowls over there."

I followed the tip of Vera's finger with my eyes, to

where half a dozen plastic bowls that had been stamped with an imitation cut-crystal design were lined up neatly on a lunch table. "Seems straight-forward."

"Keep 'em filled, and you'll be fine. Oh, and keep an eye on things throughout the night. Don't let anyone spike the punch, okay?"

"Spike the punch?" I repeated, failing to picture this happening in a room full of adults. "Aren't these people, like, middle-aged now?"

"The class of ninety-nine was notorious for its troublemakers." It was clear by her expression that Vera didn't have a high opinion of any of them.

"I'll watch the punch like a hawk, Scout's honor." I mean, I hadn't actually been a Scout, but the last thing I wanted was to be stuck babysitting a bunch of rowdy, drunk old people. I'd keep an eye out, all right.

"A professional catering company will be here tomorrow to handle the food, so mainly you'll just do what you're told when it comes to that, and otherwise, stay out of their way. Most likely they'll want you to carry an appetizer tray around the room, but if you're not comfortable with that, it's no problem. Just say the word."

"No, that'll be fine," I assured her. A serving tray was perfect for my purposes. It would give me an easy excuse to wander the room and listen in on conversations without standing out.

"Great!" Vera rummaged through a large box that

sat open on one of the benches. She pulled out a huge stack of laminated papers, which appeared to include both old and new photos of the class members. "Right now, I've been assigned to decorating duty. Want to give me a hand?"

We gathered the photos, plus rolls of tape and spools of purple and gold crepe paper, and headed back to the gym. A wall of folding bleachers had been covered in sheets of purple plastic, and Vera explained our task was to arrange the "then and now" photos along one section, and the brief bios each attendee had provided along the other. I noticed right away that the bios lacked their owners' names.

"It's a matching game," she said. "An icebreaker type of thing, where people will win prizes if they can guess which modern photo belongs to the correct yearbook picture, and then match it to the bios, and finally guess the person's name."

"Sounds difficult," I said. Out of my graduating class of 450, I doubted I could remember more than a dozen, the ones who had been my closest friends.

Vera laughed. "Not as hard as you'd think. Probably eighty percent of these folks still live on the island, and they see each other all the time."

"I hadn't thought of that." Summerhaven wasn't Cleveland; that was for sure.

"The hardest part is likely to be figuring out which of the twenty bios of lobstermen with a wife and two kids is actually the one you're looking for."

I shuffled through some of the typed sheets and could see she was right. Still, after maybe ten nearly identical ones, I came across something different. "Here we go. This person became a hairdresser in Portland."

"Oh, that *is* different." Her eyes twinkled mischievously. "I wonder if it will end up being a guy or a girl."

"Good question. What else is in here?" I flipped through a few more, then stopped as another outlier caught my eye. My heart beat faster as I read. "This one owns a shipping business on the mainland, says it went from one boat to a whole fleet of vehicles, with operations worldwide. That's pretty impressive."

"Oh, that's Phil Stanley." Vera said it as if everyone should recognize the name, though I'd never heard it before. "He's a big Summerhaven success story. Still owns a house on the island, although he doesn't get back much anymore. I'm surprised he's even coming."

"Oh." My high hopes sank just a little on that news. Phil had seemed like a perfect candidate. He'd started out small, with let's say the proceeds of selling a single novel to a classmate, and then expanded rapidly as, perhaps, the blackmail payments started rolling in. But if he was rarely on the island, he probably wasn't my guy. *My* guy needed to have been around last Saturday and able to slip something nasty into Sebastian Grenville's food, or else Grady wouldn't stop until he'd thrown me in the slammer.

"Hmm." Vera's eyes squinted, as if trying to recall something. "You know, now that I think about it, I saw Phil outside the Owl and Quill last Saturday night. He must've been going to that planning thing James was hosting over there."

"For the old student council members, you mean?" Yeah, a go-getter businessman like Phil would probably have been in student government. More importantly, if he'd been on the island since last weekend, it meant he'd had the opportunity to kill Sebastian Grenville. If he had the motive, that is, which still remained to be seen.

When I'd finished my decorating project, I met up with Cass. She'd been assigned to help the DJ set up the sound equipment and had spent the entire evening in a sound booth behind the stage.

"Did you get any leads at all?" I asked her.

She shook her head. "No, you?"

I told her about Phil Stanley and showed her the wall of photos. "Which one do you think he is?"

"Phil Stanley?" Cass looked at me like I was nuts, which would probably be appropriate in any number of circumstances, but in this case seemed a little unfair since I didn't have the long-term history on the island that she did. "Everyone knows what Phil looks like. He's donated so much money to the town over the years I think there's a portrait of him in city hall hanging right next to the mayor's. That's him, there."

She pointed to a recent photo of a man in his late

thirties but aging well, slim and muscular, with a tan
that, unlike the ruddy lobstermen hanging all around
him, was a little too perfect to have been gained by
working outside and had probably come from several
sessions in a tanning booth.

"And his yearbook photo?" I asked.

She shook her head. "I don't know. It was way
before my time. I never saw him when he was young."

I glanced at the rows of black and white yearbook
photos, then zeroed in on the eyes and nose of the
modern photo, committing them to memory as best I
could. I scanned the old photos again, more closely
this time, stopping on the third row, second photo
from the left.

"What do you think, Cass? Is this a match?"

She looked at it closely. "I think it might be."

Below the photo was a list of organizations and
honors, and as I took them in, a smile slowly spread
across my lips. "Listen to this. It says he was class
treasurer and lists one of his activities as SHS Lit
Mag."

"Summerhaven High School Literary Magazine?"

"It has to be." I looked at the yearbook photo in
triumph. As class treasurer, he would definitely have
been on the island last Saturday for the planning meeting, and the affiliation with the literary magazine told
me he had an interest in writing. I quickly filled Cass
in on my theory that, either through bribery or black-

mail, Sebastian had paid the true author of his first manuscript a hefty sum for their silence.

"I'm counting four others who list that as an activity," Cass said. "I guess it could be any one of them."

She pointed them out, and I immediately recognized one of them as James Thorne. I should've guessed he'd been involved. While Phil Stanley remained suspect number one in my mind because of the money issue, James Thorne was back on my naughty list for sure. If I had my way, he was going to tell me all about Phil, and the rest of their friends, too.

CHAPTER THIRTEEN

On Saturday morning, I rode my bike directly to the Owl and Quill, arriving as James was turning the sign around on his front window to indicate the shop was open. He caught sight of me as I was reaching the door, and I thought he was going to turn the sign back around, lock the door, and bolt. Instead, he stood aside as I opened the door, greeting me with silence and a look on his face like he'd just swallowed a lemon.

"I need to know everything you remember about the Summerhaven High Literary Magazine," I said, not seeing any need for pleasantries when we both knew this wasn't a social call.

"As I recall, the last time you burst into my shop, it was to accuse me of murder and demand I turn myself in to the sheriff." He stroked one tip of his mustache with a pinched finger and thumb. "Talk about humiliating, and then I find out it wasn't the strawberries that killed him, after all."

"You must see why I thought it was you, considering the dirty prank you played." I sighed. Antagonizing him wasn't going to get me anywhere, but maybe an appeal to his decency, or his vanity, would. "Look, James, I really am sorry about that. I hope you can forgive me, because I really need your help. I know you didn't like Sebastian much, but surely you want justice, right? And imagine how famous you'd be if you held the key to putting his killer behind bars."

He remained tense for a moment. Then his shoulders relaxed as, slowly, the fight seemed to seep out of him. "What do you need to know?"

"Your senior year, there was a literary magazine. I believe there may have been five members altogether. Do you recall who the others were?"

"Let's see." He stroked his mustache again, deep in thought. "I was the president. I remember Phil and Mike, because they were the two other officers of the club, treasurer and secretary. There were two girls, Sara and Jeanette. I feel like I'm forgetting someone, but that's five. I guess I got 'em all."

I made a mental note of the names, as I planned to find as many as possible at the reunion that night. "And do you happen to have any copies of the magazine from your year? The library has them starting at volume two, but volume one is missing."

"Yeah, it would be." A disgruntled expression

settled over his features, and I knew I'd hit a sore spot. "There was no money in the budget for printing, so we teamed up with Northport that year to do a joint publication. Sebastian Grenville was the editor."

I nodded encouragingly, suspecting I was about to find out the source of this man's dislike of the famous author. "And how did that go?"

"You know who his father is?" He let out a snort as I nodded to indicate I did. "Yeah, well, if his old man was a god in New York City literary circles, I guess they all figured Sebastian was going to be some kind of second coming."

"Did he have talent?"

"Who knows? He rarely shared his own work with us plebeians. Such a pompous private school jerk."

A harsh assessment for sure. Never had I been so grateful for someone refusing to buy into the old adage not to speak ill of the dead. "And yet, he was in charge of *your* high school's lit mag? I don't understand."

"A technicality, or at least it was supposed to be. It started out that I was the editor for Summerhaven High and he was the editor for Northport Prep, and we would have equal say on the direction of the issues and which submissions we were going to print. Pretty soon, though, he got his dad to donate a bunch of money, and he ended up with the final say. Man, he just lorded it over all of us."

"I take it he wasn't fair about whose work he chose?"

"It was supposed to be fifty-fifty between the two schools, but he rarely ran more than twenty-five percent of what Summerhaven High students sent in, and even then, he made it sound like he was doing us such a big favor."

"Did you have to be a member of the club to make submissions?"

"No, anyone could send things in, sometimes with their names on them and sometimes anonymously. As co-editor, I tried to be fair and give everyone a chance, but like I said, Sebastian had other ideas."

"Sounds like he made a lot of enemies."

"He wasn't going to win any popularity contests at Summerhaven High back in the day, but once he got famous, it's amazing how quickly a lot of people changed their tune." He shook his head ruefully. "You'd have thought half the class was his best friend right after *Magnolia Sunset* first published, the way people talked about him back then. Although a lot of that faded away after so many years went by and he never published anything else."

"And he never came back to the island until right before his death?"

"Not that I ever knew. I mean, we reached out to Northport for our ten-year reunion and invited them to join us. A few of them did, but not many. This time none at all are coming to ours, but I heard their class had decided to do a ski trip to Switzerland to mark the twentieth reunion, so I guess that sounded better than a night in a stuffy high school gymnasium. But as for Sebastian, he never showed his face here again, up until last week."

"And then ended up dead."

"Yeah, that's something, huh?" There was a certain twinkle in the man's eye that didn't quite match the solemnity of the subject, and I had to wonder if he knew something he wasn't saying or if he was just too busy reveling in the schadenfreude of his old nemesis's demise to keep up appearances. He'd been quick to admit to his strawberry-jam prank, but what if that had been to throw me off?

WHEN I CHECKED MY MESSAGES LATER THAT day, I had one from Becky at Happy Helpers, reminding me that temporary staff was expected to check in at the gymnasium no later than 5:00 p.m. The more I thought about Sebastian Grenville's death, the more I became convinced that, in addition to plagiarism, his dictator-like rule over the high school literary magazine might have been a contributing factor in more than one person on the island wanting him dead. As hunches went, my money was still on Phil Stanley, but in case I was wrong, it frustrated me that I still lacked a foolproof way to figure out who the original author of his stolen manuscript had been.

The inn was empty, as Jackie had left a note to say she and Sybil were going out for a hike around the old stone quarry on the east side of the island. It was a lovely spot, popular for swimming in the summer, and I was glad to see they were hitting it off and that my earlier stupidity hadn't ruined their budding romance. Lillian and Gus were nowhere to be seen, but I wasn't alarmed. The faint vibration that hummed between my bracelet and necklace assured me all was well in their part of the spirit realm. As for Sebastian Grenville, he remained the same, still perching on the chaise and glowing. I thought perhaps he would have changed in some way, a hint as to whether my investigation into his death was growing hot or cold, but no such luck.

Even without ghostly guidance, though, I was certain I was getting closer to an answer. In his youth, Sebastian had bullied and tormented the five members of Summerhaven High's Literary Magazine club. The odds that one of them had decided to get revenge was high, indeed. Phil Stanley was the strongest candidate, but he wasn't the sole option. If only I could figure out a way to find out for sure, instead of spending the evening guarding the punch bowls.

The punch bowls.

The plan popped into my brain fully formed, as only the truly brilliant, or the very idiotic, plans are likely to do. This one was the former type of plan, naturally. Given that all five club members would be at the reunion that night, how easy it would be to whip up a potion that would reveal which of them was the real author of *Magnolia Sunset*. I would be watching the punch bowls to keep middle-aged miscreants from boozing it up, so all I had to do was spike the punch myself. As magical schemes went, this was about as foolproof as you could get.

I called Cass, our coven's resident potions expert, but she didn't answer. I left a message, and in the meantime, I flipped through the pages of the family grimoire for inspiration. The truth spell was near the front, and I'd even completed it successfully before, if by successful I was including spells that eventually did what they were meant to while only causing limited bloodshed. In my defense, is it really my fault so many people at the Dockside Diner have such unflattering thoughts about one another or that noses bleed so profusely when punched?

I don't so much need someone to tell the truth as I need to find it, I thought, which is how the finding spell popped into my mind. My fingers caressed the silver chain around my neck. As spells went, I'd aced that one. I got back my missing amethyst pendulum, and Lillian, to boot. At least, I think it was the finding spell that ultimately brought her home. Who can really tell what works with ghosts? But I was counting that one in my personal win column, which brought me to a total of two spells I should be able to do adequately that, when combined, should yield the result I needed. Did anything ever get much more certain in life than that?

Should I wait for Cass or call Aunt Gwen? a voice in my head whispered. In a perfect world, certainly, waiting was a prudent choice. On the other hand, what good was being a witch if you couldn't, at some point, take off the training wheels and go for a ride on your own? I decided on a compromise, which was to make up a batch of potion and only use it if I wasn't explicitly told not to before the reunion started.

Recalling Vera's instructions for making the punch, I searched the refrigerator and found a partial bottle of ginger ale and a few splashes of cranberry juice left in the bottom of a pitcher. This gave me a simple base for my potion. I mixed them together in equal parts as I'd been told to do, yielding only about a cup altogether until the juice ran out, but it would be sufficient, as a little goes a long way where potions are concerned. Fetching my wand from my bedroom, I worked the finding spell first, as it was the freshest in my memory. Then I stared long and hard at the special cupboard where Aunt Gwen housed our family's collection of magical spoons.

Mine was old wood, decoratively carved, and had been passed down through the generations, most recently from my own mother. If I'd truly been the kitchen witch everyone claimed me to be, it should have felt as natural in my hand as the air I was breathing, but the truth was, it felt foreign. In fact, when I used it to stir, things tended to explode. Aunt Gwen used her spoon for every magical working—I don't think she owned a wand at all, and if she did, I'd never seen her use it—but when it came to focusing my power, I much preferred the slender piece of oak Sybil had given me at our inaugural coven meeting. Unfortunately, the spoon was a required element of the truth spell, so I took it from its resting place, muscles tensing, and tried to think happy thoughts.

The trickiest part to harnessing magic successfully, I was learning, was not getting the right ingredients or even reciting the words correctly. Those were important, but for a spell to work the way it was intended, it was vital to ask it to do what you actually needed it to do. This might sound obvious, but magic can be very literal. As I stood in front of my potion, my first instinct was to focus on finding Sebastian Grenville's killer. That was, after all, what I really wanted. As soon as it was determined not to be me, I was off the hook. However, it occurred to me just before I dipped the spoon into the potion that I was asking the wrong thing. I was assuming there was a killer, but I didn't know it for sure. He might've died by accident. What I really wanted to know was who the real author of his first manuscript had been. Whether that person was actually responsible for his death was a mystery I could deal with once I'd established who it was.

See? You are getting better at this whole witchcraft thing. I gave myself a mental pat on the back as I plunged the spoon into the pink, fizzy liquid. "Reveal the author of *Magnolia Sunset*," I muttered as I stirred. "Reveal the author of—"

"Looks like you could use this."

"Lillian!" I jumped a mile high at the unexpected voice, sending droplets of sticky punch flying in every direction. I whipped around to see her standing in the middle of the kitchen, her skirt hiked up on one side to reveal a silver flask strapped to her leg. "How many times have I asked you not to sneak up on me? And in the middle of a spell, too."

She gave a sheepish smile. "Sorry. But I thought you'd appreciate this."

"How did you know I'd need that? Have you been spying on me?" I threw my hands in the air as I realized the item in question was partially see-through. "How am I supposed to use that? It's a ghost flask. It has no substance."

"I brought the real one back with me from 1929. It should be in that drawer."

My eyes followed to where her slightly translucent finger was pointing, where I caught Gus nosing around the punch-filled measuring cup. As if knowing he was being watched, he shook his head vigorously, sending tufts of fur everywhere. Then he sneezed, directly into my potion.

I balled my hands into fists. "Both of you, out, now."

"But, the flask—"

I yanked open the drawer, where a silver flask sat, just as Lillian had predicted. "Got it. Thanks. Now go."

Lillian faded about halfway from sight, then stopped. "You could be a little more grateful."

"Your cat just sneezed all over my countertop." I pointed to where the little offender had been standing, though smartly, he'd skedaddled. "It's unhygienic."

"Gus cleans himself constantly," Lillian argued.

"With his tongue! If the Board of Health caught wind of him being in here while I was preparing food, I'd never be allowed to reopen this kitchen again."

The rest of Lillian that had remained visible blinked out in an instant. *Note to self: Next time you want to be alone, criticize her cat.*

I gave the cat-tainted potion a withering look. There was a piece of fur floating on the top. Yuck. I knew I should start from scratch, but I was out of cranberry juice and running short on time, as well. Instead of pouring it down the sink, I unscrewed the top from the flask, draped a small square of cheese-cloth over it, and slowly allowed the potion to drip through. It wasn't ideal, but it would filter out the worst of the contamination, and besides, I wasn't the one who had to drink it.

Once I'd changed into my Happy Helpers shirt and a pair of sensible khaki trousers, I studied the flask.

Sadly, my uniform didn't allow me to hide my contraband with the same finesse that my flapper friend had demonstrated. Luckily, it had deep pockets, and once I'd slipped it in, it pretty well disappeared from sight. I gave the slight bulge a pat.

Time to catch a killer.

CHAPTER FOURTEEN

It wasn't long after I arrived at the gymnasium for roll call that the first reunion guests began to trickle in, taking up seats on folding chairs surrounding tables draped in purple and gold. With one hand against my hidden hip flask, I looked for Cass, hoping to run my potion-making method past her before moving forward on my plan, but couldn't find her. Recalling my objective to circulate as freely as possible through the crowd, I went straight to the head caterer and was chosen as a volunteer to carry hors d'oeuvre trays.

If you've never carried an oversized silver tray of tiny stuffed mushroom caps and meatballs through a crowd of people who, though they've put on their best clothing and are trying to masquerade as dignified, are really ravenous beasts at heart, let me offer a word of advice: Don't. Don't even pick it up to begin with. If you're already holding it, just make an excuse, put the food down, and leave. Seriously, I wish someone had given me this advice that night. Live and learn.

My initial, brilliant plan was to head immediately for the table in the far corner, where I could see James Thorne and a man who looked very much like the photo of Phil Stanley I'd seen the day before, chatting together with a third man and two women. Members of the class of 1999 Literary Magazine club, perhaps? I needed to get close enough to find out.

This is where the tray I was holding became a problem, because with every step I took, people materialized out of thin air, reaching for cocktail napkins and toothpicks like they'd never seen food before. When the first tray ran out, I'd only made it about a quarter of the way across the gymnasium floor. I thought I would at least breeze through that portion the second time around, but the problem with the hors d'oeuvres trays was that no two appeared to be alike, so instead of letting me pass, people whom I knew had just partaken of mini egg rolls brazenly stopped me to grab shrimp cocktail. It took until the fourth attempt for me to realize the only way through was to put the tray on my head and speed walk my way across without making eye contact with anyone along the way. When I reached my target, the bronze-skinned man, who at a closer distance I could definitely tell was Phil Stanley, broke into applause.

"Well done. I was just saying I wondered what we would have to do to get some snacks over this way."

"Your classmates are hungry this evening. I wasn't sure I would make it." I lowered the tray and made eye contact with James, who was studying me warily. "So, are these the literary magazine friends you were telling me so much about earlier today?"

Before James could respond, Phil stuck out his hand. "We sure are. I'm Phil Stanley."

"Nice to meet you, Phil," I said, shaking his hand. I pretended to know nothing about him. "Are you a writer, like James?"

Phil laughed. "No, not me. I work in shipping."

"Now, he's being modest," the other man at the table broke in. "You must be new around here not to recognize Phil. He runs one of the biggest shipping companies on the eastern seaboard. I'm Mike, by the way."

"And what do you do, Mike?" I asked, trying to sound polite but not unusually interested in his response. In truth, I was hoping to see if he, too, could fit the profile of someone who had come into a large sum of money at some point in the past twenty years.

"I build houses."

"You make it sound so run-of-the-mill," said one of the women, giving his shoulder a nudge. "Mike builds mansions, more like. He's built up the biggest construction company in southern Maine."

I nodded while calculating how much money that

must require. I wasn't ready to exclude Mike from my list just yet. "Here on the island?"

"We build here, of course, but mostly I'm based on the mainland."

Mainland, huh? I'd have to see if Mike had been in town the previous week to know whether to rule him out. "So, you didn't become a writer?"

"Nah," Mike answered. "Other than James, Jeanette's the only real writer here."

The woman who had spoken earlier waved her hand, as if batting away the compliment. "Legal briefs, that's all the writing I do these days."

"You're a lawyer?"

Jeanette nodded. "I work in DC most of the year, although I still come home for the summers."

"She went to Columbia for law school," the other woman added.

Now, that was not a cheap school, by any means. Had Jeanette had some help from the sale of a certain manuscript to help her afford it? She was staying on my suspect list for the time being.

The woman who had spoken held out a hand, and when I took it, I couldn't help but notice it was covered in sparkling rings and bracelets. "Sara. I'm the English teacher at Northport Prep. Not as impressive as the rest of my peers, but it's rewarding in its own way."

Rewarding, indeed. Sybil may have been our coven's resident expert on fashion and accessories, but

I knew enough to know that nothing on Sara's fingers or wrists was fake, and her manicure was fresh, besides. A high school English teacher who could afford luxuries like that was pretty unusual in my experience. Which meant that out of the five members of the literary magazine club, James Thorne was the only one I'd managed to eliminate convincingly. I turned my attention to Phil, who remained my primary suspect.

"Now that you're so successful, you've never been tempted to take some time off to write?"

Phil's cheeks flushed as he looked across the table at Sara. "If you want the honest truth, I only ever joined the club so Sara would go to prom with me."

"Oh, Phil." Sara giggled like she was still a teenager, placing one diamond-encrusted hand to cover her lips. It occurred to me that I may have read her situation incorrectly. The way the two of them were looking at each other, I wondered if the jewelry had been a gift.

"It seems like your club members have all stayed pretty close through the years," I remarked. "It's funny, considering none of you, except maybe James, had much of an interest in pursuing writing as a career."

"That's what it's like on a small island," Phil volunteered. "The five of us were friends long before the club, and it was really just us looking for something to do together."

James sat, pinching one end of his mustache, something I'd seen him do before when he was busy thinking. "You know, this has been bothering me since earlier today. It wasn't just the five of us, was it? I feel like we've forgotten someone."

The rest of the group looked puzzled, until Jeanette sat up a little straighter. "Actually, you might be right. There was a boy, a grade or two younger than we were, who used to kind of hang around. Quiet. He didn't get involved much, but sometimes he'd say something, and it would be really profound. Does anyone else remember?"

"Oh, wait." Phil smacked his hands together, the loud sound making me jump. "Yes! He was a little guy, I think, with kind of curly, longish hair. And something about him was very *effeminate*, I think you'd call it."

Mike snorted. "I think we used a different word for it back then. But, yeah. I know who you mean now. What was his name?"

"Toby," Sara chimed in. "He was—"

"Tamsyn!"

I dropped the serving tray, which fortunately had been picked clean of food, onto the table and whirled around to see Vera, her face red and eyes flashing.

"You're on the clock. You can't just stand around and gab."

Her tone was harsh, and I was momentarily stunned. Vera had been so polite and friendly before.

What had happened? The answer, of course, was fairly obvious after a moment's thought. At the authors' tea, she'd been working for me. Now I was reporting to her, and in my eagerness to investigate Sebastian Grenville's death, I'd pretty much been the worst employee ever.

"I'm sorry, Vera. I lost track of what I was doing."

"There's been a change of plans with the punch," she said, talking as she walked and expecting me to keep up with her brisk pace. "It's too hard for people to get to the back of the room, so we're moving the bowls to the tables."

Right. The punch bowls. That was the entire reason I was there, and with all the chitchat, I'd almost forgotten. I sped up, getting a few steps ahead of Vera.

"I'll start bringing them over," I offered, reaching a hand into my pocket to make sure I would be able to grab the flask without being too obvious about it. I wished the polo shirts had long sleeves, so I could hide it there, but as long as Vera wasn't looking too closely, I thought I could manage.

"Hold on." Vera came to a halt in front of the table that held the punch bowls and scowled. "We don't have the orange garnish. There should be a big plastic container with them in the refrigerator. Can you run and get them?"

"I...uh..." I watched, helpless, as she picked up the first bowl and started toward a table. This wasn't my plan. Not at all.

"Hurry!"

I dashed down the hall toward the kitchen, determined to retrieve the orange slices and get back in time to deliver the punch to the Lit Mag club's table if it killed me. Which it almost did. I was not cut out for running. By the time I re-entered the gym, more than half the tables had been taken care of, and to my frustration, instead of asking me to carry bowls, Vera pointed to a table clear on the opposite end of the room from my goal.

"Go add the oranges to those. Don't forget gloves." She pointed to the table that had once held the punch. "They're under there, hidden by the tablecloth."

I slipped on a food service glove and plopped handfuls of fruit into punch bowls with a speed unlike the catering industry had ever seen. There was just one table left to be served when I was done, the table with James and his friends. Vera was making a beeline toward the final punch bowl from one end of the room while I did the same from the other. She reached it first.

"Here," she directed, "put the oranges in so I can bring it over."

The big, heavy bowl was already clasped to her chest, and I saw no way to pry it from her without looking suspicious. My only hope was to sprinkle the oranges with the potion and hope for the best. I improvised a plan.

"Oh, fudge berries. There's a hole in this plastic glove. Let me get a new one."

I ducked beneath the tablecloth, pretending to find a new glove, but actually, I unscrewed the stopper from the hip flask, dumped as much as I could over the remaining orange slices, and re-emerged. I took the final handful of slices and added them to Vera's bowl. There was a quick flash, like an electric spark, as the oranges hit the punch, but Vera didn't seem to notice. I assumed it meant the spell had been activated. As Vera took the enchanted punch bowl toward its intended targets, all I could do was wait.

I was pacing the perimeter of the gymnasium, keeping an eye on my suspects while trying to look busy enough that Vera wouldn't assign me something new to do, when I bumped into Cass. "Where have you been?" I demanded. "I've been trying to reach you all afternoon."

With a frown, Cass dug her phone out of her pocket and checked the screen. "Oopsies. I turned the ringer off. What's up?"

"I sort of made...a potion."

Have you ever had a time when you were so wrapped up in acting on a plan that you never gave much thought to how it would sound when you tried to explain it to someone else? Yeah, this was one of those times.

Cass blinked, one of those slow ones that said she was going to try to reserve judgment until she'd heard the whole story, but it wasn't going to be easy. "A potion? What exactly is this potion meant to do, and who is it for?"

"After talking to James Thorne this morning, I needed to figure out if Sebastian Grenville stole the manuscript for his first book from Phil Stanley."

"Phil Stanley, like the mayor's best friend and Summerhaven's hometown hero? That Phil Stanley?"

"Yeah, that's the one." I tugged at the edge of my shirt as I processed just how ludicrous it must sound. "Hear me out, though. Remember how we found out he was one of the members of the Lit Mag club back in high school?"

Cass's eyes grew wider. "Yes, but I think you got a few steps ahead of me between yesterday and today."

I crossed my arms in front of my chest. "It was an obvious conclusion."

"For you, maybe," Cass muttered. "So, let's get back to the potion."

"Right, well, I tried calling you." I paused just long enough to let whatever guilt that statement might stir up have time to take effect. "I mixed up a little bit of punch, then did a finding spell, followed by a truth spell, and put it in the bowl with the oranges."

Her eyes swept the room with obvious horror. "You've given everyone in the class of 1999 an untested potion?"

"Of course not!" Geez, how much of a newbie did she take me for? Even I knew better than that.

"Fine. So, who did you give it to?"

"Them." I nodded my head toward the table in question. "Those are the five who were in the club, and they've all had significantly more success than the average Summerhaven High graduate. You were right yesterday. Any one of them could've been the original author."

"It doesn't mean any of them were responsible for Grenville's death, though," Cass pointed out.

"I know. I thought of that. It's why I only made the potion to reveal the true author, not to say if they were the killer."

"Smart," Cass said, which made me flush just a little with pride. I was finally getting the hang of the witch thing. "So, how do we know when the potion's worked?"

"I..." My mouth remained open, but the words stopped flowing, because the truth was, I had no clue. I cleared my throat. "I didn't really think of that part."

Cass groaned. "That's the part of potions that can really trip you up. Trust me, I know. If you forget to include a way to collect them, you might never find out the results."

I buried my head in my hands, massaging my forehead, which suddenly throbbed mercilessly. "You've got to be kidding me," I said with a moan. "The perfect opportunity, and I screwed it up."

"Well, maybe not," Cass said reassuringly. "Sometimes it becomes obvious."

It only took another hour to discover that Cass was right.

"SOMEONE'S BEEN IN THE LADIES' ROOM FOR quite a while," a reunion guest informed me, her face a perfect picture of disgust. "I think she's having issues. There are some *noises* coming from inside, if you know what I mean. It's going to need a good cleaning if the rest of us are expected to use it after this."

"I'll go check," I told her, praying my temp duties with Happy Helpers didn't include providing janitorial services. "Thanks for letting me know."

The reunion was in full swing, and despite Vera watching like a hawk all night, I suspected someone had managed to spike the punch after all. No doubt one of the partygoers had over imbibed and was paying the price. I tapped on the door to the bathroom and heard a sound I wasn't quite able to identify, but which confirmed my suspicions that the person on the other side of the door was going to wake up with a lot of regrets in the morning.

"You okay in there?" I called. There was a shuffling from inside, then a click as the lock was undone. As the door cracked open, I saw it was being held by a hand covered in diamond rings. "Sara?"

The crack widened. Sara's face came into view,

pinched with pain and covered in a sheen of sweat. "My stomach. Something's not right."

Yeah, I could see that. She looked like she'd just gotten off a roller coaster or something, all dizzy and ill. On the bright side, I was pretty sure I'd just identified my author. The English teacher, of course. I should've guessed that from the start.

"Do you remember where the nurse's office is?" I asked, and she nodded in response. "Good. Let's start by going there." I wasn't sure if the door would be open, or if there would be any antacids or aspirin inside if it was, but it was the best plan I could come up with.

On the way down the hall, we ran into Jeanette. She was holding her abdomen with both hands, her lips pressed together tightly and pain etched across her face. Whatever was going on with Sara, it was clearly hitting her, too. They must've written the manuscript together. Had they teamed up to kill Sebastian Grenville, too?

"Oh no," I said when I saw her. "Not you too. Come on. We're going to look for some medicine in the nurse's office."

When we arrived at our destination, the room was not empty. The door stood open, and the lights blazed into the darkened hallway. Phil Stanley sat on one of the cots, white as a sheet, while Mike was curled up in a ball on the other. James, looking no better off than the others, rummaged through a cabinet.

"Do you think you can swallow?" James asked.

"My throat feels tight." Phil loosened his tie and undid the first button on his shirt.

I looked around the room, goose bumps breaking out on my arms. "Are you all feeling sick?"

James turned to face me, looking like death warmed over. "It came on all at once, maybe ten minutes ago. Maybe it was the egg rolls. They seemed undercooked."

Yeah, maybe. "Is anyone else out there showing symptoms?"

James shook his head, then appeared to regret it as he grasped the edge of the nurse's counter. "I don't think so."

As my brain seemed to freeze in panic, I heard footsteps approaching.

"What's going on?" It was Cass.

"They're...not well." I finished lamely.

"Call Noah," she said.

"Are you sure I should I call him, or do you think it's a different kind of emergency?" I was legitimately worried magic had caused this malady, but that might not have been my only reason to balk at the thought of calling Noah. I hadn't seen him since the night we'd had dinner, and I was mortified at what he must think of me. He'd been gone all week, so I hadn't even had a chance to apologize.

Cass thought it over for a second. "You call him,

and I'll get Sybil on the phone. That way we cover all the bases."

I NODDED AND GRABBED MY PHONE.

"Hello?" Noah's voice sounded in my ear, and I nearly started to shake with relief to hear it. I might not know where we stood on a personal basis, but when it came to anything related to his work, Noah was rock-solid. I had no reason to doubt him on that.

"It's Tamsyn. There's a problem at the reunion. Several people are sick."

"How serious?"

I glanced at the five occupants of the nurse's office, in various states of discomfort and, worse, some looking like they wouldn't be able to make it out of the building on their own. "You might need to send an ambulance."

"I'm on my way."

At this assurance, my chilled body began to thaw. If there was a medical fix to the magical mess I'd made, Noah would know the cure. Anything else that was weighing on me was just going to have to wait.

CHAPTER FIFTEEN

The sky was black as I sat in a rocking chair on the porch at the Pinecroft Inn, and though the moon that night was full, it was small and dim, as though it had been moved far away and its light reduced to little more than a faint glow. I'd just gotten an update from Noah on the five people who'd been taken to the island clinic from the reunion two hours before. Now I sat, rocking, holding the phone as if Noah's calm voice could somehow still bring me comfort even though the call had ended a minute before. It was only when Cass poked her head out the front door that I started to emerge from the trance-like state the evening's events had left me in.

"You coming in soon?" Cass asked.

I rose at her prompting and headed in, unaware how cold the night had become until the cozy warmth of the house hit my skin, sending belated shivers through my body. Cass waited just inside the entryway while Sybil sat on one of the chairs near the fireplace. They hadn't taken the time to build a fire, being too occupied with waiting on word from the clinic, but as I rubbed my hands over my icy arms, I regretted the oversight. I entered the living room, and Cass followed, choosing the chair opposite Sybil.

"Any word?" Sybil asked.

I settled onto the couch, tucking my legs up beside me and pulling a favorite blanket over my lap. "They're all resting at the clinic infirmary tonight, still very sick but expected to make a full recovery. Noah will call the mainland in the morning to expedite the lab tests."

"Excellent news," Sybil said. The lines that had creased her brow faded away, and she sat back in her chair, relaxed.

It was good news, much better than I'd expected, yet I found it impossible to relax, or even to muster any enthusiasm as I related it. No matter how upbeat their prognosis, it didn't change the facts. My magic was broken. That's why Sebastian Grenville had died, and why five more people had become ill. I'd screwed up the spells, simple as that. I was a novice at best, and distracted besides. I had no business doing magic on my own. And once my coven knew the extent of my condition, they'd probably agree I should never do magic again.

Did witches get banished, I wondered, or have

some sort of ceremony where powers could be stripped away? If so, would I still be allowed to stay in Pinecroft Cove, or would I be sent out into the world on my own? That sounded terrible. I sighed. Regardless of the consequences, I had to tell them.

"Ladies, there's something I've been keeping from you, and I think it's time I just come out with it." There was no backing out of it now.

The lines reappeared on Sybil's forehead as she leaned forward. "What is it?"

"I'm..." I swallowed hard, forcing myself to continue even as my eyes filled with tears. Once my secret was out, there was no going back. "I'm not a kitchen a witch."

"What do you mean?" Cass scooted to the edge of her seat. "Of course, you are. You're a Bassett. Bassetts are always kitchen witches."

"Well, I'm not," I insisted. "And what's more, I'm not so certain everyone else in the family was, either. My mother, for example. Or Lillian."

"Who's Lillian?" Sybil's frown lines doubled in depth, which told me exactly how distressed this conversation was making her because normally her glamor magic would never allow such a thing to be visible.

If the first revelation had been difficult, the next one was set to break me, but I knew it had to happen. "Lillian is the ghost who resides in the Pinecroft Inn."

"I've never heard of the inn being haunted before,"

Cass said. "How do you know? Have you felt cold spots or heard strange knocking noises?"

"I've talked to her."

Cass nodded slowly. "With a spirit board?"

I twisted the blanket in my lap, wadding it up in my fists. "No, like we're doing right now. Just talking. She loves to talk. She and that darn cat of hers never stop."

Sybil raised one eyebrow. "There's a ghost cat, too?"

I shook my head. "Gus isn't a ghost. He's just immortal, I think. He hasn't said."

Her eyes widened, projecting a look I took to mean I had about ten seconds left before she called Noah and asked to have me hauled away to a padded room. "The cat talks, too?"

"Of course, the cat doesn't talk," I assured her. Meows a lot, yes, but no talking. Not that I was certain he lacked the ability, mind you. At times, in fact, I was sure he was refusing to answer out of spite. But I wasn't going to tell the Head Priestess of my coven that.

"And you've actually seen this ghost?" Sybil said, as if needing to clarify just how far gone I was.

"All the time," I said. "She pretty much makes herself at home."

Sybil rubbed her temples. "And how does all this tie into you thinking you're not a kitchen witch? I'm not following."

I closed my eyes, thinking it might make it easier if I didn't have to see her or Cass's reaction to what I was about to say. "The summer my mother died, she'd started hearing things, voices that only she could hear. I thought she was crazy. And the idea that she could just fall overboard and drown seemed impossible. Deep down, I was sure she'd lost her sanity, and she'd chosen to end her own life. But now, I'm not so sure. I think whatever type of witch I really am, she was, too." Which meant that maybe things would go as badly for me as they had for her, but I couldn't bring myself to say that part out loud.

"And this Lillian," Cass said, "she's also a witch?"

"A powerful one, I think. There are things she can do that I don't think would be possible otherwise."

"Like what?" Sybil asked.

"Travel through time."

Sybil placed her hands palm to palm, like a steeple, and tapped the fingertips repeatedly against her lip. "You have a time traveling ghost. You're certain of this?"

"She's brought me along." I cringed, knowing how ridiculous it sounded. "Back to the 1920s, when she was alive."

Sybil's jaw went slack. "That's…"

"Crazy, I know." I hung my head. "If you don't want me in the coven anymore, I completely understand."

Cass spoke up. "Why would we not want you in the coven?"

"Because whatever kind of witch I am, my magic is strange. And dangerous. In the past week, I've tried to work two simple spells, and both times they were disasters." I could see Cass wanted to argue, but I put up a hand to urge her to let me finish. "I'm not talking about regular mistakes from inexperience. Five people are in the hospital tonight. A man's dead!" His ghost was also haunting the inn, which I hadn't mentioned yet, but I figured they'd had enough of a shock, and I'd had enough humiliation for one night.

"You can't believe that's your fault," Sybil said quietly.

"I don't believe it," I whispered, pulling the blanket close around me. "I know it. I'm broken, and I don't deserve to practice magic anymore. People get hurt."

After reassurances that I refused to listen to, Sybil and Cass left. Feeling restless and unable to settle down, I put on a sweater and went outside. I felt so alone, unmoored. Aunt Gwen was unreachable, and I had no one else to guide me. I knew my coven cared and wanted the best for me, but they were almost as new to being witches as I was, since formal training in the magical arts only began in earnest once a coven had been formed. What I longed for, more than anything, was for someone older and wiser to tell me what to do. But there was no one. Even Lillian—who technically qualified as older by virtue of having been born more than a hundred years ago, although I couldn't bring myself to say she was wise—was nowhere to be found.

I walked across the great expanse of green grass in the front of the house, then entered the woods and kept walking. There wasn't a well-defined trail, but there was enough space between the trees that it was easy to pass without getting hit by branches or tangled in brush. Off to my right, I could see the dark water of Pinecroft Cove, smooth as obsidian, the moon's reflection a perfect circle on its surface. The sight of it drew me closer, until I reached a clearing in a circle of trees and stood at the bank. Though the night was chilly, the air was completely still. Not so much as a single ripple marred the glassy smooth perfection.

Though I could see it from my bedroom window, I avoided looking at Pinecroft Cove. The memory of what the place represented to me was too painful. But looking now, I couldn't tear my eyes away. Had the water been like this the night my mother died? It would've been warmer, but there'd been a full moon then, too, that night when her boat was found, but she was gone. Was a pale, shining disk on the water the last thing she'd seen before she slipped beneath the surface? I would never know, just as I would never know how it had happened or why.

There was a boulder near the water's edge, low and flat on top. I sat on it, crossing my legs, rocking slightly as I continued to stare, wishing she were there. *I have the power to see ghosts, but I can't even talk to my own mother.* I let out a low, bitter laugh. I'd never been a big fan of irony.

"Why, Mom?" My words were soft but audible. At least, I could hear them. I knew she couldn't, but somehow talking to her after fifteen years brought more comfort than I'd expected it to, so I continued. "How could you just leave me here, and not even tell me who I was? I mean, I moved to Cleveland. Dad had me become an accountant. An accountant! Is that what you wanted for me?"

There was no answer. I wasn't expecting one. Even so, I didn't want the conversation to end.

"I'm in trouble, Mom. I'm a terrible witch. I can't do any of the things I'm supposed to be able to do, and the powers I do have are frightening. Dangerous." My voice was shaky, and the threat of tears made me shut my eyes. I swallowed, and my throat was scratchy and dry. "I may have killed someone, Mom, and made even more sick."

Tears ran down my cheeks as I held my breath, waiting to see what consequences would accompany this admission of guilt. I'm not sure what I expected. It's not like my mother was going to come charging out of the water after fifteen years and send me to my room. What happened was nothing. Absolutely nothing. Just the moon on the water, and the air as still as a tomb.

"I need help," I whispered. "I need you. I need

Grandma. I need Aunt Gwen. I'm all alone, and I have no idea what I'm doing. I'm in trouble. Please. Please help me."

I listened to the silence for a moment, looking out at the vast emptiness of the cove, then rose to leave. As I turned toward the trees, a rush of wind swept past me, shaking the leaves and sending a shower of them falling to the ground. Then it was still again.

I WOKE TO A BANGING SOUND, ONLY TO realize I'd never made it up to my room. Dappled, early morning light came through the living room curtains. I stretched my body on the couch, trying to remember why I was there. The last I could recall, I'd returned from my walk and sat for what was only supposed to be a minute at most. Instead, somehow I'd curled up, my favorite blanket wrapped around me, and slept the night away. From the crick in my neck, I doubted it had been a restful sleep.

The banging came again, only now I recognized it as the sound of someone knocking on the front door. I rose and opened it to find Noah standing outside. His dark hair was disheveled, as if he'd run his fingers through to straighten it instead of using a comb, and he wore the same khaki pants and plaid shirt he'd arrived at the school in the night before. Somehow, it was a look he managed to pull off.

After a quick glance downward at myself, I folded my arms across the Happy Helpers uniform shirt I still wore, and which I'd managed to spill something down the front of, too. They'd probably dock my pay for that, but considering I'd nearly killed five reunion attendees, that was the least of my concerns. I hadn't looked in the mirror, but I didn't have to. There was no doubt I was sporting an impressive halo of scarlet frizz all around my head. It was unfair that he looked so put together in the morning.

Noah wore his white lab coat, and for some reason, this puzzled me. He never wore that outside the clinic. Was he here on a professional call? Was this what it looked like when the men in white coats finally came to take you away? I stared at one long white sleeve like a total imbecile instead of saying hello.

"It was cold," he said by way of explanation once my silent focus on the garment had gone well beyond any acceptable limits on such things. "I rushed out without a jacket last night, and I haven't been home since."

Poor Noah. This was the second weekend in a row I'd ruined for him by causing a major medical emergency, to say nothing of the dinner I'd spoiled by loudly accusing our friend's date of being a murderess. Given all that, I was fairly sure he'd come by on a strictly professional errand this morning. Why would he want anything more to do with me?

"I'm so sorry, Noah. For everything." I lacked the

energy to delve into all the details, but I hoped he understood how heartfelt my regret was for all the trouble I'd caused him.

"I'm used to being on call round the clock. It's not your fault they got sick."

Wasn't it? I wasn't so sure. "I feel like all you're ever doing these days is coming to my rescue. Please, come in. Let me make you a cup of coffee, at least."

"Nonsense. You're helping me out with that bake sale, don't forget."

I looked at him with surprise. "You still want me to do that? If you don't feel like you can trust my kitchen, all things considered, I totally understand."

"I'm sure your kitchen is fine," he said, following me in that direction.

"You are?" This assertion brought an inkling of relief, though I feared it might turn out to be premature. "Does that mean you've heard some news?"

"It's too early for the lab results from last night's incident, but based on some new details from Grenville's labs, I have a hunch." He took a seat in the dining room as I prepared a cup of coffee.

"A hunch?" I'd been hoping for something more solid, honestly. Maybe a premonition, or funny tingling in his tummy. But I guess I would settle for a hunch.

"Clostridium botulinum."

"Gesundheit." If this was his hunch, I needed a hint.

"It's the bacteria that causes botulism."

I was just about to set his coffee mug down when he said this, and it slipped from my hand at the news, falling the last inch and landing with a clunk on the table top as coffee sloshed over the side. "But, that's a type of food poisoning, right? How can you be sure that wasn't my fault? I made the food for the tea, and I helped with the punch, too."

"There's no way you were responsible for this. Not unless you're running an illegal med spa out of your aunt's kitchen while she's away." There was a spark of humor in his mocha eyes that I would've found really charming, had I not still been slightly terrified Sheriff Grady would be arriving any minute to read me my rights.

"What is that supposed to mean?" It was meant to be a friendly query, but it may have come out a bit more snappish than that.

I immediately felt terrible about it as Noah's face took on a conciliatory expression. "I should've explained better. As soon as I realized what everyone's symptoms last night were pointing to, I gave the head lab tech in the medical examiner's office a call. Got him out of bed, but I hooked him up with one of my uncle's condos a few years ago, so he owes me. Anyway, he said the reporting system is all backed up, but he took a look at Sebastian Grenville's tox screen and sure enough, it was what I thought."

"Which was?" I prompted and really did make an effort to keep my cool this time.

"His death appears to be linked to the presence of a significant quantity of botulinum toxin in his system."

"That's what Sheriff Grady meant when he said they were testing for a foodborne neurotoxin?"

"Yes, only in this case, it's very unlikely that food was the source. All indications are it came from a highly concentrated, medical grade source, consistent with the type used in Botox treatments. Although since the island doesn't have any med spas licensed to administer that sort of thing, I can't imagine where it came from."

I gasped, suddenly recalling the frozen faces of the garden club under their wide-brimmed, floral-festooned hats. "Mildred's Botox party."

It was Noah's turn to look confused. "What?"

"Every year, Mildred Banning invites all her friends for an exclusive spa day over Labor Day weekend," I explained as the details flooded back. "This year, she brought in some Hollywood doctor or something to give them all Botox injections. They look ridiculous, like, completely frozen stiff."

Noah nodded. "That can happen if it isn't administered properly, and especially if the concentration is too high."

"But, wouldn't they have gotten sick?" It was a small enough island that if the garden club had all come down with an illness, we would've heard about it.

"Highly unlikely. The body simply doesn't absorb

the toxin in that way. To cause the type of illness I saw last night, or what killed Grenville, it would've had to be ingested at least a few hours before the symptoms appeared, and in a quantity that was very deliberate."

"But, why would Mildred have wanted to kill a famous author or the members of an old high school club?" I only realized I'd said this out loud when I caught the look of complete disbelief on Noah's face.

"She wouldn't have," he said, as if there weren't a doubt in his mind, which was fair, I guess, since the idea of it was a little ridiculous. Mildred was a wealthy woman in her seventies, not a serial Botox poisoner.

"Right. Of course not." But maybe someone she knew held a grudge of some sort? I made a mental note to find out.

I didn't know whether to laugh or cry. With a concrete, scientific explanation like Noah had offered, my faulty magic and questionable cooking skills were both off the hook. Now I just needed to talk to Mildred Banning to figure out how the Botox from her party could've made it into a killer's hands, and if she just might know whose hands those could be.

As important as that was, there was one other thing I needed to do first, before Noah had the chance to slip away again. "About that bake sale," I said, filling his coffee cup to the brim, "why don't you give me all the details now so I can get started?"

CHAPTER SIXTEEN

"Well, that was just rude." I scowled at the screen on my phone, which had gone blank.

"What was rude?" Lillian sat across from me at the dining room table. She wore a dress that resembled a kimono and held what appeared to be an ivory tile in one hand, roughly the same size as a domino but with a Chinese character on it instead of black dots.

"Mildred Banning just hung up on me."

"I knew a Ruth Banning, a real chippy. She was out with a different fella every night of the week and usually didn't make it home 'til morning, if you know what I mean." Lillian tapped the tile against her front tooth as she studied the completely empty stretch of table in front of her. "Think they're related?"

"Wouldn't that be funny," I said with a snort. Even Botox hadn't been able to wipe the sourpuss expression off Mildred's face. I doubted she'd ever been the type to have fun. I was about to say so but got distracted by Lillian setting the tile onto the table. Immediately, it disappeared. "What are you doing?"

"Playing Mahjong," she replied, eyes intensely focused on the spot where the tile should've been. "Do you play?"

"Never even heard of it," I replied.

"Oh, it's the cat's meow."

"I thought it was the cat's pajamas."

"Now, that just sounds stupid." She gave me a look as if to say I really should've known better. "People are the cat's pajamas. Things are the cat's meow."

"Well, isn't that grammar lesson just the bee's knees?"

She shook her head, clearly pained. "Maybe you should stick to your own vocabulary."

"So, this Mahjong game. What is it exactly?"

"Oh, it's all the rage. We played it at Davenport's all the time." Her eyes sparkled with mischief. "I'm very good."

I eyed her with suspicion. "You played for fun?"

"And money. Obviously."

Why hadn't I guessed that sooner? "So Davenports is a speakeasy and a gambling den?"

"All the best places are," she replied. "You know, I'm still a little hazy when it comes to my last days on earth, but I do believe I was owed a fair bit of money from my winnings. I just can't remember by whom."

"Maybe you were paid back right before the end," I suggested.

"Or maybe I was murdered so they wouldn't have to pay," she countered with a shrug. "I honestly don't know. Isn't life funny?"

I found it odd how lightly she treated the subject, considering we were talking about her demise, but I guess ghosts aren't like humans in that respect. "So, you play Mahjong like solitaire, by yourself?"

She frowned at the table, another tile having appeared in her hand from out of nowhere. "Nope."

My eyes widened as I looked at the seemingly empty chairs grouped around the table. "Lillian, tell me the truth. Are there other ghosts sitting here right now?"

Lillian shifted uncomfortably in her chair. "Maybe."

"But, I can't see them. I'm only able to see you and our brooding writer up there." I gave a nod toward the stairs. I squinted hard at each chair, but nothing changed. "Why can't I see them?"

"I don't know." She smacked her tile onto the table, and it ceased to be visible, just like the first had done. "I don't make the rules. But technically, they exist on a different plane. So maybe that's why."

My head swiveled to take in the room. "Are there a lot of them on this other plane?"

Lillian bit her lip. "What do you mean, a lot?"

I shook my head, grabbed my phone, and rose. "You know what? I don't want to know."

Striking out as I had with Mildred, I decided to give Sybil a call. If anyone had an in with that pretentious old bat, it was my high society High Priestess. As it was a Monday, I expected to catch her at her shop, or else at the archives desk at the library, but when she answered, the echoing quality of the sound hinted she was outside, instead.

"Where are you?" I asked.

"Heading over to your house. Why?"

My stomach knotted. Considering everything I'd told her and Cass last time I'd seen her, I wondered if she was on her way over for some kind of intervention. "First, you tell me why you're headed here instead of at work."

"Well, actually, I wanted to ask Jackie a question about Sebastian's manuscript. Is she there?"

I moved to the base of the staircase and heard the tapping of a keyboard coming from the guest room upstairs. "Hard at work, as always."

"Hmm. I hate to interrupt." Sybil was silent for a moment. "I have an idea. Can you meet me at Duffy's Wharf in twenty minutes?"

The islands of Summerhaven and Northport were so close together that you could nearly toss a stone from one and hit the other, but somehow in the several hundred years in which they've been inhabited, it never occurred to anyone to build a bridge. As a result, to get to Northport Island, you first must go to Duffy's Wharf. It was called this because it was owned by Jack Duffy, one of a long line of Duffy's who'd lived in that spot and owned a reasonably seaworthy motor-boat, and if you showed up anytime except between 2:00 and 3:00 pm, which was when Jack Duffy liked to take a nap, he would haul you across the water for seven dollars roundtrip, plus two bucks extra if you brought a bicycle. There was a similar arrangement on the Northport side, this one operating out of Sullivan's Wharf, which had gotten its name for pretty much the same reason.

When I arrived at Duffy's, Sybil was already wait-ing. She wore wide-legged white trousers and a navy blue rain coat, and her hair was covered by a blue-and-white-striped scarf that made her look like a cross between a 1960s' movie star and the world's most fashionable pirate. I straightened the visor of the base-ball cap I'd donned to protect me from the wind, then tugged at the zipper to my plain gray fleece, and reflected that, with people like Sybil and Noah in my life, I might as well give up. I would never be the good looking one in the group.

"What's this plan of yours?" I asked, but only after taking a few moments to savor her warm embrace. With the week I'd had, I needed that hug something fierce.

"I checked at the clinic, and Sara was released yesterday afternoon. According to Northport Prep, she planned to be in the classroom today, so I thought we could pay her a visit."

"So I can apologize?" I asked, still feeling guilty for her illness even after I'd been assured I hadn't played a role in it.

"Don't be silly. Noah told me all about the test results."

"That reminds me I need an in with Mildred. I need to find out more about that Botox party she hosted. Do you know her?"

Sybil made a face. "Unfortunately, yes. I'll give her a call when we get back, but first, I want to see if Sara can help us find copies of the lit mag from 1999."

"We could try another finding spell," I suggested, not sure I was ready to see any of the lit mag members again so soon, while the remnants of my guilt, however misplaced, still hung over me.

"We'd need Cass to give it the best chance for success," Sybil pointed out, "and she's busy at the tearoom all day."

This convinced me, so we set off across the water and arrived on the other side about fifteen minutes later. The campus of Northport Preparatory School was just a short walk from the wharf and looked exactly like every fancy prep school in every movie that had ever been made. The buildings were made from red brick, with stately white columns in the front and ivy growing up the sides. Inside, the mahogany banister of the main staircase had been polished to a high sheen by the countless hands of graduates who had gone on to become senators, statesmen, and captains of business. By the time we arrived, school was out and the halls were empty, but when we reached the office of the English department, Sara sat behind a stack of papers at her desk.

"Sara," I said, and she looked up, her face registering surprise. "How are you feeling?"

"Weak but better," she replied. "Luckily, Dr. Caldwell was able to administer an anti-toxin right away, so none of us suffered nearly as much as we might've otherwise."

"Any idea why it happened?" I asked, hoping she'd be willing to share her theories as to who might have wanted to harm them and that it wasn't in poor taste to press her for information so soon.

"I assume the sheriff will know more soon, but whatever type of negligence led to this, the catering company can count on a lawsuit. Phil's already calling his lawyers."

Negligence? Did that mean none of them suspected they were targets? I wanted to explore this more but decided to keep quiet for the time being.

"We're sorry to barge in like this," Sybil said once it was clear I had nothing left to ask, "but do you happen to have a copy of the lit mag from your senior year?"

Sara's brow wrinkled. "Why on earth would anyone want that?"

"My grandmother's the archivist at Summerhaven

Library, and a review of the collection showed we're missing volume one."

"James mentioned the extra copies may have been here at the school," I added.

"Oh. There might be a few in the old department files. I'll check next time I'm in there and let you know."

"I don't suppose you could have a look now?" I asked, unable to keep the urgency from my voice.

Sara gave me a puzzled look. "Now? I was just about to head home."

"Of course. We understand," Sybil soothed. "It's just, as a book lover yourself, I'm sure you must know how distressing it is to discover your collection's incomplete."

The look on her face told me Sybil had struck a chord, and Sara nodded in understanding. "Let's just have a quick look."

The search turned out to be much easier than expected, and after opening the second drawer, Sara pulled out a thick file. "This should be it."

Inside the folder were multiple copies of a book with thick, glossy pages that were filled with both print and illustrations. I thumbed through the pages, impressed. "I'm surprised you didn't all keep copies of this. For a high school literary magazine, it's stunning."

"It is, but it would be better if it actually contained any of our work," Sara replied. "If you look closely, you'll see that despite James's best efforts, almost none of it is credited to Summerhaven students."

"Except for this one." As I'd continued scanning the pages, one name stood out. "Toby Rivers."

"Yes, that's the boy we were talking about at the reunion. He was a junior, though, I think."

After thanking Sara for the magazine, Sybil and I headed back to Summerhaven. We needed to find out more about Toby Rivers, but our first stop was Mildred Banning's house. Unlike when I'd called her, Sybil had been invited right over. Mildred was just going to have to deal with the fact that I was tagging along.

"Sybil, darling, how are you?" Mildred rested her hands on Sybil's shoulders and peppered the air in the vicinity of her cheeks with kisses. "How's your mother?"

"Mother's fine, thank you," Sybil replied in a charming but fake, rich socialite voice I don't think I'd ever heard her use before, which Mildred appeared to be eating up. "I'm sure she'd love to see you next time you're in Manhattan."

Stepping through the front door of the garden club president's miniature seaside chateau, I found it reminiscent of Cliffside Manor, only smaller. Though still impressive, it had obviously been made with a smaller budget and less skilled artisans than the old Davenport estate, and I had the impression that whichever member of the Banning family had built it years back probably suffered from quite the inferiority complex. Judging by the way Mildred was nearly getting the vapors over the possibility of dropping in on Sybil's mother, I could only assume the apple hadn't fallen far from the tree.

"Now what was it you wanted to talk about, dear?" Mildred asked, looking directly at Sybil and ignoring me completely.

Sybil glanced my way. "Actually, my friend Tamsyn tried calling you earlier about it, but somehow you must've gotten disconnected."

"Oh, was that you?" Mildred finally made eye contact, and it annoyed me to no end that I detected not even a hint of remorse over hanging up on me. "Reception's been terrible lately."

"Ms. Banning," I began, pausing long enough for her to urge me to call her Mildred. She didn't. "I understand you had a Botox party here a few weeks ago?"

"Botox? Oh, I would never use that kind of thing." The fact that her face was still mostly paralyzed as she spoke suggested otherwise.

"Really?" Sybil frowned. "You see, Mother was really hoping—"

"Oh, your mother wanted to know?" Though Mildred's lips barely twitched upward, I was fairly certain this was her attempt at grinning like a

Cheshire Cat. "Okay, I'll let you in on a little secret. Some of my girls in the garden club and I had a little spa day, with an aesthetician I brought in from one of the best clinics in Hollywood."

"Would you recommend them?" Sybil asked. "Could you tell me their name?"

"Well, normally I would share," Mildred began, a claim which I very much doubted, "but I'm not sure that I *would* recommend them."

"Why's that?" I asked. I expected her to say because they'd turned her and her friends into living stone, but her answer was much more intriguing.

"I'm not certain they're on the up-and-up. You see, I ended up being charged for four extra vials of Botox, which let's just say isn't cheap. I'm certain we didn't use that many, but they insisted they'd checked the aesthetician's stock both before and after, so I couldn't argue."

My heart beat faster as a possibility occurred to me. "Is it possible someone stole them?"

"My girls would never steal."

I did a quick roll call in my head of the other garden club members and had to admit the prospect of any one of them being a thief was unlikely. And the more I thought about it, the less likely it seemed that any of the old ladies in question would hold a grudge worth killing over. It had to be someone else. "What about the staff?"

"I trust my household like they're family."

Mildred's nose inched upward haughtily, but then a wavering look came over her. "Although, I did hire a few extra servers that day, to help with the food. They came from that new temp agency, Merry Minions, or something like that."

She knew nothing about the servers, naturally, as she was the type to find temporary help beneath her notice. Even so, my wheels were busily turning over what few details she'd provided. Once we'd left her house, I turned to Sybil, barely able to contain my excitement. "Do you think she meant Happy Helpers?"

"I assume so," Sybil said, squinting at me as I clapped my hands together. "Why?"

"I may not know who murdered Sebastian Grenville or poisoned the lit mag club yet, but I do think I just solved the string of thefts that's been plaguing the island."

"How so?"

"Mildred hired Happy Helpers, and her Botox went missing. Cass said they were using the agency over the summer, and her potion ingredients were stolen. And when Noah's medicine cabinet keys disappeared from the clinic, didn't he say his usual receptionist was on vacation and he had a temp? I'm betting she came from Happy Helpers, too."

"I'm betting you're right. You know what this means?"

"That I'm a crime solving machine?" I ventured.

"It means you're going to have to call Sheriff Grady and tell him what we found out."

My face fell. "But—"

"But, what? You can't go charging into Happy Helpers headquarters and arrest everyone on the spot because you think they're thieves. You're an innkeeper, not a deputy."

I crossed my arms in a huff, but of course, she was right. Still, I couldn't give in without one final argument. "He'll take all the credit."

"Maybe he won't," she said, but her tone lacked conviction.

I gave her a look to let her know I thought she was full of it, but I didn't say anything more. She knew as well as I did that he would, and because of that, I was even more determined to keep a few details to myself. For example, I believed someone in Happy Helpers was a murderer. The Botox that had been stolen from Mildred's party had to be what was used in the poisonings. Once I knew who had worked at that party, I would be that much closer to figuring out who was responsible for the attacks on Grenville and the lit mag members. If I was ever going to be able to rid the inn of Sebastian Grenville's ghost, the one to bring that person to justice had to be me.

CHAPTER SEVENTEEN

On Tuesday evening, we had another official gathering of the coven in the tower room at Cass's house. Once again, the altar had been set, only this time I was slightly less creeped out by all the witchy paraphernalia since I knew what to expect. When I arrived, Sybil was busy bemoaning our lack of ceremonial robes.

"I guess I just always pictured having them, okay?" she said when I asked what the big deal was. "Ever since I was a little girl and my mother used to tell me stories about when I grew up to be in a coven of my own, I assumed we would have robes."

"I know." Cass nodded with an understanding I obviously lacked since my childhood bedtime stories had been more centered around princesses and castles. All the witches in those books had been evil, which in retrospect made me wonder what my mother had been thinking when she read them to me. "I always pictured meeting in the sacred grove and casting love spells all night long. Instead, we're meeting in my attic and we don't even have homemade honey cakes for the wine and cake ritual."

"I'm sorry about that." My cheeks turned hot as I glanced at the pathetic box of graham crackers that sat on the altar. I'd been in charge of making the cakes, naturally, but it was a new recipe and I'd gotten distracted, burning them until they were little more than charcoal blobs. Thank goodness I wasn't really a kitchen witch or my magical future would be doomed. Honey grahams from the island grocery store were the best I could do. I'd thought the bear-shaped ones would help make up for it, but I could understand why the others were disappointed.

"Being a full-fledged witch isn't nearly as much fun as any of us were led to believe," Sybil said sympathetically.

I'd been raised with precisely zero expectations about becoming a witch, but it appeared it was a lot like every other thing about being an adult. Not all it was cracked up to be. I sighed. "What are we going to do about the ghost in my guest room? It's been over a week, and he hasn't spoken a word. I have no idea what he even wants at this point, other than justice, which, let's be honest, is a little bit vague."

"We could try a summoning spell," Cass suggested.

"Isn't he already summoned?" I asked. "I mean, he's literally parked on my chaise lounge."

"Cass might be onto something," Sybil said slowly. "He's there, but he's also kind of not there. He's not communicating. I have an idea that might fix that, but right off the bat, I see two problems with it."

Only two? She was lucky. My ideas usually had way more than that. "Let's hear it, anyway."

"I was thinking we could modify a summoning spell, like the one we tried with Douglas Strong's ghost, to see if we could talk to him."

I frowned. "Why not just use a spirit board?"

"I thought of that," Sybil replied, "but I think there would be too much interference. You said he's already present, protected by or projecting a sphere of energy. Spirit boards work best when the intended target is fully in the spirit realm."

"So, like, that blue energy ball he's sitting in would cause bad reception, like a cell phone?"

Sybil nodded. "Pretty much."

"Okay, well, we can definitely ask Jackie for something that belonged to him to use for the spell," I said. "All his stuff's still in the inn."

Again, Sybil looked doubtful. "I'm not sure that will be enough. For this to work, I think we need two things, and both are tricky. First, we need Jackie to participate in the ritual. She's the closest person to him that we have, and he might be able to use her voice to speak through her."

My mouth hung open. "Did you just suggest we out ourselves as a coven of witches, then use your new girlfriend as bait to lure her dead fiancé?"

"She's not exactly my girlfriend, but when you put it like that..." Sybil let out a loud puff of breath. "That wasn't even the most challenging part of the plan."

"I'm afraid to ask," I muttered.

"In this case, location is key. Holding the seance here, or even in the inn, probably wouldn't work. We need someplace with more power."

"We need the sacred grove," Cass chimed in.

"Okay." I looked from one woman to the other. "So, where is that?"

Cass shrugged. "Don't know, exactly."

Sybil shook her head. "Not sure, either. Only fully initiated witches are granted admission to the sacred grove by their family elders. I know it's somewhere in the woods, near the banks of Pinecroft Cove, but that's it."

A memory flashed into my head of a grove of trees, and a rock, and a moonlit night on the water's edge. "Is there sort of a flat boulder, close to the water?"

They exchanged glances, and then Sybil said, "Yes. The high altar."

Oops. I was guessing right about then that a high altar wasn't the type of thing you should admit to sitting on. "If we're really going to do this, I think I know where it is."

"I'm in," Cass said.

"Me, too," said Sybil.

After looking at Cass and then Sybil, I gave a solemn nod. "Then so am I."

Sybil headed toward the door. "Okay, let's go to the inn and get Jackie onboard."

"Sure thing," I replied, "but I'm just going to say right now, Sybil, that explaining to her about the whole witch thing is strictly your job."

WHILE CASS STAYED BEHIND TO GATHER THE necessary supplies for the ritual, Sybil and I returned to the inn. When she went to speak with Jackie, I took the safer approach and hid in my bedroom. It's not that I anticipated a big blowup on Jackie's part, but I really wasn't sure what to expect. I mean, what was the appropriate response to finding out the woman you've been dating is a witch? I suppose it might've been wise for me to listen in and see, just in case I ever found myself in a similar position, but in the end, I did the next best thing and sent Lillian to find out what was going on.

"How's she taking it?' I asked when Lillian remerged in my bedroom after what felt like a very long stretch away.

"Better than I thought she would," Lillian admitted. She hadn't outright expressed doubt in our plan, but she'd been uncharacteristically quiet about it. Now

I knew why. "She seems open to the idea that witches exist, anyway."

"That's a start. Do you think she'll do it?"

"I think she might."

Too nervous to sit, I paced my bedroom floor. "What's going on with Sebastian?"

"He doesn't like it when I get too close," Lillian said. She chewed on her lip for a moment before continuing. "So, I sent Gus to check."

"He won't let you get near him, but he's okay with the cat?"

"Gus can be very charming."

I snorted. I had a lot of words to describe Gus, but charming wasn't one of them. "Does Gus have anything to report?"

"I don't know," Lillian replied. "It's not like he can tell me."

"Right," I said, rolling my eyes. "That was a great plan, then."

Lillian pouted. "You don't have to be so snippy about it, especially considering what's hanging in your closet right now."

I stopped my pacing in front of the closet door and pulled it open, seeing nothing but the usual assortment of clothing inside. "What am I missing?"

Lillian looked inside with a frown. "Oh. Try the dresser."

I opened each dresser drawer, staring at an assortment of socks, underwear, and folded sweaters. "Any other ideas?"

"The hall closet," Lillian said with a snap of her fingers.

We ventured downstairs, me by actually walking down them and her by sort of appearing there. I opened the hall closet to find three cape-like garments hanging from the rod. I took them out one by one to inspect. The first was made of camel-colored velvet with a paisley floral print in tones of aqua and burgundy. The second was a luxurious crimson silk with an apple green lining and wide kimono sleeves. It had a printed band of gold Celtic knot work across the hem. The third was a deep turquoise blue with an intricate pattern of intertwined vines traced in silver and a simple corded tie at the neck. They were beautiful and, though pristine in their appearance, had clearly traveled here from some long-ago time.

"What is this?" I asked, unable to tear my eyes away from Lillian's gift.

"I know you're planning a ritual tonight at the sacred grove. I thought your coven could use some proper ceremonial robes." Lillian reached out as if to stroke the fabric with her finger, which, of course, she couldn't actually do, but the sentiment was clear. "These were not the ones we used for that, but they did belong to three of my coven sisters who were very dear to me. I thought you might like them."

"I don't know what to say." Just when I thought I

had Lillian figured out, she went and did something truly unexpected and thoughtful. "Thank you."

I put the robes carefully inside a large shopping bag for easy transport, then waited to find out if the ritual was going to happen. After a few more minutes had passed, I heard the bedroom door upstairs open, and Sybil and Jackie emerged. As she came down the stairs, Jackie looked shaken yet oddly resolute. When she reached the bottom, she turned to face me.

"Sybil's explained everything, and I'm ready to help." She straightened her shoulders, pulling them back as if to emphasize what she'd said. "She also showed me the samples of Toby's writing from the old literary magazine, and I'd say with absolute certainty it's a style match for *Magnolia Sunset*. I studied that book for nearly a year before I was allowed to start writing anything, so I can spot the original author's work a mile away."

I nodded. "Now we just need to confirm it with Sebastian's spirit, if we can."

"And we need to find out if Toby is on the island and whether he might have been looking for revenge," Sybil added.

"There are a lot of unknowns," I conceded. "But if we can answer even a few of these questions, it could really help."

Once Cass arrived, toting a canvas bag filled with everything we needed to set up the altar in the grove, I led the way from the house, tracing the same path I'd taken a few days before. It seemed easy enough, but when we reached the clearing with the large, flat rock, both of my coven mates—or coven sisters, as Lillian had called hers, which I thought had a nice ring to it—regarded me with something akin to awe.

"How did you find this spot?" Cass asked, her eyes wide and sparkling in the moonlight.

"I just walked here," I said, feeling confused. After all, the path hadn't been hard to find.

"Both Cass and I have played in these woods for years," Sybil said, "and we've honestly never been here before."

"It was just…here." I shrugged, not knowing what else to say.

"No incantations?" Cass pressed. "No finding spells to locate it?"

"No. I just went for a walk, and this is where I ended up." I felt the sudden urge to drop the topic. I'd done nothing special. I really didn't know what the big deal was, and it was making me jittery to question what it might mean if it turned out the ability to stumble across the sacred grove wasn't normal after all. I set down the shopping bag and reached inside, searching for a distraction. "I don't want to forget these. They're from Lillian."

Cass and Sybil were speechless when I held up the antique cloaks. As if by instinct, Cass reached for the red one while Sybil took the turquoise, leaving me with my favorite, the camel-colored velvet. After an appropriate amount of time spent admiring the new garments, Sybil asked a question, which clearly had been percolating in her mind for some time.

"When you say they're from Lillian, you mean your resident ghost BFF?"

"That's the one." Why hadn't I realized that if I'd wanted a normal topic of conversation to distract us, presents from poltergeists probably wasn't the smartest way to go?

Fortunately, everything was set for the ritual, and our attention shifted quickly from other things. It was time to begin. A pentacle had been traced on the top of the rock altar in white salt with a lit candle placed at each of the five points, making the salt shine like tiny diamonds. A bowl of extra salt had been placed beside a chalice filled with wine and a plate of very tasty looking petit fours that Cass must have swiped from the kitchen at the tearoom. They really did put my Teddy Graham contribution at our last meeting to shame, and kitchen witch or not, I made a mental note to step up my game for next time.

Also on the altar sat a candle, a large seashell filled with water, a feather, and a cloudy white crystal, which represented the four elements. The only thing that remained was to cast a circle and begin. While we three witches donned our cloaks, Jackie stood back and took in the scene with a look that hovered between awe and fear. I remembered the feeling well from the first magical circle I'd witnessed, and to be honest, I still felt the same, though I tried to project more confidence than I felt.

Once we were done, Jackie came closer, holding out her hand. "Sybil said that to reach Sebastian's spirit, we needed something that was important to him." In her palm sat a heavy gold ring with a center stone of deep purple, in the style that was common for a high school class ring. "In all the years I knew him, he never took it off."

Sybil took the ring and brought it to the altar, setting it in the very center of the pentacle. Then, calling us forward one by one, she directed each of us to choose one of the elements from the altar and to stand in the corresponding corner, each of which had been marked by a large, white rock positioned a few feet from the altar in the correct compass direction. Cass took the feather, representing air, and stood beside the marker for east. Sybil gave the candle to Jackie and showed her to the southern corner. Then I chose the seashell, for water, and stood to the west. Finally, Sybil, as High Priestess, picked up the crystal, representing earth, and took her position in the northern corner.

Raising her crystal to the sky, Sybil called out in a clear, strong voice, "Guardians of the Watchtower of the North, Spirit of Earth, we call upon you!" She took a step forward and placed her crystal on the altar.

Beneath my feet, I felt a slight trembling.

Cass lifted her feather into the air with both hands.

"Guardians of the Watchtower of the East, Spirit of Air, we call upon you!" She took a step forward and placed her feather on the altar.

All at once, a gust of wind whipped around us like a tiny tornado, then went still.

I glanced to my right, where Jackie stood frozen, eyes wide. "Raise up your candle," I whispered, "and call on the Spirit of Fire."

She nodded, and to her credit, her hands only shook a little as she raised the unlit candle and announced in a faltering voice, "Guardians of the Watchtower of the…South? Spirit of Fire…we, uh, call upon you."

The wick of her candle burst into flames. Jackie let out a yelp and nearly dropped it, managing to rescue it at the last second without catching her hair, or anything else, on fire. She took a stumbling step forward and put the candle on the altar. Honestly, for a newbie and a non-witch, I had to give her credit. She'd handled the whole thing much better than I would've.

Turning my attention back to the ritual, I raised my seashell and said, "Guardian of the Watchtowers of the West, Spirit of Water, we call upon you!" I stepped forward and placed the shell on the altar.

A second later, a glowing white circle of light shone up from the sandy ground, enveloping us in its radiance, then dimmed.

"Our sacred circle is cast," Sybil intoned. "Blessed be."

As Sybil took a step toward the altar, my heart pounded like a hammer against my chest. By now, the ritual of casting a circle had become familiar to me, but I had no idea what to expect next. I was about to find out.

First, Sybil took a pinch of salt from the bowl and sprinkled it over Sebastian's ring. Then, she waved the feather over it, followed by a pass from the lit candle. Finally, she sprinkled it with some of the water from the shell. Covering her face with her palms, she kneeled and recited some sort of incantation, but it was too quiet for me to hear. Then she stepped back into place and motioned for all of us to join hands, which we did.

"We open the door to the spirit realm, with love and light. Spirit of Sebastian Grenville," Sybil said, her voice echoing through the trees, "we call upon you to join our circle."

The first sign that the spell was working came when the wind began to pick up, gently at first, then stronger, until our hair flew in wisps around our faces while the leaves crackled on the trees. Then a sort of bluish fog formed in the center of the rock altar, seemingly streaming from the gold ring, and eventually taking human shape and coloring. Our apparition did not appear as solid to me as Lillian usually did, but he had the unmistakable features of the deceased author and lacked the glassy quality I'd seen in the second-floor guest room. A quick glance around the circle at three slightly shocked faces told me that, unlike other ghosts I'd encountered, I was definitely not the only one who could see this one.

"Welcome, Sebastian," Sybil greeted when the spirit was fully formed. "We're sorry for the terrible tragedy that took you from this world, and we'd like to help you find peace. Do you know why you're still here?"

The ghost didn't speak but slowly shook his head.

"Do you know who was responsible for your death?"

Again, he shook his head.

To my surprise, before Sybil could ask another question, Jackie spoke with a voice that was clear and commanding. "Sebastian, you need to talk to us. You need to tell us everything about the manuscript, about the literary club and the true author. Everything. It's okay. You can use my voice."

As all of us looked on in shock, Jackie closed her eyes and drew a deep breath. At the same moment, the ghostly figure's chest puffed up, as if he had done the same. When Jackie opened her mouth to speak, it was her voice, yet I knew right away she was not the one in control. The words belonged to Sebastian Grenville.

"The manuscript I published, the one the world revered me for, was never mine. It was Toby's. It was written by a gentle soul, a genius, that no one understood, except maybe me. I loved him with all of my heart."

"What happened to Toby?" Sybil asked. "Why did you steal his work?"

But already, Sebastian's spirit was fading, returning to fog. "Please. I cannot take this secret to my grave. Please."

Then he was gone.

CHAPTER EIGHTEEN

It was after midnight when we made it back to the inn, one moment buzzing from the success of the summoning ritual we'd just performed and the next exhausted from the drain that working such powerful magic always entails. As we approached the old gray-shingled house, I noticed all the lights were on. Had I left them this way when we'd headed out in search of the grove? I was usually in the habit of turning them off, but with all the excitement, I supposed there was always the possibility that I'd forgotten.

Just as I'd convinced myself that must be the case, the front door opened, and a very familiar, but most unexpected, figure burst through and onto the porch. Her plump body was still clothed in her most brightly colored vacation attire, and beside the door, I belatedly registered a pile of suitcases. My heart skipped a beat. She was back!

"Aunt Gwen?" Breaking away from the others, I ran up the porch steps and pulled the old lady into a tight embrace. "What are you doing home? You're not supposed to be back until next week."

She held me close for a moment, then pulled away just far enough to see my face. "There was a sudden storm that kicked up on Saturday night, just as we were celebrating a full moon ritual on the cruise ship deck. It was so strong, it blew us right out of the Bermuda Triangle."

I squinted in confusion. "Bermuda *Triangle*? I thought you said the cruise was to Bermuda."

"Bermuda. Bermuda Triangle. Whatever." She waved a hand as if there were no difference whatsoever between those destinations. "I'm not the one who needs to explain anything right now, young lady. You are."

My stomach dropped like a broken elevator. "I am?"

"You and all your friends here," she said, pointing down to the lawn where Sybil, Cass, and Jackie stood huddled, looking uncertain what to do. "Or do you think I'm not aware that you were all just out in the sacred grove performing who knows what kind of forbidden magic?"

"Forbidden?" I gulped. "I don't think we were doing anything forbidden." I mean, not like *outright* forbidden. More of that gray area of magic that was probably better not to attempt on your own, but no one in charge ever thought you'd be dumb enough to try, so they didn't bother coming right out and telling you not to do it. You know, if you want to get technical about it.

"In the house, now. All of you." Aunt Gwen used that stern, motherly voice she had that prompted all of us to do exactly as we were told immediately and without argument.

No sooner had I stepped foot inside the house than my nostrils were engulfed by some sort of cinnamon and vanilla goodness that wafted through the air like a cloud sent directly from heaven. I looked at my aunt in astonishment. "Aunt Gwen, are you baking? You haven't even brought your luggage inside yet."

"I couldn't exactly grill you about this evening's activities in the woods without a snack, now could I?"

"Grill?" Normally, if Aunt Gwen was talking about grilling things, I would've been the first in line, but in this particular context, I didn't care for the sound of it one bit.

"Everyone into the living room," Aunt Gwen directed, ushering each of us toward an empty couch or chair. She frowned when she caught sight of Jackie, who was heading toward the stairs as if to retreat to her bedroom when no one was looking. "Including you, whoever you are."

Jackie nodded mutely and scurried back into the

room, taking a seat alongside the rest of us. A few moments later, Aunt Gwen came in from the kitchen, bearing a tray full of cookies and cake. She set it on the coffee table, along with small plates and cocktail napkins, and as I helped myself to a treat, I really wasn't sure what to expect next. Was I in trouble? Did getting in trouble with Aunt Gwen always involve baked goods? If so, was this not an incentive to misbehave? Frankly, as I sank my teeth into a still-warm snickerdoodle, I just didn't care. Of course, it was only after I swallowed a few bites that I remembered the truth spell.

Oops.

Aunt Gwen pulled a rocking chair from a corner into the center of the room and settled her round bottom onto the cushion with a slight *oof*. "So, what have you ladies been up to this fine evening?"

"We've been summoning the ghost of my dead fiancé in the woods," Jackie volunteered.

As the words came out, her eyes grew wider, and I could tell the effects of the truth spell were going to hit her especially hard since she, as a non-witch, was the one among us with the lowest tolerance to magic. Oh, the rest of us would crack, too, but since we knew what lay in store, we could at least fight to keep our mouths closed for a minute or two. I'm not sure why, though. Aunt Gwen would win in the end.

"And who are you, dear?" Aunt Gwen asked sweetly.

"Jacqueline Cortez, ma'am. I'm Sebastian Grenville's ghostwriter, only I'm not allowed to tell anyone that or to ever let on that he was gay. So am I, by the way." Jackie's hand belatedly flew to her mouth, like closing a barn door when the horses were already out.

"Aren't you a helpful child?" Aunt Gwen nudged the tray a little closer. "Have another cookie?"

"I wouldn't if I were you," I mumbled.

Aunt Gwen shot me a look. "Having another isn't going to strengthen the effects of the spell, Tamsyn. But it does make a nice snack."

"What spell?" Jackie asked, sounding thoroughly bewildered.

"It's a truth charm," I explained, reaching for another cookie. "But she's right. Damage is done. We might as well eat up."

"Now, girls…" Aunt Gwen swiveled in her chair, turning her attention to Sybil and Cass, but before she could launch in, I cleared my throat.

"Leave the rest of them out of this. I'll tell you everything."

She turned to face me with a satisfied expression that made it clear she'd been hoping for that outcome all along. "I'm all ears."

I took a few minutes to recap all that had happened since she left, explaining in detail the string of events that had led first to the death of a famous author on our front lawn, and then to the hospitalization for poisoning of five of his former high school friends. Finally, I reached the moment of my own confession. Part of me knew I could probably fight it off, maybe keep the secret as long as she didn't ask me any direct questions that would draw it out, but at that point, I realized I didn't want to keep the truth hidden any longer.

"Aunt Gwen, I'm not a kitchen witch. I'm something else, and I'm not sure what it is exactly, but it's much more powerful and frightening. I'm sorry I didn't tell you before."

She sat quietly for a moment, rocking her chair forward and backward. "You're certain of this?"

I nodded. "I know Bassett women have always been kitchen witches, and this must come as quite a shock, but I'm positive."

"Wait here."

Aunt Gwen rose, and when she left the room and headed upstairs, I was afraid the news had upset her so much she'd had to take some time to herself. However, a few minutes later, she reappeared, dry-eyed and totally composed, carrying a very old looking wooden box. She set it on the table beside the cookie tray—which, full confession, was mostly empty at this point because, as she'd already mentioned, the damage was done, and also have I ever told you I'm a stress eater? Aunt Gwen unclasped the lock but did not open the lid.

"This trunk has been in our family for generations, so many I couldn't even tell you how far back. It's much older than this house and probably goes all the way back to the founding days of Pinecroft Cove as a haven for witches who were escaping persecution in Massachusetts." She reached out and took my hand, placing it on the box. "Go ahead and look inside."

Though my fingers felt all at once shaky and weak, I managed to open the lid, cringing at the deafening squeak emitted from its rusty hinges. Inside was an odd assortment of magical-looking instruments, bird feathers, and a crystal ball. What I didn't see were any items related to cooking, which seemed odd for an heirloom belonging to a family of kitchen witches.

"What is this?" I asked. "What does it mean?"

"It means, my dear, that things aren't always how they appear." Aunt Gwen rested her gnarled hand on my shoulder, flooding my insides with warmth and comfort. "The fact that you're different doesn't mean you don't belong. Our family's magical legacy is filled with mysteries I've never understood and have always been just as happy to look past. I see now that may not have been wise. Perhaps you'll be the one to shine some light on the past and figure out exactly who you are in the process."

WITH AUNT GWEN'S REASSURANCES TO bolster me, I woke up the next morning determined to find out as much as I could about the mysterious Toby Rivers. I found white pages in the desk drawer in my bedroom—and if you are asking right now, as I was to Aunt Gwen then, what exactly white pages are, it turns out they're what people used to use to find telephone numbers before the internet—and found a listing for a family with the last name of Rivers on Davenport Drive. The phone number was disconnected, but I hoped that a trip to the neighborhood might yield some clues.

When I went downstairs, it was immediately obvious how much the atmosphere of the inn had changed now that Aunt Gwen had returned. For one thing, Jackie, who had been a virtual hermit for the past week and a half, was sitting at the dining room table with a stack of sweet potato waffles as high as her head on a plate in front of her looking for all the world like she'd been starving for days. Okay, technically, I hadn't actually fed her. But first of all, she's a grown-up, and second, I'd been forbidden from cooking by the Board of Health. I hadn't explained that part to Aunt Gwen yet, and I'd never been more grateful to know the effects of truth charms were extremely limited in duration.

Aunt Gwen was bustling around, cooking and cleaning, as if she'd never left. As much as she'd been looking forward to her cruise, she seemed happy to be home. This made me feel better, because ever since she'd mentioned her ship being blown off course by a powerful wind, I'd been feeling a tremendous amount of guilt. Thinking back on the night of the full moon, how I'd stumbled into the sacred grove and cried out for help, I was pretty sure I was the cause of that storm. But I didn't have time to worry about that now, as I was a woman on a mission to right the wrongs of a spirit's past so he could cross over to the other side.

*Speaking of spirits...*I eyed Jackie, overcome with a sense of how unfair it had been for me to let her stay in that room for so many days when I'd known it was haunted. Of course, in the beginning, I hadn't cared because I'd kind of thought she was responsible for the man's death, but I'd moved past that, and now I felt pretty lousy over the whole thing. To make up for it, I decided to invite her along on my morning's adventure. She agreed, and we both piled into Ms. Josephine as soon as Jackie had finished her breakfast.

"Do you know anything else about Toby?" I asked as we rounded the curve to Davenport Drive. The road followed the edge of the island, and offered a nice view of Cliffside Light, the island's most famous lighthouse. That it happened to be on the property of the first ghost whose death I'd helped solve, a house which was now in the keeping of the good-looking doctor whom I definitely kept tripping over myself around, brought up all sorts of uneasy associations with the landmark, but from a distance, it was nice to look at.

"He never mentioned him by name," Jackie said. "I knew he'd been in love with someone back in his high school days, but I never asked questions, and I didn't realize it had anything to do with the manuscript. Do you think Toby still lives on the island?"

"I've never heard of him," I answered, "but that doesn't mean much. The population's small, but it's still over a thousand people, and I'm pretty new here."

However, when we pulled up in front of the address that had been listed in the old phone book, it was apparent that neither Toby, nor anyone else, lived in the small Cape Cod style house. What was left of its white paint seemed to have been in need of a new coat for at least the past decade, and weeds thick as a forest grew where the lawn once had been. Even so, we got out of the car and took a look around. When we'd completed a loop around the property without discovering anything of interest, a neighbor was waiting by the car, watching with interest.

"You thinking of buying the place?" the man asked when we were within easy earshot.

"Oh, is it on the market?" I asked, figuring remaining vague about our purpose for visiting might be in our best interests.

"Don't rightly know, but it's been empty for years." He shot a disgusted look toward the waist-high weeds. "Used to be a nice family house, too."

"Did you know the family that lived here?" Jackie asked, and I appreciated how she'd changed the conversation from *a* family to *the* family so smoothly. Must've been the writer in her.

"Sure. Rivers was the name. There was a dad, I think. Don't recall a mom. And there were two kids, a boy and a girl."

"Do you know if any of them still live on the island?" I asked.

"Sad story, that. The boy, he was a quiet one as a teen, but always respectful. I think the kids at school bullied him, though, on account of he was a little... different. One day, he headed off to the lighthouse"— the man nodded in the direction of Cliffside Light —"and whether he did it on purpose or just lost his footing, well..." He shrugged.

"I take it he died?" Jackie asked.

"Ayuh," he replied in his thoroughly island-like way. "As for the dad and the sister, not sure what happened to them, but I think they left for the mainland right after. Dunno if they ever came back, but no one's been in this house since."

"How long ago was that?" I asked.

"Eighteen years, maybe?" His expression changed, and he put up his hands quickly, as if he'd suddenly realized he might be driving away a potential buyer. "Now, I don't want to scare you away. It's been rented out to summer people and the like. I'm sure the inside's in fine condition, if you're interested in the place. It sure would be nice to see it fixed up."

"Well, I'll certainly keep it in mind," I assured him

before Jackie and I got back into the car. I turned to her as we pulled away. "Another dead end."

"Literally," she remarked, "as Toby's been dead for years."

I sighed, the implication only just then dawning on me. "Which means he wasn't the one who killed Sebastian or poisoned the club, no matter how good a motive he would've had for it."

"Unless ghosts can commit murder."

"Not that I've ever heard of," I replied. "I guess we're back to square one. Shall we go back to the inn?"

"Actually, would you mind dropping me off at the library? Sybil asked if I'd come by to meet her grand-mother, now that she's back."

I was just rolling past the sheriff's office when I spotted the island's news van parked along the curb. Don't start picturing anything fancy. This wasn't a news van like they have in a big city, or even a typical small town on the mainland, with antennas and a satellite dish on it. This was a white minivan with the logo of the public access television station hand sten-ciled along one side, owned by an elderly lobsterman named Earl and driven around by his not-quite-as-old son Jasper, on account of Earl having recently gone blind in one eye. In addition to a fifteen-minute news program twice per week, these news anchors were best known for the morning tide reports and a special segment on where to find the best buffalo wings on the island.

A small crowd had gathered outside the station, and Sheriff Grady stood behind a podium as if getting ready to deliver a speech. I parked the car, and we both got out, joining Sybil and Cass, whom I spotted among the crowd, just as the sheriff took the microphone. He looked prouder than a peacock, and I held my breath, absolutely certain he was about to announce they'd caught Sebastian Grenville's killer. How could he have figured it out when I was fresh out of clues?

"Good afternoon, ladies and gentlemen of Summerhaven. I am here to confirm that at noon today, my deputies took into custody Ms. Rebecca Morris of the Happy Helpers temporary agency, on suspicion of grand larceny. We believe the agency staff has been responsible for a number of thefts on the island in recent weeks, and we know everyone will breathe easier now that the culprits will all soon be behind bars."

I tried to hold in my laughter. Only on Summerhaven Island would the capture of a few petty criminals be described in terms usually reserved for major crime syndicates, and merit a full press conference to boot. But then again, with the exception of a couple of recent murders that were jarringly out of place, the island was the kind of place where serious crimes were rare. To be fair, other than the recent murder of a real estate developer, which was quite an anomaly for the island, the Happy Helpers case might've been one of the biggest things to land on Sheriff Grady's desk in a decade. As for the breathing easy part, I don't know about the rest of the island's residents, but I was certainly breathing easier at that moment, knowing that the world's most inept sheriff hadn't scooped me on the case. Not that I didn't want the killer caught, of course. I just didn't feel Grady, with all his bumbling and chauvinism, ought to be the one to accomplish it. As for the Happy Helper's crime ring, I was happy to hear my hunch had been right, even if I wasn't at all surprised not to get any credit for the tip.

"I wonder who else they're arresting," I commented as Cass, Sybil, Jackie, and I wandered away from the press conference.

"I don't know," Cass said, "but I might be able to find out."

She pulled out her phone and dialed a number. She was silent for a moment. Then her breath hitched, and she ended the call without saying a word.

"What is it?" I asked.

"What was Toby's last name again?" Cass asked, seemingly out of nowhere.

"Rivers," I replied. "Cass, what's going on?"

"I just called the number for Happy Helper's, and Vera answered."

"So?" Cass was a lovely girl but flighty, and some-times, I really wished she would get to the point.

"She answered using her full name."

"Yeah, Stone." I supplied the name impatiently, wondering what she could be getting at that had left her so shaken, and wishing she would share the details instead of worrying about Vera's name. "I think that's what she told me when we met. Vera Stone."

"Vera *Rivers* Stone."

Now I understood, and when I looked at Jackie, I could see she did, too.

"Toby's sister," Jackie said.

"Vera is Toby's sister," I confirmed.

I was stunned. Vera had been my right-hand helper at the tea, and of course, she'd overseen the punch at the reunion. I had a feeling the employment records would show she was one of the staff at Mildred's Botox party, too. She'd had the opportunity, certainly, to carry out the crimes, and possibly the means if she was in possession of the vials of Botox that had disappeared from the aesthetician's stash, but it had never occurred to me until that moment that she would have motive.

I shut my eyes, suddenly recalling a detail from the night Sebastian and Jackie had arrived. "The night he arrived, he did a reading from *Magnolia Sunset*. She seemed upset and left before it was over. I had no idea why."

"Maybe she realized it was her brother's work," Jackie suggested.

I nodded. "Maybe so. I remember her asking me if I thought a person who could write like that was a genius. Not if I thought Sebastian was a genius. Even then, the wording struck me as weird, but I didn't give it much thought. Then she took him his tea."

"She only brought one cup," Jackie said, her face going pale. "She poured the tea and handed it to him on the chaise. I asked for another cup for myself, but she never brought it. Then he started to feel sick and went to bed. Do you think the poison was in the cup?"

I swallowed hard, certain of it. "Noah said the toxin needs several hours, or even days, in the system to become deadly. It's how we knew my food couldn't be responsible. He may have collapsed at the podium, but he'd ingested the Botox the night before."

"Maybe that's why the club members at the reunion didn't die," Sybil added. "She must've put it in the punch, and it made them sick enough that they got help right away instead of going to sleep."

"But, why would Vera want to harm the literary magazine club?" Jackie asked. "They had nothing to do with the theft of Toby's manuscript."

"She got really upset at one point." I pictured the anger in Vera's eyes that night. "She caught me talking to the club members instead of working, and I thought that's why she was mad. But now I remember they were making fun of her brother. Then she decided out of the blue to rearrange the punch bowls and put them on the tables. She must've spiked theirs when I was in the kitchen getting the garnish."

The hunt for Sebastian Grenville's killer had taken

a shocking turn. It all made perfect sense, but as I looked across to where Sheriff Grady was still grandstanding, basking in the glow of the theft I'd solved for him, something told me he wasn't going to see it that way. If there was going to be any justice for these crimes, I was going to have to figure out a way to get Vera to confess.

CHAPTER NINETEEN

The problem with getting a killer to confess her misdeeds is that, when she's also wanted by the sheriff for questioning with regards to her possible involvement in a local crime syndicate, she has every reason to skip town. At least, this is what I discovered to be true when I went looking for Vera shortly after Grady's big press conference. As soon as word of their boss, Becky's, arrest had gotten back to the Happy Helpers headquarters, Vera and the rest of the workers had fled, leaving behind wastebaskets full of shredded time sheets and other documents that could tie particular staffers to the thefts. Though many of the others were rounded up by the end of the day, by sundown that night, Vera remained at large.

After serving a home-cooked supper of Yankee pot roast, at which I was surprised not to see Jackie since she'd seemed to enjoy breakfast so much, Aunt Gwen retired to bed early. If the clicking of the keyboard was any clue, Jackie was back to the grindstone of her manuscript edits, so I headed up to my bedroom to see if I could come up with any new ideas for finding Vera. I stretched out on my bed and closed my eyes. Seconds later, a furry lead weight landed in the middle of my stomach.

"*Oof,*" I grunted. "Am I going to have to put you on a diet, Gus?"

I opened my eyes, and the cat stared into them as if to communicate he knew I was full of hot air, because I wasn't responsible for feeding him and, therefore, couldn't put him on a diet, no matter how hard I tried. It was true, but it didn't mean I appreciated his sassiness.

"Meow."

"What is it, huh? Did Lillian leave you here all by your lonesome?"

He hopped onto the floor, spring boarding himself off my belly with all the enthusiasm, but none of the grace, of an Olympic diver. When he landed, he looked back at me through the fluff of his oversized tail. "Meow."

I groaned. He was a persistent little devil, and when he got like this, there was no ignoring him. "You want me to get up? Fine, I'll get up."

I followed him into the hall and down the stairs to the second floor. The typing from inside Jackie's room had ceased, but the light shining from beneath her door indicated she hadn't yet gone to bed. Gus strutted across the floor, stretched himself to full height, and began to bat her doorknob.

"Gus, get away from there. Leave the poor lady alone, would you?"

He would not. In fact, he doubled his efforts, clearly just to show me who was running the show. After something approaching forty-seven-thousand attempts, he succeeded in turning the knob just enough to send the door crashing inward.

"Meow." He disappeared into the room.

"I'm so sorry, Jackie," I called out, then froze as I stepped across the threshold of the bedroom.

I knew for a fact Jackie had stopped working at the desk in the suite's office a week prior, if not longer, due to a creepiness she had picked up on, even if she was unable to see the sphere of ghostly energy that had engulfed it since Sebastian Grenville's spirit had taken up residence on the chaise nearby. That was why it came as such a shock to see her seated at the desk, staring blankly ahead, with all trace of the energy field and its ghostly source gone. "Jackie?"

She didn't answer, nor did she blink, or possibly even breathe. On her thumb, she wore Sebastian's golden ring with the deep purple stone.

Not wanting to face the truth just yet, I looked anxiously around the room, checking behind closet doors and even beneath the bed for a sign of

Grenville's ghost. "Come on, Sebastian," I muttered. "Where are you hiding?"

"I'm right here."

The voice was Jackie's, and yet it wasn't. It was coming from her mouth, but the words didn't belong to her. I'd heard it once before, that night in the sacred grove. I spun around and gave the Jackie who wasn't quite Jackie a long, hard stare. "What have you done to her, Sebastian?"

"There isn't much time." Despite the urgent message, the tone was muted, almost robotic in its lack of emotion.

I, however, was livid and had no problem showing it. I rushed toward the desk, fists clenched. "You bet there isn't, buddy. You get out of there right now, and leave her alone."

"Lighthouse."

"Now you're just talking nonsense."

"Toby's sister. Lighthouse. Go."

"Are you seriously ordering me around right now?" I put my hands on my hips, so tired of bossy, know-it-all men. In life, Sebastian may have thought he could get away with talking like that, but I wasn't about to take any lip from a ghost. "You expect me to just hop to it and go out to the lighthouse after dark because you say so?"

"Go. Now." Jackie-who-wasn't-Jackie rose and reached out, taking my arm in a vice-like grip.

"Ouch!"

She tugged, and though I fought to remain in my spot, it was a battle I was rapidly losing. After a few seconds of resistance, I found myself being dragged toward the door.

"Okay, you win. We'll go. Just let me grab my keys, will ya?"

For the second time that day, I found myself driving Ms. Josephine, with Jackie in the passenger's seat, in the direction of Cliffside Light. This time, instead of turning off onto Davenport Road, we continued on until we reached the massive gates of Cliffside Manor. The house was dark and empty, on account of my having sent one of the occupants to prison and the other to the mainland to sort out the legal implications of some very questionable financial choices. I got out of the car and approached the gates, expecting them to be locked, but instead I found the chain that usually held them shut had been cut and the gates stood slightly ajar. I pushed them the rest of the way open, then drove onto the grounds.

I turned to Jackie, who still stared straight ahead with the glassy eyes of a person possessed. "Where to now? Is she in the house?"

"Cliff."

I'd been afraid she was going to say that.

I parked the car at the end of the gravel driveway and started out across the backyard on foot, with Jackie following closely behind. In the daytime, the gently sloping lawn offered a breathtaking view of the sea, but in the darkness, all I could see were varying shades of black, punctuated by the occasional, rhythmic movement of the beam from the lighthouse as it circled onto land. I had a bad feeling about this whole thing, and the closer we got to the cliff, the stronger it became. As the light swept past again, I could just make out a shadow in the distance, at what had to be the very edge of land. It was impossible to make out any features, but I knew it had to be Vera.

"Hold on." I stopped and pulled out my phone, dialing Noah from my contact list. It went to voice mail, but though my first instinct was to hang up, I decided to leave a message. "Hello, Noah, this is Tamsyn. I'm at Cliffside Light, and I really can't explain why right now because you wouldn't believe me anyway, but if you get this message, maybe you could come out here."

I put away the phone and crept slowly toward the figure, urging Jackie to do the same. I didn't want to make any startling noises. The cliff's edge was treacherous, and a wrong move on the loose rocks could spell disaster. It was only when I was within close range that I spoke softly and soothingly. "Vera?"

The figure turned, though I couldn't see a face, just more darkness. "You're not the sheriff. What do you want?"

"No, I'm not the sheriff, Vera. It's Tamsyn." I inched closer, weighing my next words carefully. I wasn't sure what her intention was in coming out here, but I knew there couldn't be much ground between her and a sudden drop. "I needed to talk to you. About Toby."

"What do you know about my brother?" There was so much pain in her voice I could almost feel it slicing through me.

"I know he was a brilliant writer. A genius," I added, borrowing her own word for him.

"No one ever knew." Her tone grew hard as steel. "Sebastian Grenville stole that from him."

"Yes, he did. How long have you known?" Out of the corner of my eye, I caught a faint blue glow emanating from Jackie's body, separating from her and then bouncing back as if a struggle was going on inside her for control. I forced my attention back to Vera. "Did you take the job at the inn so you could get close enough to kill him?"

"Of course not." It sounded like the truth. "I had no idea until he did the reading."

"Then why did you have the Botox?"

Vera sighed. "I stole it from the garden club party, but you probably already figured that out. Becky had tasked several of her most trusted workers with that type of thing, finding valuable items on our temp jobs that could easily disappear with being noticed. I only had the vials of Botox on me because I hadn't had a chance to give them to her yet."

"Did you steal anything from the Pinecroft Inn?"

"No. I got distracted by Grenville's reading and

didn't have a chance to case the place in my usual way."

"And you really had no idea who he was when you arrived?"

"None. I'd never read *Magnolia Sunset*. I'd barely heard of it. I mean, it's not like I went to college. Toby was the smart one. But I'd read my brother's journals and the pieces he had published in the high school literary magazine. When I heard Grenville read it, I knew."

The blue glow had intensified and seemed to be half peeled away from Jackie's body. I had no idea what would happen when it got free, but I knew we would all be better off being far away from the edge of the cliff.

"Maybe we can move this conversation back toward the house," I urged, "and you can explain everything to me."

"I'm not going anywhere," Vera said, "but down there."

"No!" The voice was half Jackie's and half something else completely as the blue light ripped away from her and became the ghost of Sebastian Grenville, more fully formed than I had ever seen him before. Jackie fell backward onto the grass, landing on her bottom, stunned but seemingly unharmed. The gold ring flew from her hand and came to rest just inches from Vera, who picked it up.

"Where did you get this?" Her voice sounded strangled and unnatural. "This belonged to Toby."

Sebastian kneeled on the lawn between me and Vera, looking pleadingly at me. "Tell her he gave it to me." He reached out to me, and with a jolt, I could see every detail clearly in my mind.

"Your brother sent that ring, along with the manuscript that eventually became *Magnolia Sunset,* to Sebastian Grenville not long before he died. They were friends. More than friends. They were in love."

"Then why did Toby throw himself off this cliff?" Vera's words were steeped in bitterness. "He didn't have friends. No one understood him. No one knew how wonderful he was, except me."

"He had one friend. A friend who loved him so much that after your brother died, he tried to get his book published, only no one would give it a chance." I looked at Sebastian to see if I was getting it right. He nodded, and I continued. "Not until he said it was his. By the time the book came out, the lie had gone too far. He was afraid to tell the truth. It tormented him every day."

"It doesn't matter. None of it matters now." Vera turned to face the sea. "I just want to go wherever it is my brother went and leave all of this behind."

"No!" Sebastian called out, his voice low and tormented. I thought I was the only one who could hear it, until Vera turned around.

"What was that?"

I needed to act quickly, rattling off everything I'd put together from what Sebastian had shown me. "Your brother didn't kill himself, Vera. He had no reason to. He'd been planning to run away. He was supposed to meet up with Sebastian on the mainland, and they were going to go to New York to be together. Whatever happened out here with Toby, it was a tragic accident. He was finally going to be happy."

"They'll send me to jail." I couldn't see her face in the blackness, but I could hear Vera's sobs. "I didn't mean to kill him. It's just that I was so mad. And then again at the reunion when those people who were supposed to be his friends were making fun of him, I just snapped."

"I know, Vera," I soothed. "I'm sure everyone will understand. Let's just move back toward the house and figure it out."

I almost thought that had been enough to sway her, but in an instant, Vera was slipping backward off the ledge. Before I could react, Sebastian lunged toward her, somehow concentrating all of his energy and grabbing her by the wrists, holding her for the necessary seconds before Jackie and I could scramble to the edge and pull her back up. Together, we pinned her to the ground. When I looked back, Sebastian's ghost had become little more than blue mist.

I watched, dazed, as a light shone on my face. I thought it was coming from the lighthouse until I realized the blue mist was moving toward it, joining with it. Then both were gone. Had Toby been there, somewhere inside the light, to greet him? I would never know, but the possibility filled me with hope. Whatever mistakes he'd made in his life, Sebastian Grenville deserved to rest in peace.

"Hello?" I recognized Noah's voice and mustered all the energy I had left to respond.

"Noah! We're over here."

Noah came running across the lawn, quickly hunkering down beside Vera. Jackie and I still had her pinned down, but she'd stopped struggling, and I feared she was in shock.

"Her pulse is off the charts," Noah said after checking her vital signs. "But I think she'll be okay. What are you doing out here?"

"It's a long story." I gave a shaky laugh.

"When isn't it with you?" I wasn't positive, but I thought I detected affection in his tone.

"Vera's the one who's responsible for Sebastian's death," Jackie said. "And the illnesses at the reunion, too. Tamsyn's right. It's a long story, but I think she'll be willing to make a full confession when the time comes."

"That time should be coming pretty soon," Noah said, checking his phone. "Sheriff Grady's about ten minutes away."

I gave Noah a sharp as daggers look, and it was probably a good thing it was too dark for him to see. "You called the sheriff?"

"Of course, I did." This time, there was the unmistakable sound of laughter in his words. "Don't you think I've figured out by now that when you go wandering off by yourself around the island at night, leaving cryptic voice mails for me, that it's a good idea to call in reinforcements?"

I opened my mouth to argue, but what could I say? Annoyingly, the man had a point. Instead, I just stuck my tongue out at him.

"Real mature, Tamsyn," he said.

Cheese and rice!

I bit down on my tongue and winced. Apparently, Dr. Perfect had x-ray vision. I should've known.

THE SHERIFF ARRIVED AND TOOK VERA INTO custody. She didn't put up a fight. She may have been overwhelmed by what she'd learned about her brother, or maybe she was still reeling from being physically touched by a spirit. I had no idea how that would feel, but it couldn't have been pleasant. In any case, she got into the squad car without further incident.

Once Vera was gone, I drove Jackie and myself back to the inn, though Noah insisted on following behind us to make sure we made it okay. He didn't come in, just pulled up to the driveway and waited for us to make it through the front door. He was chivalrous like that, and it left me all topsy-turvy inside because for the life of me, I couldn't figure out what it meant. We were friends, of course, but he had a lot of friends. So, what did that mean for me? Did he swoop in to rescue me because he liked me or just because I needed rescuing? I wondered if I'd ever know for sure.

But I had other things to deal with at the moment, starting with Jackie. Sebastian had revealed something to me that she needed to know. The poor woman was completely drained, dragging herself from the front door to the stairs as if using her last ounce of strength. She'd spent several hours being possessed by a ghost, so who could blame her? I felt guilty keeping her up any longer, but it had to be done.

"Jackie, before you head up, can we talk?"

She paused, one hand gripping the banister. "Can it wait until morning?"

"Not really." I went to the living room and took a seat. She followed, and when I saw her hollow eyes and trembling body in the light, it was jarring. "Before I say anything, are you okay? You must be confused by what happened tonight."

"I was in the bedroom, and for some reason, I wanted to sit down at the desk. It's weird because I've been avoiding that area for days, but I felt drawn to it. And then, for some reason, I put on Sebastian's ring, and after that, I can't remember anything until I was sitting on the grass near the lighthouse."

"It was Sebastian. He took control of you for a while."

Jackie shuddered. "Why would he do that?"

"He had a message he needed to get out. It doesn't excuse possessing you, but it was urgent and I doubt he saw any other way."

She swallowed, and her eyes brimmed with tears. "Will he do it again?"

I shook my head emphatically. "No. He's gone now."

"Gone?"

"Gone to wherever spirits go," I said. "I saw it myself. After saying what he needed to say, and saving Vera from making a terrible mistake, he went into the light and disappeared."

She sat quietly for a while. "I'm glad he's at peace, and that he saved Vera, but I'm not sure I'm ready to forgive him for using me like that."

"That's totally understandable," I assured her. "And even after I tell you what he wanted me to tell you, you might feel that way for a long time, and that's okay."

"Sebastian had a message for me?" Jackie looked confused. "I don't understand. We worked closely together, but it was just a business arrangement. We didn't have the kind of relationship where I expected any dying words."

I closed my eyes, trying to collect my thoughts. Sebastian hadn't relayed the information in words so much as put the information into my brain, like some kind of download from a psychic cloud storage. "He felt tremendous guilt for what he did with Toby's manuscript and about the deal he had with you. He documented everything and put it in a lockbox. Do you know who his lawyer is?"

Jackie nodded. "Yes, I've worked with him before."

"Good. Contact him tomorrow if you can. I don't know all the details, but I think once you see the contents of that box, you'll find your life is going to change significantly for the better."

We rose, and on impulse, I gave Jackie a quick hug. I think I needed one as much as she did. It had been a difficult night. I thought that getting justice and helping Sebastian's spirit cross over would feel good, but there was a heaviness inside that I couldn't shake. I was sad Vera ended up being the killer. I'd liked her, and if it hadn't been for me, perhaps she wouldn't have done what she did. On the other hand, she wouldn't have discovered the truth about her brother, so I had to hope that had brought her comfort. As I watched Jackie head up the stairs, my spirits lifted a bit. Exciting things were in store for her, and I was glad to know something good would come out of this night.

CHAPTER TWENTY

The beginning of a new week rolled around, and for the first time in quite a while, life started to feel normal again. That night would be the start of the festival of Mabon, and all the generations of Pinecroft Cove witches were expected at the inn for a celebration, along with many of the neighbors. It was a long-standing Bassett family tradition. Before that, however, it was time to say goodbye to a guest whom I felt had become a friend.

Jackie's cheeks were rosy as she stood with her luggage on the porch, waiting for Sybil to arrive and give her a ride to the ferry. She'd been in good spirits for a few days, ever since talking to Sebastian's lawyer. It turned out she was set to inherit the bulk of his estate, and instead of having nowhere to go when she left the island as she'd once feared, she would soon be taking up residence in a Manhattan penthouse over-looking Central Park.

I waved as Sybil's car pulled down the driveway, then gave Jackie a hug. "Good luck with everything."

"I still can't believe it," she said, a smile beaming from ear to ear. "*Azalea Nightfall* is going to be published under my name, and Sebastian's publisher has offered me a three-book deal."

"It's the least they could do," I pointed out as I grabbed the handle of one of her suitcases. "That tell-all confession he wrote is going to earn them millions."

"It was good of him to set the record straight, even if he didn't have the courage to do it while he was alive."

"Hey there!" Sybil called out, reaching for one of Jackie's bags with one hand while grabbing Jackie's hand with the other. "You ready for all this?"

"As ready as I'll ever be. My publicist—" Jackie let out a shaky breath and laughed. "I have a publicist! Who would've thought that would ever happen. Anyway, she says there's already a whole bank of news vans waiting on the mainland to snag interviews. I guess I can't put it off any longer."

I nodded, feeling both happy and nervous for her over what was ahead. I guessed those news crews would be a bit more intimidating than Earl, Jasper, and their beat-up old van. "Make sure to stay in touch."

"I will," she assured me, then gave Sybil a warm look. "And, next time you're in Manhattan…"

"You're my first stop. You can count on it," Sybil said.

Once they'd gone, I went back inside and found myself completely at a loss for what to do. Aunt Gwen was hard at work in the kitchen. Mabon is a harvest festival, which means food is front and center in its celebration. I mean, food is always front and center when Aunt Gwen's around, but from what I'd gathered, this was like Christmas, Thanksgiving, and an all-island potluck rolled into one night. I made a mental note to search the closet for my stretchiest pants.

The weird thing, though, was that for the first time since I'd arrived, Aunt Gwen wasn't trying to tutor me in how each recipe was prepared. Don't get me wrong, I wasn't off the hook for cooking lessons. A big part of being a witch, any type of witch, was to work spells, and they often involved food. Besides, the Bassett family grimoire was part of my heritage, and I needed to be familiar with it. But ever since I'd confessed I wasn't a true, bred-in-the-bone kitchen witch, Aunt Gwen had dialed back her expectations. We would focus on one recipe at a time, slowly adding to my magical repertoire at a pace I could handle, which would leave ample opportunity for me to explore the vast array of magic that lay beyond the realm of hearth and spoon. I still had no idea what the nature or extent of my powers really were, but the prospect of exploring all the possibilities in more depth until I discovered them was something that brought a flutter of excitement to my belly.

Even so, my conscience wouldn't have been clear if I didn't at least poke my head into the kitchen to see if my aunt needed help. "Is there anything I can do?"

"What's that, dear?" She looked up from her steaming pot, wisps of red hair that had escaped her bun curling around her face. She was so in her element at the stove that happiness just about radiated from every pore. Try as I might, I couldn't imagine magic ever making me feel quite so fulfilled. Heck, I doubted if anything in life ever could.

"Can I help with setting up anything for tonight?"

"You know, if you wouldn't mind checking the grape arbor and seeing if the table's clear, that would be a huge help."

I headed out the back door and down the sloping lawn to the grape arbor, a place I didn't usually pay much attention to because the only thing that would have come as a bigger shock to me than being told I was a kitchen witch would've been if I were supposed to have power over plants. My only ability where green things were concerned was to send them to the great beyond. I'd seen the vegetable garden and the wide, green grape leaves stretched across the top of the arbor from my window but never bothered with a closer inspection. Now that I did, it was a surprisingly lovely space.

A series of posts and beams, just a bit above head height, provided support for the grapes that grew along their tops, as well as a hidden and cool space beneath large enough to hold a long, rustic table and a dozen chairs. Twinkling lights had been threaded through the vines, and I could only imagine how magical it would look when night came. It was especially appropriate for Mabon, which occurred on the autumnal equinox. It was one of two times during the year when the day and night were exactly equal, and it marked the balance between light and dark. We would eat outside during the evening, under the twinkling lights, and enjoy mild weather, fresh food, and good wine before the winter came.

It was shady under the canopy of leaves, and in fact, along the entire table, there was only one spot where a significant amount of sunlight shone through. In this spot lounged a fat, furry, black cat. I shook my head. "Gus, I see you've made yourself at home."

He stretched his paws out in front of him, flexing each toe to its fullest, then yawned without opening his eyes. He flicked his tail, and I got the distinct impression he was disappointed in me. It wasn't the first time.

"Is this because I forgot to say thank you for alerting me to what Sebastian's ghost was up to the other day?"

Gus rolled so his back was to me. I grimaced. For a usually grumpy cat, he was taking it to a new level. I ducked out from under the arbor and quickly perused the offerings in my aunt's herb garden, my eyes falling on the one labeled catnip. I broke off several sprigs and brought them to him, placing the bouquet beneath his nose.

"I'm sorry. I should've said thank you before." I sucked in a breath and steeled myself to admit the rest. "In this particular instance, I couldn't have managed without you."

Gus snuffled the catnip, then batted it with his hind paws. Soon, he was spinning himself in circles as he tried to both eat the catnip and capture his tail at the same time. I decided this meant I was forgiven.

"I wonder where Lillian is." Though I said it just above a whisper, no sooner had the words been spoken than she was under the arbor, sitting in one of the chairs. No matter how many times it happened, it always caught me by surprise.

"The arbor! Oh, how I loved celebrating Mabon here," Lillian said, eyes shining as she looked around. "Mother would host the best parties."

"I thought you and your mother didn't get along."

"We didn't, but that doesn't mean I can't appreciate her better qualities. She was an amazing hostess."

I pulled out the chair across from Lillian and took a seat. There was something I'd been meaning to ask, though I wasn't sure how to bring it up. "Lillian, is your mother here?"

"Here?" She swiveled her head back and forth. "No."

"I mean, is she somewhere at the inn?" I pressed my lips together. I had more to ask, but did I really want to know? "Remember when you said there were other spirits, existing on planes I couldn't see?"

"Yes, there are many," Lillian said with a nod. "Our worlds overlap. There are things in yours I can't see, and things in mine you can't see. But we help each other. I can't leave the property without you, and you can't see the past without me."

"And between the two of us, we can see it all?"

Lillian laughed. "Oh, I doubt that. There's a lot going on at the Pinecroft Inn. Between the two of us, I think we only scratch the surface."

I wasn't sure what she meant and was even less convinced I wanted to know. "Can you ask something else?"

"Sure."

My stomach tightened and my throat went dry, but I pressed on. I had to know. "Is my mother here?"

Lillian thought for a moment. "I don't think so. There are so many spirits here. Some I can see, and others I can only feel. I don't think hers is one of them, though."

"Why are there so many, do you think?"

Lillian shrugged. "It's a magical place. Where else would they want to be?"

I sat back in my chair, closing my eyes as a light breeze blew across my cheeks. The sound of waves lapping against the shores of the cove rang softly in my ears, along with the rustle of leaves and the happy chirping of birds. I breathed deeply, and the air was perfumed with roses and freshly cut grass, plus a hint of salt from the sea. Maybe she was right. There was magic all around us. Where else would a spirit want to be?

"Can I show you something?" Lillian asked, rousing me from the nap I was very close to falling into.

I opened my eyes. "I guess so."

A look of total concentration came over her face, and all around us there was that wobbly quality to my vision that told me time was changing around me. When it stopped, there were people walking across the lawn and lounging in chairs either by the house or the shore. They were dressed in clothing from Lillian's era, men in suits and women in dresses, casual but chic, like they were headed to a fancy picnic. We were alone, hidden beneath the arbor, which remained exactly as it had been before.

"What is this?" I whispered.

"One of mother's parties," she replied, her eyes twinkling. "Mabon, 1927, I think. Maybe 1926."

"This is amazing," I said breathlessly. "Is this what it was like when you showed Sybil your bedroom?"

She shook her head, fixing me with an earnest look. "No, it was little more than lights and shadows with her. You're the only one I can travel through time with. I think it's a combination of our powers that makes it work."

A chill crept into me, and I looked away, eager to put the possible implications of that statement out of my mind. "Look at all the food on the tables beneath the tents." I pointed at the spread of sandwiches and pastries laid out beneath two large tents of striped canvas that sat a few yards away. There was lemonade, too, and fresh fruit, plus little dishes of ice cream with fresh raspberries and sprigs of mint on top. "You weren't kidding about her being a great hostess."

A group of children were playing croquet on a flat part of the lawn, and I watched them for quite some time. I wondered for a moment if one of them could be my own grandmother, but if Lillian was right about the time, she wouldn't have been born yet. I was just about to look away when I saw a familiar figure coming toward us, the one from her time who looked so oddly similar to a certain doctor in mine. I pointed as he drew closer. "Oh, look. Isn't that your friend, Teddy Davenport?"

No sooner had I said it but it was as if a switch had been flipped, the party scene blinking out and replaced by the present day. Lillian was nowhere to be seen, and

Gus had long since run off. Only, inexplicably, Teddy Davenport was still coming my way.

No, not Teddy Davenport. Noah Caldwell.

He reached the arbor and bent to duck beneath the leaves. "Tamsyn?"

"Over here," I said. I rushed over to the edge of the arbor and reached out to hold the vines back to make it easier for him. As I did, my hand brushed against his, and a jolt of electricity traveled the length of my arm, sending my pulse skyrocketing.

Woah, there, Tamsyn, I thought. *Easy girl.* Sure, Noah was a handsome guy, and the arbor was a lovely, secluded space, but we were just friends. It wasn't wise to let my imagination run away with me. Even so, I couldn't keep from picturing how it could be, if this were some sort of Hollywood movie. That moment when he would turn to me, and...

At exactly that moment, he did turn his head toward me, but instead of love in his eyes or a declaration of devotion on his lips, there was a look of utter bewilderment on his face. He looked back out at the yard from under the arbor once more before joining me at the table. "Is your aunt hosting a party?"

"Yes," I said with a laugh that was a little sillier than usual since I was still trying to rein in my fantasies. "Tonight, for the harvest festival. She invited you, I'm sure." I called it a harvest festival because the term Mabon held little meaning outside witchy circles.

"No, I mean has it already started or something?"

He scratched his head. "It's just I could've sworn I saw some people on the lawn as I was heading back here."

"People?" My pulse quickened as he nodded, not from attraction this time but from something very different.

"In costumes, like for an old-fashioned picnic." As I stared at him, Noah shifted uncomfortably in his seat. "I must've been imagining things."

"Yes, that must've been it," I replied.

Only, of course, that hadn't been it. My heart was really racing now, beating a mile a minute. It was a really good thing I had a doctor close by, because if it went any faster, there was a good chance it would give out. I took a deep breath. I needed to calm down, but how could I?

Lillian had said herself that time travel was a tricky thing. It took great power and skill. Few witches ever got the hang of it, even with years of practice. Lillian said I was the only one she knew who'd managed to do it.

Now I had reason to believe that Noah could do it, too.

Don't miss Tamsyn's next magical mystery in *Magic, Lead, and Gingerbread,* coming soon.

A NOTE FROM NICOLE

The weather has turned chilly here in New England this week. Pumpkins are dotting the fields and Halloween decorations are starting to crop up on lawns. As for me, I'm enjoying spending time in the world of Pinecroft Cove even more than in the summer months because of all the fun and mysterious adventures that come along with shorter days. I hope you've enjoyed this latest book in the Witches of Pinecroft Cove series!

Thank you to Em and Kelly for all your wonderful editing help. Also, a big shout out to Victoria for the amazing cover art, and Stephanie for the audio narration.

The next book in the series, *Magic, Lead, and Gingerbread*, will be coming very soon. Be sure to sign up for my newsletter to be notified of new releases, subscriber-only giveaways of signed paperbacks, ebooks, and audio, plus special behind-the-scenes articles, and more.

Subscribers also receive a free PDF replica of the Bassett family grimoire, filled with all the recipes featured in the series, plus fun hints about the Bassett family and the enchanted island of Summerhaven, Maine.

Visit me at NicoleStClaire.com

ABOUT THE AUTHOR

Nicole St Claire lives in Massachusetts where she writes paranormal cozy mysteries when not at the beck and call of her three fluffy feline fur balls. You can often find her dressed in vintage costume on her way to a ball, or perusing antique cookbooks for the perfect recipe to make when hosting her next Victorian afternoon tea. Yes, her hobbies are a little odd.

Made in United States
North Haven, CT
22 October 2022